The Last Necromancer

THE MINISTRY OF CURIOSITIES SERIES
#1

C.J. ARCHER

Series by C.J. Archer:

The Emily Chambers Spirit Medium Trilogy

The 1st Freak House Trilogy

The 2nd Freak House Trilogy

The 3rd Freak House Trilogy

The Ministry of Curiosities

Lord Hawkesbury's Players

The Assassins Guild

The Witchblade Chronicles

Stand-alone books by C.J. Archer:

Redemption

Surrender

Courting His Countess

The Mercenary's Price

DEDICATION

To Samantha and Declan, for a million reasons.

CHAPTER 1

London, summer 1889

The other prisoners eyed me as if I were a piece of tender meat. I was someone new to distract them from their boredom, and small enough that I couldn't stop one—let alone four—from doing what they wanted. It was only a matter of who would be the first to *enjoy* me.

"He's mine." Thc prisoner's tongue darted out through his tangled beard and licked what I supposed were lips, hidden beneath all that wiry black hair. "Come here, boy."

I shuffled away from him but instead of the brick wall of the cell, I smacked into a soft body. "Looks like he wants *me*, Dobby. Don't ye, lad?" Large hands clamped around my arms, and thick fingers dug into my flesh through my jacket and shirt. The man spun me round and I gaped up at the brute grinning toothlessly at me. My heart rose and dove, rose and dove, and cold sweat trickled down my spine. He was massive. He wore no jacket or waistcoat, only a shirt stained with blood, sweat and grime. The top buttons had popped open, most likely from the strain of containing his enormous chest, and a thatch of gray hair sprouted through the gap and crept up to his neck rolls. Hot, foul breath assaulted my nostrils.

I tried to turn my face away but he grasped my jaw. The wrenching motion caused my hair to slide off my forehead and eyes, revealing more of my face than I had in a long time. A new fear spread through me, as sickening as the man I faced. Only two prisoners seemed interested in a boy, but if they realized I was a girl, the others would likely want me too.

"Anyone ever tell you you're too pretty for a boy?" My tormentor chuckled, but he didn't seem like he'd discovered my secret. "Pretty boys can get themselves into trouble."

Girls even more so. It was just my ill luck to get caught stealing an apple from the costermonger's cart outside the cemetery and wind up in the overcrowded holding cell at Highgate Police Station. The irony wasn't lost on me, but it wasn't in the least amusing. As an eighteen year-old girl, I should be separated from the men, but I'd been passing myself off as a thirteen year-old boy for so long it hadn't even occurred to me to tell the policemen. With my half-starved body, and mop of hair covering most of my face, nobody had questioned my gender or age.

The big brute jerked me forward, slamming me against his body. My nose smacked into a particularly filthy patch of his shirt and I gagged at the combined stenches of sweat, vomit, excrement and gin. I wasn't too clean myself, but this fellow's odor was overpowering. Bile burned my throat but I swallowed it quickly. Showing weakness would only make it worse for me. I knew that from experience.

"Come here and keep old Badger warm."

Warm? It was summer, and the cell was hotter than a furnace with four adult men and myself crammed into a space designed for one.

"I'm next," said the bearded Dobby, closing in to get a better look at me.

"If there's anything left of him after old Badger's broken him in." Badger chuckled again and fumbled with the front of his trousers.

I closed my hands into fists and clamped down on my fear. Shouting for the constable wouldn't help. He'd told the other prisoners to "Enjoy," when he'd tossed me into the cell. It had only been a few minutes since he'd walked off, whistling. It felt like hours. I had to fight now. It was the only way left. Not that I stood a chance against the men, but they might beat me unconscious, with any luck. It was best not to be awake while they took their liberties.

I swung my fist, but Badger was faster than he looked. He caught my wrist and sneered. "That ain't going to help you." The sneer vanished and he shoved me into the wall.

I put my hands up and managed to stop myself smashing into the whitewashed bricks, but my wrists and arms jarred from the force. I gasped in pain, but smothered the cry that welled up my throat.

"Leave the boy alone." The voice wasn't one I'd heard yet. It didn't come from outside the cell but from another prisoner to my right.

"What'd you say?" Badger snarled.

"I said leave the boy alone. He's just a child."

I turned and pressed my back into the wall. My rescuer stood in a similar position, his arms crossed over his chest. He was perhaps late twenties, with fair hair and cloudy gray eyes circled by red-rimmed lids. He wasn't nearly as tall as Badger, nor as solid, and I doubted he could defeat either Badger or Dobby in a fight. My heart sank.

"You going to make us?" Dobby asked.

The man shrugged then winced, as if the movement hurt. He sported a bruise on his cheek, and his blond hair was matted with blood. "One must try. It's the decent thing to do."

"'One must try.'" Badger mimicked the other man's toff accent to perfection. Dobby and the fourth prisoner, lounging on the cot bed, laughed.

Dobby straightened his back, threw out his chest, and affected a feminine walk to where the man stood. The prisoner on the bed laughed even harder at the hairy beast's acting. "Oh, protect me from these brutes, sir," whimpered Dobby in a high voice. "You're my hero."

The blond man lowered his hands to his sides and curled them into fists. I held my breath and waited for the first punch to be thrown. The man smiled instead. It held no humor.

Dobby tugged on the lapels of the blond man's jacket, pretending to straighten it, then fidgeted with the high, stiff shirt collar. The gentleman wore no tie, and his hat and gloves were also missing. The fine cut of his clothes reminded me of my father, always so perfectly groomed. Even the fellow's aristocratic bearing was very much like my father's. Whether it was also an affectation this gentleman had developed, it was difficult to tell. I wasn't as experienced with the upper members of society and their ways as I used to be.

"Finished?" the blond man drawled. I wondered why the gentleman had landed in jail and why he was defending me, a stranger. He'd get himself killed if he didn't keep quiet.

His fun spoiled by the gentleman's lack of fear, Dobby snorted and moved away. He turned back to me and licked his lips. Badger wiped the back of his hand over his mouth and eyed me with renewed interest. He reached for me, but the blond man smacked his hand away. Neither Badger nor I had noticed him approach.

Badger bared his teeth in a snarl. "You don't get to ruin Badger's fun!" He smashed his fist into the blond man's face, sending him reeling back into the bed.

The prisoner lounging there had to quickly pull up his legs or be sat on. The blond man recovered, and with a growl of rage, lunged at Badger. But he swung his fists wildly and his blows merely glanced off the bigger, meaner prisoner. Badger responded with another punch to the gentleman's jaw. Blood splattered from the blond man's mouth as he careened backward and slammed into the wall. His head smacked into the bricks, and the *crack* of his skull turned my stomach.

Dobby laughed, sending spittle flying from the slit in his beard. Badger dusted off his hands and watched as the gentleman folded in on himself and crumpled to the floor like a ragdoll. My heart sank, and it was only then that I realized I'd let it rise in hope.

My rescuer was dead.

A sickening fear assaulted me along with the memories of that terrible night five years ago when my mother had died. I could still hear my father's accusation, still feel the sting of his belt across my back, and the icy rain he'd sent me into with the order never to return home.

Yet those awful memories could help me now. If the prisoners reacted to my strange ability as my father had… It was my only hope.

I knelt alongside the gentleman's lifeless form and placed my hands on either side of his face, as I had done to my mother after she'd breathed her last. While I'd been overset by tears then, I wasn't now, and I could see the gray pallor of death consuming his youthful face. I stroked his jaw. It was still warm and his short whiskers felt rough on my palms.

Someone behind me snickered. "You can't do nothing for him now, boy. Let old Badger comfort you, eh?"

I didn't move and he didn't rip me away from the body, thank goodness. I needed to touch it. At least, I think I did. I'd only ever done this once before. What if I couldn't repeat it? What if my connection to my mother had been the key that time, and it wouldn't work on a stranger?

I caressed his face as if we'd been the most intimate of lovers, and willed his spirit to rise. *Please speak to me. Do this for me and help me to live. I don't want to die here like this.*

I didn't want to die at all. That in itself was something of a revelation, but I had no chance to think about it further. A pale wisp rose from the body. At first it looked like a slender ribbon of smoke, then it grew larger and took on the shape of the dead man. It was still as thin as a veil of silk chiffon, but it moved as if it held solid form.

The spirit frowned at me from his floating position then settled his gaze on his own lifeless figure. He sighed. "And so it ends."

My heart ground to a halt. "I'm sorry," I whispered.

The spirit blinked at me, as if surprised that we were communicating. "Not your fault. I brought it on myself. I'd had enough of living, you see." He sighed again. "My parents said I would amount to nothing and they were right. Couldn't even get in a good punch." He nodded at Badger, who was standing behind me.

"What's he saying?" Dobby asked.

"He's talking to the dead," Badger said. "Boy's mad." He snorted and spat a glob of green mucus on the floor near my feet. "Get up, lad. It won't go well for you if I have to drag you over here."

The spirit's face twisted with disgust. "Wish I could have done something to help you, child. I haven't accomplished much in my life, but my hatred of bullies is well known. Just ask my father." He laughed at a joke I wasn't privy to. "That's something, eh? A legacy I can leave behind?"

I didn't think it was much of a legacy, but I didn't say so. He was my only friend in that cell, and I needed him. "There is one thing you can do for me before you go," I whispered.

"What's he saying?" Dobby repeated.

"I don't bloody care." Badger's hand closed around my shoulder and he wrenched me away from the body. He fumbled with the front of his trousers again. I had only seconds.

"Get back into your body," I told the spirit. I no longer kept my voice low. He needed to hear me, and it didn't matter who else did now. The die was already cast.

The spirit didn't move. "How?"

I wasn't entirely sure. When my mother had done it, she'd simply floated back down into her body when I'd asked her to. "Lie on your…self," I told him.

Badger's fingers gripped my jaw, smashing the inside of my mouth into my teeth. "Shut it," he snapped. "I don't want to hear no lunatic talk. Do ye hear me?"

"He's soft in the head." Dobby bent to get a better look at me. If Badger hadn't been holding my jaw, I would have smashed my forehead into his nose.

"Bloody hell!" The other prisoner leapt off the bed, his eyes huge. "He's still alive!"

Badger let me go. He stumbled back and stared at the now standing body. It wasn't alive, but the spirit had re-entered it and was controlling it. Even though I knew what was happening, the sight still made my blood run cold.

The body turned to Badger. The insipid, blank eyes of the dead man were as lifeless as they had been moments ago, and I wasn't certain how the spirit could see through them.

The third prisoner crossed himself. Dobby mewled. Badger continued to stumble backward until he fell over his own feet and landed heavily on his backside.

"What…me…do?" The brittle, thin voice coming from the corpse startled me as much as it did the prisoners. It was nothing like the spirit's smooth one. It was as if he labored to get the dead vocal organs working.

"I don't know," I said.

"Jesus christ," Dobby muttered. He joined the other prisoner in the cell corner, as far away from the body and me as possible.

"You…control…me." The body bent over the cowering, sweating Badger. The brute looked like he'd pee his trousers if the dead man got any closer. "Kill?"

"Can you?" I asked. It wasn't a request but an honest question, since the gentleman hadn't been able to so much as punch Badger when he'd been alive. As the color drained from Badger's face, I realized how it must have sounded. I didn't correct myself.

"Constable!" Badger screamed. "Constable, get this madman out of here!"

Was he referring to the reanimated corpse or me? I laughed. I couldn't help it. Perhaps I *was* mad, but seeing the cruel Badger frightened out of his wits was the most gratifying experience of my life, and I was going to enjoy it while it lasted.

Unfortunately that wasn't long. The constable's face appeared at the slit in the door. "What's all this noise about?"

"Get it out! Get it out!" Badger threw his arms over his face, like a child hiding under the sheets at night.

"Shut up in there!"

"He's gone mad," I said to the guard.

Badger kept screaming at the constable to remove "the devil," and the other prisoner joined in. Dobby slunk back against the wall, away from us. Away from the door.

The door that was now opening. "Bloody hell, don't make me come in there, you bleedin' idiot," said the constable, as he stepped into the cell. He wasn't armed, and his attention was distracted by Badger and the others. "What's got up your arse, anyway?"

"Let's get out of here," I said quietly to the corpse.

Like an automaton, the body turned stiffly toward the door. The constable took one look at those dead eyes and fell to his knees. "Devil," he muttered before launching into an earnest prayer.

I almost didn't move, so stunned was I at the similarity to my father's reaction when he'd first seen Mama's corpse rise. But a nudge from the dead man got my feet working. I slipped past the constable and out the door. The body lumbered after me with jerky, awkward steps, as if the swift movement was too difficult for its dead, uncoordinated limbs.

"Hoy there! Stop!" Another policeman ran toward us, his truncheon raised.

The body pulled back bloodless lips and hissed. The constable dropped the truncheon then took off in the opposite direction.

"Hurry," I urged the body.

"If you wish." His voice sounded stronger, not as strained, and his steps were more sure now. He seemed to have adjusted to his deceased state.

We ran along a corridor, past another two holding cells. Three more constables fell back from us with gasps and terrified mutterings. Only one challenged us, and the corpse under my command pushed him away. Easily. It seemed he was stronger, now he was dead, than when he was alive.

"You there!" shouted the constable behind the desk in the reception room. "What's—?" He stumbled back as the corpse turned vacant eyes and white face toward him.

The clang of a bell sounded from behind us, warning of a prisoner escape. Ordinarily it would signal for all available constabulary at the station to chase us, but none did. Their fear of "the devil" overrode any sense of duty.

The dead man pushed me toward the door. We ran, but he stopped before reaching freedom. I stopped too.

"Do not let them catch you, child!"

"And you?" I asked.

"When you are safe, release my spirit."

"How?"

"Speak the command. Now go!"

The desk constable approached uncertainly, his shaking hand clutching a revolver. He swallowed heavily and pointed it at the corpse.

I slipped out the door and into South Grove. The street was surprisingly empty, but then I realized any passersby would have scattered when they heard the bell. I darted into a nearby lane as a gunshot joined the cacophony.

"I release you," I said softly. "Go to your afterlife."

I never found out if my words, spoken from some distance, were enough to release the spirit from his body and send him on his way. I hoped so. He'd died for me, and I owed him whatever peace was in my power to give.

I kept running, not daring to stop or steal anything, despite my hunger. I hadn't eaten in three days, and then it had been only some strawberries. My last experience at thieving had got me arrested. It was the one and only time I'd been caught. I prided myself on being one of the best thieves on the north side of London, but I wasn't sure I'd ever be able to trust myself again. For now, it didn't matter. I was too intent on getting as far away from the police as possible to think of food.

When I finally reached Clerkenwell, I slowed. My throat and lungs burned, my heart crashed against my ribs. But I was far from Highgate Police Station and there'd been no sign of pursuit. I took the long route to the rookery, just in case, and stopped outside the old, crumbling house with the rotten window sashes and door. I glanced up and down the lane, and seeing no one about I pulled aside the loose boards at knee height. I squeezed through the hole and let the boards flap closed behind me.

"Charlie's back!" shouted Mink, standing lookout near the trapdoor that led down to the cellar. The boy lifted his chin at me in greeting. It was as much as he ever acknowledged me. He wasn't much of a talker.

"'Bout bloody time!" came the gruff voice of Stringer, from down in Hell. That's what we called the cellar. It was an apt name for our crowded living quarters where we ate, slept and passed the time. It was cold and damp in winter, hot and airless in summer, but it kept us off the streets and out of danger.

"Thought you'd scarpered." Stringer popped his head through the trapdoor. His face and hair were dirty, and I could smell the stink of the sewers on him from where I stood near the entrance. He must have gone wandering down there again.

"I got arrested," I said.

Both Stringer and Mink blinked at me. Then Stringer roared with laughter, almost propelling himself off the ladder. "You! Fleet-foot Charlie, caught by the filth! Well, well, never thought I'd see the day. Oi, lads, listen to this—Charlie got himself arrested!"

"How'd you get out?" asked Mink in his quiet voice. He was a serious boy, compared to the others, and watchful. He didn't join in with the annoying pranks they liked to pull, and he could read well enough too. I liked him more than the rest of the gang members, but that wasn't saying much. I'd almost asked him how he'd learned to read and where he'd lived before he found himself part of Stringer's gang, but decided against it.

I didn't know any of the children's pasts, and they didn't know mine. Nor did I get too friendly with them. It would make it easier to leave, when the time came. No goodbyes, no sorrows, no ties; that was my motto. I moved on twice a year, every year, and had done so since that wet night Mama died. I couldn't have lived as a thirteen year-old boy for over five years if I'd stayed with one gang the entire time.

"Bit of luck," was all I said to Mink. "Move it, Stringer, and let me past." I thumped his shoulder.

He descended the ladder and I followed, leaving Mink to watch the entrance.

"Charlie!" cried another boy named Finley. Mink, Stringer, Finley…they weren't real names but, like mine, they were probably near enough. "How'd they catch *you,* then? Dangle a clean pair of britches in front of ya nose?"

The eight lads lounging in the cellar fell over each other laughing. Ever since I'd mentioned wanting to steal clean clothes to replace my reeking ones, I'd been the butt of their jokes. It made a change from them teasing me for refusing to strip off so much as my shirt in front of them.

"Pigs were hiding near the costermonger's cart," I said, lying down on the rags I used as a mattress. It was cleaner than the actual mattress that had been dragged down from the upstairs bedroom before the roof caved in. Cleaner, but not free of lice. I scratched my head absently. "I think the costermonger told them to look out for me."

"Serves you bloody right for getting slack," Stringer said, kicking my bare foot. I didn't rub the spot, despite the pain. It was never a good idea to show weakness, even among boys from my own gang. Perhaps especially to them. "And for going back there. Again."

One of the other boys snorted. "What you going there all the time for, anyway, Charlie? What's in Highgate?"

"Idiot. Don't you know nothing?" Stringer leaned against the wall and crossed his arms. In that pose, he reminded me of the gentleman in the holding cell. Both blond and slender, there was a certain bravado and defiance about them.

My heart pinched. I regretted that the man had lost his life because of me. I sent a silent word of thanks to Heaven, Hell, or wherever he'd ended up. I wouldn't forget his sacrifice, nor would I make the same mistake again and allow myself to be caught. Life was precarious for homeless children. And women.

Stringer rubbed his thumb along his smirking lower lip. "He goes to the cemetery."

I went very still. He must have followed me once. How much did he know? Did he see me visit Mama's grave? Or wander around the other headstones, imagining what the deceased had once looked like and how they'd lived? Did he know I liked to sit beneath the cedar trees and dream the day away?

Finley pulled a face. "Blimey, Charlie, that's a bit mordid, ain't it?"

"Morbid," I corrected him automatically.

Stringer's smirk turned to a sneer. "Shut your hole, Charlie. No one cares what you been doing, anyway. You got caught today. You got slow." He leaned down and poked me in the shoulder. "Never forget that." He hated when I corrected them. It always seemed to bring out the worst in him. I supposed it was because it made him feel inferior to me, when in fact he was the eldest and the leader. Well, not actually the eldest, but no one there knew it.

The boys were aged from eight to fifteen. Stringer was not only the eldest but also the biggest. He was already the size of a grown man, and there were rumblings about him leaving the gang of children to take up with a band of more ruthless men who lived in the neighborhood. Two of the boys had even approached me to take over from him, but I'd refused. It would probably mean I'd have to fight Stringer, and there was no way I could win against him. Besides, it was coming time for me to move on again. Mink in particular was beginning to look at me like he was trying to solve a puzzle. Sometimes I wondered if he already knew that I wasn't who I said I was.

"Anything to eat?" I asked to distract Stringer.

"Some bread," he said, jerking his head at the boy nearest the board we used as a table.

The boy tossed a hunk of bread to me. I caught it. Not a crumb flaked off the hard crust. I set it aside with a sigh, not wanting to break my teeth.

The afternoon wore on. Boys came and went, some bringing food and water that I didn't touch. While I was hungry, they were hungrier. They always were. That was the problem with boys. I had at least finished my growing. Not that I had much to show for it. Sometimes I wondered if I would have been taller with a more womanly figure if I'd had plenty to eat in the last five years. I would never know now. My size helped me to blend in, so I wasn't overly disappointed.

I slept until it was my turn to watch the entrance, then slept again after Finley relieved me. It was mid-morning on a dreary day when I got the first inkling that something was amiss. The boys who returned from foraging—as we called our thieving stints—eyed me warily. They whispered behind their hands and tittered nervously.

"What is it?" I said as one boy crossed himself when he passed me. "Why is everyone staring at me like I've got two heads?"

He wouldn't answer.

"Mink? You'll tell me."

But even Mink kept his distance and wouldn't speak to me. I did overhear him tell a group of boys that it wasn't possible and the devil didn't exist, nor did God. That earned him an eye-roll.

When Stringer returned around midday, and also gave me a wide berth and strange looks, I decided it was time to go for a walk. I wasn't getting answers. I didn't need them anyway. I knew what they'd heard. The gossip network among the gangs was more efficient than any telegraph.

I left through the hole in the wall and made my way north out of Clerkenwell. I felt no fear walking among people who were little better off than me. It was safer in the downtrodden suburb than the holding cell at the police station. My patched up clothing and shoeless feet marked me as not worth robbing, and if a man wanted to rape someone, he would wait for dark, and choose someone slower and most likely female. There were easier pickings than a small, quick youth.

I wandered for hours, not really heading anywhere. Or so I thought. When I found myself at the top of a familiar Tufnell Park street, I realized long-buried habit had taken me home.

Home. The detached red brick house with the white trim couldn't be called that anymore. Home was where you slept at night, and where people who loved you welcomed you with open arms. My father still lived there, but I doubted he would let me in if I knocked on the door. I had visited from time to time, but never ventured further than the shrubs inside the front gate behind which I hid as I waited for my father to make an appearance. Most times he didn't. I'd seen him only twice in five years, when he'd invited in a parishioner who'd come to his door. He'd welcomed *them* with smiles and a warm handshake.

I checked up and down the street and, seeing no one, opened the gate. I cringed at the squeak of hinges and quickly ducked behind the shrubbery. Spindly twigs grabbed at my hair and the patch sewn over my jacket elbow tore. The bush was in need of pruning. Mama had been the gardener, not Father. There were signs of neglect everywhere, now that I looked closer. Weeds sprouted along the flowerbeds and moss grew between the brick pavers. The gate needed oiling and the front steps needed sweeping. I wondered if the housekeeper had kept the inside clean or if she'd let her standards lapse too, now that Mama wasn't there.

I adjusted my position to alleviate the cramping in my legs. After a few more minutes, I needed to shift my weight again. What was I doing here? Why did I need to see him? He'd made it clear that he didn't want me. "The devil's daughter," he'd called me, right before he hustled me outside into the rain.

I'd stood near this very bush, crying, hoping he'd change his mind when his temper cooled, but knowing he would not. Then, like now, I knew I would never be forgiven for making Mama's corpse come to life. I was an unholy abomination against God, according to my father. He should know, being a vicar.

I was about to get up when the gate squeaked. I peered through the shrubbery leaves to see a gentleman in a gray suit closing it. He was of medium height and slender build, with brown hair poking out from beneath his top hat. I caught only a glimpse of his face, but it was enough to know that he was about forty with a strong jaw and nose. I didn't recognize him, so if he was a parishioner, he must be new to the area.

I couldn't leave now. I might catch a glimpse of my father. Perhaps it was foolish to want to see a man who did not want to see me, yet I did. I never claimed to be anything but a fool.

The stranger knocked, and the housekeeper opened the door. The stranger introduced himself, but all I heard was "Doctor," the rest was taken by the wind. Was father ill? I was trying to decide how I felt about that when the housekeeper asked him to wait then disappeared. A moment later, *he* appeared in her place. Father.

Emotion washed through me like tidal waves, threatening to overwhelm me. First happiness at seeing him alive and healthy, then sadness that he didn't want me, and finally anger for the manner in which he had disowned me at the age of only thirteen. I'd heard much later that he told his parishioners I'd been kidnapped. The police had even searched for me. I wondered how long a person needed to be missing for them to be declared dead. Did I even officially exist anymore?

My emotions and thoughts stopped tumbling in all directions with the next words spoken by the stranger. "I'm seeking a particular girl of eighteen years of age. I believe one lives here."

The look on my father's face probably matched mine. His mouth opened and closed, wobbling jowls that had gone pale. When he finally found his voice, it came to me clearly across the garden. "You're mistaken. There're no girls here."

He went to shut the door, but the stranger thrust his foot into the gap. I strained to hear. "Are you Mr. Anselm Holloway?"

"Kindly leave my premises," my father said.

"Not until I have answers. I believe you have a daughter, Miss Charlotte Holloway, who is eighteen."

"I told you." My father's voice had taken on that stern, commanding tone he used in his sermons, and when banishing daughters. "There are no girls living here. Kindly remove yourself from my premises, Doctor."

For one long moment I thought the stranger would force his way into the house, but he did as asked and removed his foot. My father slammed the door and the doctor walked back down the footpath. I was sure to get a better look at him this time. He was quite handsome, for a man of middle age, with the smooth face of someone who spent most of his time indoors. He wore his whiskers very short and only on the sides. The flecks of gray in them gave him an air of authority that his soft cheeks did not.

Should I announce myself to him now, or wait until I could slip away from the house undetected and catch up further along the street? I abandoned the idea altogether when I saw his eyes. They were filled with fury. Rage pulsed from him with every determined step. The muscles in his jaw twitched and his lips peeled back from his teeth as he muttered something under his breath that I couldn't quite hear. He uncurled one fist to open the gate then slammed it shut behind him. He stalked off down the pavement, stopping a few feet away to cast a piercing glare back at my father's house. Then he continued on, around the corner, and was gone from sight.

No, I would not reveal myself to him yet. Not until I knew if he was as dangerous as he looked.

I considered how best to find out more about him as I walked back to Clerkenwell. Perhaps the housekeeper would tell me his full name if I asked. But she might alert Father to my visit. Perhaps I could return to the house tomorrow and wait again. The doctor might also return, looking for me. I could then follow him home and question his neighbors as to his nature.

But what if he caught me and was indeed up to no good? I had the horrible feeling that his searching for me was connected to the gossip my gang had been hearing that morning, and the thing I'd done in the Highgate holding cell. It might be wise to avoid him and lay low for a while. Or leave the gang altogether.

Yes. I would do it that afternoon, while there was still enough daylight. After I retrieved my few belongings, I would set off and get far away from Clerkenwell and Stringer's gang.

I pulled the loose boards back from the hole in the wall, but someone blocked the entrance from the other side. Stringer came through, followed by Finley and the others. They spilled onto the street like rats escaping a sinking ship via the porthole.

"This is him!" Stringer shouted.

I blinked at him. "Who're you talking to?"

"You need to come with us." Someone gripped my elbow, but not hard. It was easy enough to wrench free.

I spun round and backed away from the two burly men. "Don't touch me," I snapped.

One of them held up his hands. "Apologies, boy, but we need to speak to you."

"No, he needs to come with us," the other man countered with a roll of his eyes. He was a little taller than the first fellow, and a lot uglier. His features were put together like a roughly hewn cliff beneath the craggy ridge of his brow. A curved scar sliced across his cheek and pulled down the corner of one eye. His small mouth and thin lips seemed out of proportion to the rest of him.

"Right," said the first man. His handsome face was a stark contrast to his friend's. Fair hair flopped down from beneath his hat and fell into wide gray eyes that blinked at me without guile. He smiled a dazzling smile. "Come on, lad. We'll see that you get a hot meal." He sniffed and wrinkled his nose. "And a bath."

"I don't want food and a bath," I said, hoping they couldn't detect my lie. "I want to know where I'm going and why."

"Can't tell you that," said the bigger man. "Orders are to bring you back."

They seemed harmless enough, and the offer of food and a bath sounded wonderful. Too wonderful. I'd heard of street children being lured into slavery and prostitution in just such a manner. I lived by the rule that if something sounded too good to be true, it usually was. That rule had kept me safe so far, and I wasn't about to abandon it now.

"Why me?" I asked them. Had they heard what had happened in the holding cell? If so, how had they traced me here so quickly? Money must have changed hands, and a few key questions asked of the right people. The police weren't well enough connected, so these fellows weren't officials. Whoever they were, I doubted they had good intentions.

"Dunno," said the ugly one with a shrug of his heavy shoulders. "We just carry out orders."

Convenient. "What did they offer you to rat on me?" I asked Stringer.

"Enough." Stringer shoved me in the back. "Go on. Go. We don't want you round here no more. You're trouble, Charlie, and your freak tricks will bring more people to our den if you don't bugger off. Word's out now, so you gotta go. Right, lads?"

"Right," chimed in the other boys, even Mink. I shot them all withering glares then turned back to the two newcomers. They'd taken a step closer to me and they held themselves tense, as if ready to spring. If I were going to avoid being caught, I would have to be quick.

"I'm not going anywhere with you until you tell me why," I said.

The ugly one blew out an exasperated breath. "Bloody hell, stop being a stubborn little turd and just come with us."

The pretty one rolled his eyes. "What my friend is trying to say is that we mean you no harm."

"Unless you don't copperate."

"It's co-operate, idiot, and well done. You've just made the boy soil his trousers."

"I'm not afraid of you," I told him.

"You should be. Death won't be as civil as us."

Death? They meant to kill me if I didn't go with them?

Pretty held up his hands. "I didn't mean to frighten you, lad, but—"

"Bloody hell," muttered Ugly. "We ain't got time for this. Grab him and let's go. Death'll have our guts if we take too long."

"Death will come and do the job himself, like he always does when you mess up."

"Me?"

I turned and ran.

"Jesus," growled Pretty. "Get back here! It won't go well for you, that way."

Their footsteps pounded behind me, but they were slow and I managed to streak ahead. "*You* should've grabbed him," I heard Ugly say.

"You're not in charge here, I am."

"You bloody well are not. He is."

"He's not here!"

"Oh yeah? Who's that, then, eh?"

Just as he said it, I tripped over something thrust in my path. I landed on the pavement on my hands and knees, scraping off several layers of skin. There was no time to wallow in the pain or assess the damage. I scrambled up, only to find two strong hands clamping down on my arms, pinning them to my sides. I struggled, but it was useless. The man behind me was far stronger. I stopped struggling to lull him, but his grip didn't relax. Damn, damn and hell. I heard Ugly and Pretty approaching and knew I had to act immediately or it would be three against one.

I kicked backward, smashing my foot as hard as I could into my captor's shin, then jerked my head back hard. Unfortunately, his height worked against me and I only managed to hit ribs instead of a throat, chin or nose. The kick earned a sharp intake of breath from my abductor, but otherwise he didn't make a sound. Nor did he loosen his grip.

I was out of ideas. I was good at avoiding capture—usually—but not so good at freeing myself afterward. The panic seizing my breath and overriding my brain wasn't helping either. Should I scream? Would anyone come to my rescue if I did?

Instinct took over and I struggled again, trying to wrench myself free. But that only made his fingers dig further into my flesh with bruising strength.

"Stay still," he snarled, in a voice that welled up from the depths of his chest.

"Or what?" I was pleased that I sounded defiant. If I couldn't have my liberty, I could at least hold onto some dignity.

"Or I'll be forced to hurt you."

As if he wasn't already.

"Want me to shoot him, sir?" That was Ugly's voice.

"Idiot," said Pretty. "What'll that achieve?"

"His copperation."

"Doubt he'll feel very *co-operative* with a bullet wound."

The grip of the man holding me changed, but before I could use the opportunity to my advantage, I was rendered immobile once more. He wrenched my arms behind my back and pinned them there.

I winced as pain shot down to my wrists and numbed my fingers. "You're hurting me!"

The man they called Sir didn't answer.

"To be fair, he did warn you," said Pretty.

Ugly snorted a laugh.

Sir shoved me forward, but I refused to walk. I wasn't going to make this easy for him.

"Move," he said, his voice surprisingly calm in my ear.

I pulled my knees up so that my feet were clear of the pavement. He didn't so much as grunt with the effort of suddenly taking all my weight. I, however, gasped as my arms screamed in agony and my left shoulder popped out of its socket. I bit my lip to stop myself crying out and tried kicking again, but it only served to put more pressure on my already burning arms and shoulders.

"Fool," Pretty muttered. He appeared in front of me and, walking backward to keep pace, went to push my hair off my face.

I jerked my head from side to side then when that didn't work, spat at him. Ugly laughed.

"Little blighter." Pretty raised a hand to strike me, but Sir's steely, "Don't," stopped him.

"Go on ahead," Sir said. "Let me know if someone comes."

Pretty glared at me then he and Ugly strode off around the corner.

"Stop resisting," Sir said to me. "Nobody wants to harm you."

"Your name Mr. Nobody, eh?" I laughed at my joke although I didn't find it funny. "I'm not going anywhere with you until you tell me what you want with me."

"We can't talk here."

"Then we won't be talking at all, Mr. Nobody."

He continued to carry me forward, only to stop when Ugly's face appeared around the corner. "Gang of rough looking types coming this way!"

A gang? They might be willing to help me, but it was unlikely. Most of the "rough looking types" in Clerkenwell only helped when there was something in it for them. Yet I had to try and get them on my side. I could claim Sir and his men were police. "Rough looking types" hated the constabulary. I opened my mouth to scream, but before a sound came out, Sir clamped a large hand over my mouth *and* my nose. He pulled me back against his body, one arm now bracing me around my waist, still pinning my arms, the other smothering me.

I couldn't breathe. I couldn't move to scratch at his hand. The harder I tried to breathe, the quicker I used up the remaining air in my lungs. My chest burned, my throat closed, and blackness crept in from the edges of my vision.

He was going to kill me and there wasn't a thing I could do about it. Fog clouded my thoughts. I felt my strength drain away. He finally let me go, but I could not have run even if I'd had my wits about me.

The darkness swallowed me. I felt my body being lifted, but I was unsure if it were by human arms or the Reaper's, come to take my soul to the afterlife. All I did know was that everything was about to change.

CHAPTER 2

I didn't need to open my eyes to know that I was inside a coach. It had been many years since I'd ridden in one but the rocking sensation was unmistakable, as was the subtle scent of the leather seat on which I lay. My hands and feet were tied and I lay on a bench seat, facing forward. My shoulder still hurt, but not as badly as before. It had popped back into the socket while I was unconscious. By luck or by my captors?

At least one of them was with me in the cabin. I could hear soft breathing and feel a gaze upon me. My hair still covered half my face, reaching past my nose. A small mercy.

"I wasn't expecting him to put up a fight." That was Pretty's cultured voice, coming from the seat opposite. Unless he was talking to himself, there must be another beside him.

Nobody answered.

"The lad's got some fire in his belly," Pretty went on. He paused, yet there was still no response from his companion. I suspected it was the one they called Sir then, not Ugly. Ugly was more talkative. "Do you think he'll have answers?"

"Some." Yes, definitely Sir. I recognized his rich, velvety tones.

"Do you think he knows where she is?"

She? Who was he talking about?

"Perhaps," Sir said.

Pretty grunted. "Think he'll tell us where to find her, if he does?"

"I'll see to it."

A cold lump of dread lodged in the pit of my stomach. He had no qualms rendering me unconscious to capture me, so what methods would he employ to get answers? Answers to what? I didn't know the whereabouts of any missing women—

Unless he meant me, Charlotte Holloway. If so, it seemed he hadn't connected Charlie the boy to Charlotte the missing girl. Yet. I needed to get away from him as soon as possible, before he worked it out. With my hands and feet tied, escape was not going to be easy.

The men didn't speak for some time and the silence between them felt awkward. They weren't friends then, but more likely master and servant. A good ten or fifteen minutes passed before the leather seat creaked beneath the shifting weight of one of them.

Pretty cleared his throat. "Odd that he hasn't woken up yet."

"He's awake," Sir said.

How had he known?

The leather seat creaked again and I felt warm breath on my chin. I opened my eyes, startling Pretty. "How long have you been awake?" he asked.

I didn't answer. I didn't want him knowing I'd overheard their conversation.

The man sitting beside him spoke instead. "Since we drove off."

Sir was not what I expected. He was strikingly handsome, although he seemed to want to downplay his good looks. His black wavy hair reached to his shoulders, a few errant strands spilling over one sharp cheek. No gentleman I'd ever seen kept his hair that length or in such disarray. Nor was the hair on his face the latest fashion. Instead of being styled and oiled to a sheen, it shadowed his jaw as if he'd forgotten to shave for two days. If he didn't wear such a fine, well-fitting suit, I would not have thought him a gentleman at all. He didn't even wear a hat or gloves.

I sat up, which was not an easy task, trussed up as I was. Neither man assisted me. I shrank into the corner then remembered I was trying to look defiant and unafraid. I tilted my chin and stared into Sir's black, black eyes.

That was a mistake. He met my gaze with his own fiercely direct one, and I felt like I was being sucked into a well so endless it would take a lifetime to reach the bottom. He gave away nothing through his eyes, yet I felt he could see everything in mine. Surely he must know I was not who I claimed to be. I wanted to look away before he saw too much, but I could not. He was much too compelling.

It was only because the carriage slowed that I was released. He glanced out the window and my own gaze followed. We drove through a set of enormous iron gates spiked with spearhead finials, then along a drive. Lawn carpeted the landscape, the occasional tree or shrub interrupting the smooth surface. I craned my neck and finally caught a glimpse of our destination as we rounded a gentle bend.

I gaped at the mansion. It sat atop a low rise like a crow with wings spread out in either direction. The building was a mad collection of shapes. Tall, narrow pinnacles shot from the centers of square towers positioned between the triangular gables and rectangular chimneys. But it was the central tower that caught my attention. At almost twice the height of the rest of the house, it was an imposing entrance. Beneath the three cones at its crown was a small window, then nothing but dark stone plunging down to the large arched door. Rapunzel wouldn't look out of place in that high window, but it would take more than a lifetime for her hair to grow long enough to reach the ground.

I recoiled and suppressed a shiver. Sir watched me with those all-seeing eyes of his. His expression remained cool, detached, unreadable. It was unlikely he cared what I thought about our destination, unless he could use that fear against me.

"Is this Bedlam?" I asked. I could well imagine the mansion was the infamous insane asylum. It looked bleak enough to house those miserable, mad people. People like me.

Pretty snorted. "An apt assessment, but no."

The coach pulled to a stop and Sir opened the door himself. No servants emerged from the house to do it for him. The cabin dipped as he stepped off, then dipped again as someone jumped down from the driver's seat.

Ugly came into view beside Sir. "How's he going to walk with his feet all bound up like that?"

"You're going to carry him," Pretty said.

Ugly looked to Sir, but he merely walked off. "Put him in the tower room," he said. "See that he's fed and bathed."

"Don't just stand there, pizzle head." Pretty signaled to Ugly. "Come get him."

Ugly grimaced, revealing two rows of broken, jagged teeth. "Why don't you do it?"

"Because I'm in charge, and the one in charge doesn't do any hard labor."

"You're not in charge, Death is." Ugly jerked his head at the retreating figure of Sir. They called him Death behind his back and Sir to his face? I wondered if he knew.

"I'm second in command, and since he's no longer here, I am in charge. Grab the little blighter and get him up to the tower room."

Ugly sighed and reached for me. I scooted along the seat into the back corner. "I'm covered in lice," I told him.

Ugly scratched his bushy sideburns. "Do I have to touch him, Seth? Couldn't we just untie him and let him walk up?"

"And risk him running off? I'd like to see you explain that to Death." Pretty—Seth—grabbed my arm and dragged me to the cabin door. Without warning, he shoved me into Ugly's waiting hands.

The big man caught me easily. "You stink."

I managed to dig my elbow into his ribs and received an *oomph* for my troubles. "Compared to your sweet smell, you mean?"

Seth chuckled. "I think I'm going to like you, lad."

"Don't get too attached to him." Ugly hoisted me under his arm and carried me toward the house like a roll of fabric. "Death'll get what he wants out of him then send him back to the sewer."

"What information is that?" I spat.

"Stop moving," Ugly said. His arm tightened around me and I thought he'd cut me in half.

"You're hurting me!" I wriggled and kicked out with my bound legs, but connected with nothing but air.

"Calm down, lad," Seth said. "Co-operate and you will not be harmed. Fight and it will not go well for you. Death doesn't like it when his orders aren't followed."

"I don't have to follow his orders. He's not my master."

"Yet he will get what he needs from you nevertheless. He's good at that."

I gulped at his ominous tone as much as the promise in his words. I imagined the man they called Death extracting my real name from me with the use of medieval torture devices. He probably kept them in the dungeon. Surely a place as grim as the one we were now entering had a dungeon, with walls so thick that no one would hear my screams.

"What you shivering for, boy?" Ugly said, hoisting me higher on his hip. "It ain't cold."

"This is uncomfortable," I told him. "Can't you put me down and let me walk?"

"No," Seth said.

"Where are we?"

"Lichfield Towers."

"Are we still in London?"

"Yes. Highgate."

I knew Highgate had some big homes, but estates of the scale of this one weren't common. I could picture only two that I knew of, both behind high fences and rows of trees. Now that I thought about it, the front gate had looked familiar. We weren't too far from the cemetery.

Knowing my location buoyed me somewhat. If I did escape, finding my way back to Clerkenwell wouldn't be too difficult. The first thing I'd do when I returned to our basement Hell would be gather my few belongings and find a new place to live, somewhere where nobody knew me. Somewhere far away from Stringer and his gang.

I got to see very little of my surroundings, facing downward as I was. The floor tiles in the entrance hall were mostly covered by a crimson Oriental rug and the walls were paneled in dark wood. Ugly carried me up a grand staircase, his footfalls deadened by a carpet runner. Despite being daytime, the lack of windows meant it was dark in the stairwell without the chandelier lit. We continued up and up, Seth following behind us. We passed many doors, all closed, until we finally reached what must have been the highest room in the central tower.

Seth slipped past us and pushed open the door. The room was larger than I expected, with more furniture than I'd seen in one place for a long time. Still, it was bare compared to my childhood room in Tufnell Park. It contained only a small bed, a dresser, table and chair. There were no knickknacks on the table or dresser, no pictures adorning the deep red walls, and the bedspread was plain gray. Yet I loved the room. Once Ugly and Seth left, I would be alone inside four walls for the first time in an age. It was a luxury I'd feared never to experience again.

Not that I would experience it for long this time. If I could tie together the sheets and blankets, I wouldn't need Rapunzel's hair. I could simply attach one end to the bed and climb out the window. I glanced at the window and bit my lip. Perhaps not. It was a long way down.

Ugly dropped me onto the bed. I bounced on the mattress and had to suppress a smile before they saw it. The mattress was *soft.*

"How're we supposed to bathe him up here?" Ugly said.

"I don't need a bath."

"Smelled yourself lately?"

Seth looked me over and I made sure to keep my face dipped so that my hair hid it. "You stink worse than Gus."

"Oi!" Gus protested. "I ain't that bad."

"Besides, our orders are to get you bathed."

My face flushed and I was glad my hair covered it. My filth was a foolish thing to be ashamed of, but I couldn't help it. My mother had been a stickler for cleanliness, scrubbing my skin with carbolic soap and my fingernails with a slice of lemon every day. She would have a fit if she saw the grime that had been deeply ingrained into my nails and skin now.

"Fetch a washstand and bowl of water," Ugly—Gus—said.

"It won't be enough," Seth said. "The water will be black before he's even half clean."

"Take him to the bathroom and fill up the tub."

"The bathroom's two levels down. Besides, Death didn't tell us to take him to the *bathroom.* He said to bring him here."

"Then what'll we do?"

"A jug of water and a bowl will do me well enough," I said, sitting up. "There's no need to bother with a bath."

Seth jerked his head at Gus. "You get it. I'll strip those rags off him."

"No!"

They both blinked at my vehemence. "Why not?" Gus asked. "You ain't got nothing we ain't seen before. Only smaller." He chuckled as his gaze focused on my crotch.

"You'll be perfectly safe with us," Seth said, somewhat soothingly. "Neither of us care what you look like."

They would if they knew I looked like a girl. "I've got scars. I don't like folk seeing them."

"Me too." Gus began to unbutton his jacket. "I'll show you mine first. Ain't no reason to hide scars. Shows you're a fighter."

"Or careless, in your case." Seth's eyes gleamed with humor. I almost found myself smiling along with him.

"Weren't my fault the water got spilled." Gus didn't continue to unbutton his jacket, nor did he do them up again.

"No, but it was your fault there was still hot water in the pot. You were supposed to empty it."

Gus gave Seth a rude hand gesture. Seth ignored him and bent to untie me. "Guard the door," he told Gus.

Gus did. He was a solid man, a wall of brawn that I would never get past without a distraction.

"Don't think about running off," Seth said. "Death will get you before you even leave the house."

I tilted my chin. "How will he know I've escaped?"

"He'll know. He knows everything. That's how we found you."

"Death's a machine," Gus chimed in. "And like God, too. A god-machine. Don't push him or he'll come down on you like a ton of bibles."

"He probably knows you just said that," Seth said with a wink at me.

Gus swallowed heavily and glanced around the ceiling, as if looking for the god-machine himself up there.

With my hands and ankles finally free, I felt more human. I stood and walked around the room, checking the drawers in the dresser—they were empty—and looking out the window. Definitely too far to climb down.

"Go get the water," Seth said. "I'll fetch him something to eat."

Gus narrowed his eyes at me. "He'll escape."

Seth grinned and pulled a key out of his waistcoat pocket. "Now, why would he want to leave this comfortable room and return to the sewers anyway?"

"I didn't live in the sewers," I growled at him.

"You lived in a cramped, dark cellar that stank like a sewer. You're better off here, lad. Don't forget it."

"Do I have my freedom here?" I snapped. "Can I come and go as I please? No? Doesn't seem like I'm better off."

Seth's mouth flattened into a sympathetic grimace. Gus shook his head and opened the door. The two of them filed out and quickly shut it again. The lock tumbled and I was left alone.

I suddenly felt weary to the bone. I stared at the bed, so soft and inviting. The pillow was plump too, like a cloud. But it was too clean for the likes of me. I didn't want to get any lice on it. Same with the chair. It was upholstered in nice brocade fabric patterned with gray and crimson flowers.

I stood by the window instead and looked out upon the garden and lawn. Large trees rimmed the edge of the property, and beyond that I could see buildings in one direction and parkland in another. It was a lovely vista, and one I could have happily stared at, yet my stomach wouldn't let me enjoy the view. It churned with worry. The last time I'd been locked away had been the morning before and men had tried to rape me in the police cell. While I didn't think Death and his men had that in store for me, their reasons for abducting me couldn't be good. Nothing associated with my reanimation of dead bodies had turned out to be good, on the two occasions I'd done it. The first time I had been thrown out of my house by my father, and the second time, scary people came looking for me. First the doctor, then Death.

I sank down onto the floor and drew my knees up to my chest. I had a sickening feeling that I wouldn't be going anywhere for a long time.

***

Death visited me after I'd washed and eaten. Seth and Gus allowed me to bathe in private when I asked to be left alone. Still, I didn't undress entirely, nor did I put on the clean clothes provided for me. For one thing, the trousers and shirt were too big. For another, I didn't want to get comfortable at Lichfield Towers. If I succumbed to the comforts, I might never want to leave. And I *had* to leave. Death had something in store for me, the re-animator of corpses. Something I suspected I wanted no part of.

He stood with his back to the closed door, arms folded across his chest. He'd dispensed with jacket, tie and waistcoat, and the informality made him seem less like a gentleman and more like a wastrel. Indeed, his dark, disheveled looks wouldn't have been out of place on a carnival gypsy.

"What's your name?" he asked me.

I scowled at him from my position by the window. I'd not yet sat down on the chair, since I hadn't changed out of my filthy clothing, and I stood with my arms crossed over my chest too.

"They called you Charlie."

I wished I'd gone by a name that wasn't so close to Charlotte. Fortunately, Death didn't seem to notice the similarity. Perhaps I'd been mistaken, and he wasn't looking for me—Charlotte Holloway—after all, but another girl that he thought I knew.

"My name is Lincoln Fitzroy," he went on.

"I thought it was Death." I didn't care if my retort got Seth and Gus into trouble. They were nothing to me.

One corner of Fitzroy's mouth twitched in what would have been a smile on anyone else. On him, it was probably just a twitch. His face didn't lighten in any other way, but remained stern. I wondered if the man ever smiled or laughed. I doubted it.

"Are you going to kill me, Mr. Death?"

"That would be foolish, since I want answers from you."

"And if I refuse to answer? Will you kill me then?"

"Have I given any indication that I would?"

"You nearly killed me when you kidnapped me."

"You were not in danger."

"I fainted from lack of air! How could you have known I wouldn't die?"

"Ladies faint all the time and do not die."

I recoiled. Did he suspect? I dipped my head to ensure my face remained covered by my hair. "I am not a lady."

"Clearly." He came toward me and regarded me levelly. "I know how long a person your size can be deprived of air before death takes him."

"How do you know? Trial and error?"

He lifted a hand. I ducked out of his reach and put my arms up to shield my face.

"I only want to get a better look at your face," he said.

That was precisely why I'd darted away, but I realized my action could have been mistaken for fear that he'd hit me. "This ain't right," I told him. "You can't keep me here."

"Who will stop me?" He shrugged one shoulder. "Nobody will look for you. Your friends gave you up for a few coins. You have no family, no one to worry about you. For all the world cares, you might as well not exist, Charlie Whoever You Are."

Tears burned the backs of my eyes. He was right, but hearing it put so baldly stung. I was truly alone. Not a single soul cared whether I lived or died.

Except me. Sometimes, I wasn't even sure why I did care. It wasn't as if I was adding value to society. Even the blond man whose spirit had saved me in the cell had left behind a reputation for defending the weak from bullies. The only impression I would leave behind would be my freakish way of communicating with the dead.

"Tell me how you did it," Fitzroy said.

"I don't know what you're on about, and I don't want to know. Let me go. I don't want to be here."

His gaze flicked to the clothes still folded on the bed and the food I'd left largely untouched. I'd nibbled at the bread and cheese, but the butterflies fluttering in my stomach wouldn't let me eat more. "Is there something else you desire?"

"My freedom."

He waited, as if he expected me to add something of a material nature that he could command Seth or Gus to deliver to my room. "I will grant you your freedom when you tell me how you became a necromancer."

Necromancer. Was that the name for me? It was quite an improvement over devil's daughter. "I don't know nothing about necromancing." I clenched my jaw, folded my arms and sat on the floor.

After a moment, he crouched by my side. I'd not heard his approach. The man was light on his feet. Even more surprising was that he had no smell. No hint of any soap or hair oil, no body odor, nothing. It was the oddest thing, and more unnerving than his quiet step.

"There is another who can bring the dead back to life," he said. "A young woman of eighteen. Are you related to her?"

"I don't know no women, and I ain't related to nobody." I hugged my knees and pressed my forehead against them. "I don't know anything about bringing dead bodies back to life, neither."

Another long pause then, "Where are you from?"

I didn't answer.

"How long have you lived on the street?"

I hugged my knees tighter. He didn't go on and when I glanced up, I saw that he'd moved away. He watched me from the window, his arms once more crossed. The window was on the opposite side of the room to the door—the door that he'd left unlocked.

"He saved you, didn't he?" Fitzroy didn't pose it as a question. "The prisoners were going to hurt you, but the spirit frightened them off by re-entering his body. At your command."

If he knew that much already, what else did he know?

"How did you do it?"

I snorted. "You've got the wrong boy."

"No."

"I don't know what you're talking about."

"You do." He said it with the utmost conviction that I knew I could never get him to doubt himself. "Is it something you've always been able to do?"

"You're a tosspot."

He grunted. "I expect a gutter dweller to come up with something more offensive than that."

"A fucking tosspot."

"Better. Now answer my question." He leaned a hip and shoulder against the wall and glanced out the window. A small frown connected his brows.

His distraction gave me the opportunity I needed. I sprang up and sprinted for the door.

But he reached it first. His palm slammed against the wood at my head height, the sound reverberating around the tower room. I watched him through the curtain of my hair, searching for signs that he would use that hand on me. His only movement was a small tightening of his lips.

"I have tried asking nicely," he said in a voice that was much too calm. "I have fed you and clothed you, provided a soft bed for you."

"I need none of that." It was a bold thing to say, considering the man's nickname was Death, but while I was the person with answers, he wouldn't kill me. That didn't mean he wouldn't hurt me.

He straightened to his full height—an impressive size. Not as tall or broad as Gus, but big nevertheless. It would be easy for him to beat me senseless or break my bones.

I shrank away from him, regretting my impulsive actions and words. It might be wiser to bite my tongue in future.

"Then what do you need?" he said.

I glanced at the door.

"You will be worse off out there than in here."

I shrugged a shoulder.

His black brows drew together and his gaze drilled into me. "Who is out there for you? Who do you want to see again?"

My father.

I edged away from him and sat on the floor again, my back to the wall. I pulled up my knees and curled into the tightest, smallest ball possible. He watched me from beneath that severe brow. His anger seemed to have dissolved somewhat, but I still didn't trust him. He was too quick and too hard to read. He could haul me up by my shirt in a heartbeat and thrash the answers he sought out of me.

A knock on the door made me jerk. "Mr. Fitzroy, sir," said Seth from the other side. "Lord Gillingham is here to see you."

A lord? A real live *lord* was under the same roof as me? I suddenly wanted to look out the window and catch a glimpse of this lord's carriage and horses. I'd wager it was magnificent and the animals fine.

"Tell him I'm unavailable," Fitzroy said.

"Er…" Seth cleared his throat. "He already knows you're in here talking to the boy. Gus told him, not me."

I would not have known Fitzroy was irritated if it weren't for the curling of his right hand into a fist. His face remained unchanged from its glowering severity. Without a word, he opened the door and left. The lock clicked into place, and I was once more a prisoner and alone.

I expelled a long breath and got up to look out the window. A gleaming black coach pulled by two grays was indeed waiting down below. I unlatched the window and pulled up the sash.

"You there!" My loud whisper didn't so much as cause the horses' ears to twitch. "You there!" I called.

The driver glanced around, but seeing no one, shook his head.

"Up here!"

He tilted his head back and touched the brim of his hat in acknowledgment.

"Help me! I am being held prisoner. Tell the—" Not the police. They wanted me over the theft and escape. "You must help me get out!"

The driver merely stared up at me. Then, with a shake of his head, he turned back to the horses. My heart sank. It was hopeless. He probably thought me a mischievous child, having a lark. It would be impossible to convince him otherwise from such a distance.

With a sigh, I picked up the wedge of cheese and bit off the corner. It tasted delicious, not like my usual fare of stale crumbs that even the rats turned their noses up at. I devoured the rest, shoveling it in, unable to eat fast enough.

Then I promptly threw up in the corner. What a waste. I should have opened the window and deposited the contents of my guts on the front steps. That notion made me smile.

The lock clicked in the door. Fitzroy must have finished his business with Lord Gillingham already and come to question me again. I steeled myself and took courage in the fact that he'd not yet hit me.

But instead of my captor, another man entered. I guessed him to be about forty, with rust-colored hair starting high on his forehead and a short beard of a redder hue. He cut a fine form in a dark suit, with shoes polished to a high sheen and a gold watch chain hanging from his waistcoat pocket. He clutched a walking stick in one hand, and I caught a glimpse of the tiger shaped head as he adjusted his grip. It wasn't his clothing that told me he was Lord Gillingham, however, but his bearing. His body was ramrod straight, his mouth turned down in disapproval, and his head tilted back so that he looked down his nose at me, even though he wasn't very tall. Fitzroy may be a gentleman, but this man was a cut above—and he knew it.

"Close the door," he said over his shoulder to Gus.

Gus and Seth, standing in the hallway outside the room, frowned at one another, then Gus closed the door. I was alone with the stranger.

I debated whether I should bow to Lord Gillingham, nod, or take his hand. I was still trying to remember the proper etiquette for when a boy met a lord—and whether I wanted to conform—when he spoke.

"You are the child." He sounded as if his mouth were full of strawberries that he didn't want to spill. It was quite ridiculous. I had to press my lips together to suppress a laugh.

"Don't see no other in here, do you?" I said.

"My lord."

"Name's Charlie, but 'my lord' will do just as well." I winked, warming to my bit of fun. Mimicking and mocking the upper classes had always been a popular pastime in the slums, no matter if it were Stringer's gang or any of the others I'd lived with over the years.

Gillingham's wide nostrils flared and his pale blue eyes flashed. "Do not play the fool with me."

"Yes, my lord." Perhaps riling him wasn't a good idea when he could prove an ally. I knelt on the carpet and clutched my hands together. "Please, my lord, will you help me? The man named Fitzroy has kidnapped me and is keeping me prisoner here. Against my will," I added when he gave no sign of concern or surprise.

He stalked around the room, pinching his nose when he spotted my sick, then came back to stand in front of me. "He tells me you have not yet answered any of his questions."

I went to stand, but he poked his walking stick into my shoulder. "Stay."

"I am not a dog," I spat.

His top lip curled up. "No. A dog would do as his master bid and be thankful for what he's been given. People like you are fit only for picking up the shit of dogs."

Charming fellow, although hearing "shit" said in his toff accent was quite amusing. Stringer and the others would laugh if I mimicked this conversation for them.

"Where is the girl?" he asked.

"I already told Mr. Fitzroy, I don't know no girls, I ain't got no relatives, and I don't know what happened in no prison cell. My answers ain't changed."

"Not yet."

"Huh?"

His top lip curled again and he circled me slowly. He didn't lean on his stick, and I wondered why he carried it. It was part of his nobleman's image, I supposed, like the accent and sneer. "Fitzroy is too lenient this time," he said quietly, as if speaking to himself. "I do not pretend to understand why, when a good beating ought to produce answers. He rarely shows mercy, so why start now?"

I gulped. "Where is Mr. Fitzroy?"

"I will ask the questions. Where are you from? Who are your parents?"

I swiveled to keep him in my sights.

His face turned pink then a mottled red, and his lips quivered. "Answer me!"

I clenched my jaw and held the man's gaze with my own. I would not let him intimidate me. He might be a lord, but he wasn't my master. "Buckingham Palace, and her majesty the queen. I call her Mum."

The walking stick smacked across my back. I arched forward and gasped as hot pain bloomed. I gathered my nerves and steadied my breathing to control the agony. If I let it rule me, I would give in, and I didn't want to give in to this man. I went to stand, but he shoved me so hard with his boot that I fell onto my side. I scrambled away, but he followed me, stick raised. Glacial eyes pinned me to the carpet as thoroughly as his boot did.

"I'll ask again," he snarled. "Where are you from and who are your parents?"

I hesitated, trying to think of the ramifications if I told him the truth about my Tufnell Park home and Father. But I couldn't think. The fierce pumping of blood through my veins and the knot of anxiety in my stomach were playing havoc with my mind.

He raised the stick again and I braced myself. It cracked across my shoulder with bruising force. He raised it again and I scampered further, only to hit the wall. Gillingham stalked toward me like a hunter tracking his prey. With a gleam in his eye, he brought the cane down on me again. And again. And again.

CHAPTER 3

I endured each blow, managing to protect my face, but my left arm, shoulder, side and leg took the full force of his strikes.

And then they suddenly stopped.

"What the blazes are you doing, Fitzroy?"

I peeked through my fingers to see Fitzroy holding the stick and glaring at Gillingham like he wanted to smash him with it. I hadn't heard him enter. Over by the door, Gus and Seth stared like simpletons at the lord and their master, their lips apart, their eyes wide.

I wiped my tears and snot on my sleeve to remove the evidence of my fear and pain. But I couldn't stop the shaking.

"Don't touch him," Fitzroy said in a low voice that I had to strain to hear.

Gillingham tugged on his jacket lapels and tilted his chin even further. "The ministry hasn't become what it is today without laying a corrective hand or two on little rats like him."

"He is a child." Fitzroy spoke through a jaw so tight that it barely moved.

Gillingham wrinkled his nose at me. "Children are capable of duplicitous thoughts and behavior, just as adults are. Children like that one are vermin, not fit for the comforts you offered him. Of course he won't tell you anything useful. Look at that." He nodded at the clothes still folded on the bed, untouched. "He doesn't want to help himself. Filthy creatures like him are a scab on a decent, God-fearing society. He even threw up the food you provided, the ungrateful little wretch."

The angles on Fitzroy's face sharpened. His eyes narrowed to pinpoints. The air in the room stretched thin, taut. I held my breath, waiting for his temper to explode. "I am in charge of the ministry now, and I say how we treat our informants." Fitzroy's voice was cool and ominously quiet.

Either Gillingham didn't fear his temper, or he wasn't terribly observant, because he didn't back out of the room as I would have done if I were him. He straightened and squared his shoulders. "You are only in charge because the committee put you there. And the committee do as *I* say, Fitzroy."

"No."

"No?" Gillingham spluttered a humorless laugh. "What is that supposed to mean?"

"It means that you need to get out of Lichfield Towers before I turn your stick on you."

Gillingham did take a step back then. His gaze flicked from the stick to Fitzroy's menacing face, where it settled with renewed determination. "You get above yourself again, *Fitzroy*. Do not forget who I am, and do not forget what I know. I can crush you."

"Seth," Fitzroy said.

Seth stood to attention. "Yes, sir?"

"See that Lord Gillingham finds his way safely to his coach."

"Certainly, sir." Seth didn't bat an eyelid at the tense exchange, but Gus, just behind him, gawped openly as Gillingham and Fitzroy glared daggers at one another.

Seth cleared his throat. "My lord, the, er, stairs are this way."

Gillingham pushed past the men without a backward glance at me. "The committee will hear of this!" His heavy footsteps echoed for some time until they muted into nothing.

The tension in the bedroom relaxed somewhat, but a sense of awkwardness lingered. Or perhaps it was me who felt awkward, as all eyes focused on me now. I wished they would ignore me. I preferred to go undetected, blending in with the other boys when I could, or simply vanishing altogether when I could not. This attention was far too unnerving.

"He forgot his stick," Gus said with a nod at the cane still in Fitzroy's hand. "Not that he needed it. Bloody toff walked out of here without a limp."

Fitzroy had been watching me from beneath lowered lids, but now he grasped the stick with both hands and snapped it over his knee. He opened the window and threw both pieces out.

Someone below cursed loudly. I hoped it was Gillingham.

Fitzroy shut the window. "Help him out of his shirt."

"Don't come near me," I snarled at Gus and Seth.

Seth frowned, but Gus approached. He reached for the top button on my shirt. I slapped his hand away.

"I'm only trying to help!"

"Don't come near me," I said again.

"I ain't going to hurt you, Half Pint," Gus said. "Just get your shirt off and let us look at your sores." He reached for me again and this time I grabbed his hand and bit it.

He yelped and went to slap me. I jerked away and he made no connection. It was just an empty threat.

"Leave him," Fitzroy said.

"I weren't going to hit him," Gus grumbled. "Just scare him into doing as he's told."

"Fetch clean water, a salve and bandages."

Seth hurried out of the room. Gus regarded me with hands on hips. "Saying we get him to take his own shirt off, do you think he'll let you tend his wounds, sir? I wish Lady Harcourt were here," he added before Fitzroy answered. "She'd know how to get the lad to trust us."

A lady? That was all I needed—another bloody toff. I'd only met one, but that had proved to be enough for me to thoroughly dislike the lot of them. "I can tend my own wounds," I said before one of them got ideas that they would do it.

"You cannot *see* all your wounds," Fitzroy said.

"I don't need to."

Fitzroy's eyes narrowed. "Help him stand."

Gus came forward, but I put my hand up. "I don't need help."

To prove my point, I got to my knees. Pain spiked through my body and made my head spin. I put a hand to the wall and concentrated on controlling my breathing. Everything hurt, but I couldn't let the men know, or Fitzroy would insist on inspecting my wounds.

The breathing helped and although the pain didn't lessen, I could endure it. I got to my feet and raised my brows in triumph at Fitzroy.

"Sit on the bed," was all he said.

I eyed the bed. "I have lice."

Gus pulled a face and scratched his head.

"That's why you were given clean clothes," Fitzroy said. "Remove your rags and throw them in the fireplace. We'll shave your head. Gus—"

"No!" I inched away from both men. "I'll change into them clothes myself when you're not looking. And you're not touching my hair." I'd had beautiful hair as a child. Long golden curls had reached down to my lower back. Now it was above my shoulders, with a long fringe, and it was light brown. Shaving it off meant losing a little bit more of the real me, as well as losing the veil it provided.

"Why d'you care?" Gus said with a shrug. "It's just hair."

"Can you walk?" Fitzroy asked. I nodded. "Then come with me. Gus, fetch salt from the pantry. Lots of it. And kerosene."

"Cook won't like me taking his salt, sir."

Fitzroy picked up the pile of fresh clothes from the bed then stood by the door. Gus slumped out and I followed at a slower pace that still made me wince as I put pressure on my leg. At least no bones had been broken, but it damn well hurt. Gus trotted down the stairs ahead of us.

"What's the salt for?" I asked Fitzroy.

"Your bath."

"But that'll hurt!"

"And heal."

I stopped and folded my arms, but that only made the bruises down my left side ache more. "I'm not having no salt bath."

"Then you can succumb to either Gus or Seth rubbing salve into your wounds."

"It's just some bruises. Salt won't do much for them."

"There's blood on your back and shoulder."

I tugged the shirt at my shoulder to get a better look at it. There wasn't a lot of blood, but even small cuts could fester.

"You have a choice," Fitzroy said. "A salt bath or Gus will play doctor." He continued down the stairs without watching to see if I followed. "You cannot reach the cuts yourself."

With a sigh, I trailed after him. He was right, and my wounds needed tending, but I couldn't let anyone see my body. "And the kerosene? I ain't putting that on my sores."

"For the lice."

It was what my mother had used on my hair the one time I'd picked up head lice. "I'll need a narrow toothed comb too."

I followed Fitzroy down two flights of stairs and along a corridor. We passed no one, and I heard no sounds of life coming from elsewhere in the house. Gus had mentioned a cook, and the absent Lady Harcourt perhaps lived there, but what about other servants? A house on the scale of Lichfield Towers ought to have footmen and maids, a housekeeper and butler. Perhaps their duties were done for the day and they were downstairs in the service area with the cook. I didn't know the routine of grand households.

In the bathroom, Fitzroy opened the taps and the cast iron tub began to fill with hot and cold water. My father's house didn't have indoor plumbing, and the ease with which the bath was drawn amazed me. I dipped my hand in and suppressed a smile. The water felt wonderfully warm.

Seth arrived with the salve, then Gus brought in a bag of salt and a bottle of kerosene. He added the entire bag to the bathtub as Seth poured the kerosene into the washbasin and added some water. He pulled a comb out of his jacket pocket and placed it on the washstand.

Fitzroy ushered them out. "You will not be disturbed. A guard will remain outside and that window needs a key to unlock it. We are also two floors up with no means of climbing down. There is no escape." With his unspoken warning hanging in the air, he left.

I slid the lock home and stared at the door, half expecting someone to bang on it and order me to open up. Nobody did. Seth and Gus's voices rumbled in conversation as they quietly discussed Gillingham's behavior and Fitzroy's cold ire. I understood that to mean Fitzroy had left.

I washed the hair on my head and nether regions first. The diluted kerosene burned my skin, but I knew it ought to kill any of the crawlies. I didn't rush combing my hair, even though I wanted to climb into the bath. My mother had told me the lice would return if the eggs weren't completely removed. It wasn't easy to de-louse my own hair, even with the mirror, but I was as thorough as possible. I tried not to think about being around lice-infested bedding and children again after I escaped Lichfield. At least I would be itch-free for a few days.

Finally I peeled off my clothes and stepped into the bath. The salt bit into the cuts, but the thought of being clean again was so alluring that I bore down on the pain and plunged in. I gasped as my body burned. It felt like thousands of pins were being stabbed into the cuts. The urge to leap out of the bath was overwhelming, but I resisted. The salt would heal me faster, and I needed to be healed for when I returned to the filthy, germ infested streets.

After a long few minutes, the agony subsided until my cuts merely stung. I embraced it, welcoming the salt into my skin, and closed my eyes. For a long time I simply soaked. My earlier wash in the tower bedroom had taken much of the filth off, but immersing myself in the bath seemed more thorough. I could *feel* years of dirt leaching out of me. I used the exotic smelling soap on my skin and hair until the odor of salt and kerosene no longer filled my nostrils, and then I washed myself again with it.

Earlier, I'd thought bathing would make me too comfortable at Lichfield Towers, but now I wished I hadn't resisted. Surely one bath and a little food didn't mean I would give up my secrets. There was no reason I couldn't enjoy the comforts until I found a way to escape.

I remained in the bath even when the water cooled. Getting out meant returning to the tower room and being questioned by Fitzroy. While he hadn't hurt me, I didn't trust him not to snap when my refusal to answer stretched his patience too thin. I would need to watch him carefully for signs that his hard exterior was about to crack. Keeping my life and my identity safe had meant learning to read even the subtlest of cues given by those around me. Fitzroy, however, was more difficult. He seemed to have few expressions and held himself with stillness. A machine, Gus had called him. I could well see why.

The banging on the door startled me. "Oi!" Gus called. "You drowned or what?"

"Go away!"

"We can't stand round here all day. It's almost dinner time."

Was it that late already? The water was getting cold anyway so I climbed out and dried myself off. I dabbed some of the salve on the cuts I could reach, then finally dressed in the clean clothes. I left my old ones in a puddle in the corner. They were fit only for burning.

I went to adjust my long fringe over my face in front of the mirror, then paused. My skin was no longer dirty and my hair was already drying into waves. I brushed it back with my fingers and stared at the woman in the reflection. There was no way I could fool anyone now that I was clean. My features were too fine and feminine, the plumpness of the thirteen year-old gone. I had changed so much that I hardly recognized myself.

I dipped into an awkward curtsy and smiled at an imaginary gentleman come to ask me to dance. "Why, thank you, sir," I whispered. "My hair is my crowning glory, so everyone says."

I sounded ridiculous. I looked it too with the short ends of my hair sticking out between my fingers. With a sigh, I let it fall back to cover my eyes, cheeks and nose.

"Farewell, Charlotte," I whispered, biting back tears. "It was a pleasure to see you again."

I unlocked the door and held my breath as both Seth and Gus looked me over.

Gus sniffed. "You smell better."

"The clothes are a little big," Seth said. "At least they're clean." He chuckled and ruffled my hair.

I smacked his hand away, but I was relieved that they still saw me as a boy.

"Come on, back to the tower room with you." Gus prodded one of my new bruises and I hissed in pain. "Sorry, Half Pint. Forgot."

They marched me up the stairs and led me back into the tower room. I eyed the bed, this time allowing myself to imagine what it would be like to sink into the mattress.

"Sure you don't want me to check you over, make sure nothing's broken?" Seth asked.

"I'm sure."

"Suit yourself. I'll bring you some dinner soon."

"What d'you think's wrong with him?" I heard Gus whisper to Seth as they left. "Deformed pizzle? Only one plum? Third nipple?"

I didn't hear Seth's response as he shut the door and locked it. It didn't matter what they thought, only that they left me alone. They had, and the bed was calling me. I climbed onto it and peeled back the covers. The sheets smelled like sunshine and lavender, and were as white as snow. I lay down and my head sank into the pillow. Heaven. Nothing had ever felt so soft.

I suddenly felt exhausted. The warm bath, warm room and big bed all conspired against me. There would be no attempted escapes tonight, while my body was weary and half broken. Tonight, there would only be blissful sleep.

Tomorrow, however, was a new day.

***

I woke up to morning sunlight shooting through the crack between the closed curtains. A cold supper sat on the dressing table. I pulled the curtains aside and threw open the window. It was the sort of summer day I used to appreciate when I was a child. Father would drive us to the countryside for a picnic after church, or Mama and I would pick flowers from the garden and take them to poor parishioners along with loaves of bread. I'd forgotten how to enjoy summer since then. Probably because warm days meant the smell from the sewers became overpowering, and the rats and lice multiplied.

I ate the cold beef and carrots, but left the rest. I didn't want to throw up again and I already felt full. Someone had cleaned up the sick from the previous day and set out a clean shirt. I'd have to remember to take it with me when I left.

Seth and Gus came mid-morning. One carried books and the other paper and ink. I almost fell off my chair in my haste to touch them. I took the topmost book from the stack that Gus set down. It was a novel titled *A Study In Scarlet* by Conan Doyle.

It had been an age since I'd held a book. I used to love to read, although Father didn't allow novels at home. It seemed rather scandalous to simply hold one. I wondered what was so wicked about *A Study In Scarlet.* I couldn't wait to find out.

But…*why* were they delivering books to me?

I returned the book to the stack and backed away. "I don't know how to read," I told the men. "I don't know why you'd bring them in here."

Gus flipped through the pages of the novel then carelessly tossed it on the bed. "Death's orders. Don't know why he thinks you'd want 'em. Wasted on you, if you ask me."

"Wasted on you, too," Seth said.

"I can read."

"Barely." Seth turned to me. "Death says you're to have whatever you want."

"I want my freedom."

"Except that."

Gus picked up a cold green bean from my plate, tilted his head back and deposited it like a worm being fed to a bird. "He thinks boys want books and writing paper," he said as he chewed. "I reckon he's forgotten what it were like, being a lad."

"Just because you have no use for these things doesn't mean Charlie doesn't want them." Seth winked at me.

I worried he'd seen my reaction to the book and knew I could read. "I don't want them," I said. "Take them away."

"Can't," Gus said. "Death said to bring 'em to you, so we did." He picked up the plate and headed for the door.

"Wait!"

Both men stopped and blinked at me.

Now that I had their attention, I wasn't entirely sure what I wanted to say to them. No, that wasn't quite right. There was a great deal I wanted to say to them. I just wasn't sure where to *start.* "Where's Mr. Fitzroy?"

"Out."

Good. That was one less person I had to worry about, and going on previous experience, I could outrun Gus and Seth. "Who else is in the house?"

"Never you mind," Seth said before Gus could answer. "You'll only see us while you're in here."

"Who is Lady Harcourt?"

"Death's mistress," Gus said.

Seth slapped Gus's shoulder. "He won't like you telling the lad that."

"The boy's thirteen and been living on the street! He's probably had more girls than you. Unlike you toffs, lads like Charlie and me dipped our wicks soon as we could. Eh, Half Pint? Talk about lovers ain't going to shock you, is it?"

"I wasn't referring to educating the boy in the ways of romantic relationships. I meant Death won't like you calling Lady Harcourt his mistress."

Gus sniffed. "Because she's a toff?"

"Yes, but also because she may or may not be his lover anymore. He seems a little cooler toward her lately."

"Don't know how you know the difference. He's always showed as much warmth as an icicle to anyone, including her, far as I can tell."

"That's because you're an unobservant nitwit."

I only half listened to their bantering. I couldn't stop thinking about Fitzroy having a lover. Like Gus, I couldn't imagine their leader capable of a romantic relationship, as Seth had called it. He seemed as passionate as a stone.

"What is the ministry?" I said, cutting through their bickering.

"Save your questions for Death," Seth said.

"When will he be back?"

"Later."

"And what am I to do until then?"

He nodded at the books. "Teach yourself to read."

The men left. They continued to bicker outside, until one set of footsteps receded. The other must have remained to guard me. I didn't think it necessary, since I was locked in.

I sighed. Escaping would have to wait. Perhaps the next time they delivered provisions, I could slip past them and out through the unlocked door. Until then, I had a book to read.

I pulled the chair over to the door and set it against the wall. I stuffed the spare shirt down the front of the one I wore then sat on the chair to read. I was ready to spring up the moment the door opened.

After the first ten pages, I'd decided to take the book with me when I escaped. My reading was a little rusty, but I managed to follow the story, despite not understanding some of the more complicated words. I read several more pages before the door opened.

"Luncheon is—"

I sprang up, ducked under the tray Seth carried, and darted through the door and past Gus.

"Get him!" Seth shouted.

Gus let out a string of curses that would have made a lady blush, then lumbered down the stairs after me. My bruised left side throbbed in protest, but I outpaced the bigger, slower guard easily enough. I took the stairs two at a time, and leaped over bannister handrails to avoid the landings altogether. On the final flight, I slid down the bannister to the floor.

Momentum propelled me forward toward the front door. I hoped it was unlocked, and that I was fast enough to outrun Gus and Seth and got to the trees before them. Once there, I could hide or climb the fence. I knew how to disappear in Highgate, as long as I wasn't captured before I reached the street.

"Get back here!" Gus shouted. Two sets of footsteps pounded behind me now, but I'd outstripped them by a considerable margin.

I was almost free.

"Halt or I'll shoot."

I glanced toward the voice to see a beautiful woman aiming a small pistol at me. My heart and feet stopped dead.

I was not free.

CHAPTER 4

"Remove the book," the woman commanded. "We don't want him using it as a weapon."

Gus went to snatch the book from my hand, but I refused to give it up. It was a silly thing to worry about, while a gun was pointed at my head, but the thought of permanently losing the book weighed heavily on my heart. With a click of his tongue and an almighty wrench, Gus freed it from my clutches. He tucked it under his arm, where I worried his sweaty pits would stain the cover.

"Bring him into the parlor." The woman turned her back on me. The hand that held the muff pistol dipped into the folds of her lustrous black skirts and came out empty.

Seth and Gus glanced at one another, their brows raised. "Shouldn't we take him back to the tower room, my lady?" Gus asked.

"He will be fine with me." The woman's gliding steps reminded me of a sleek, unhurried cat. Perhaps it was the tight corset that slowed her movements. Having worn the undergarment before my banishment, I knew how restrictive they could be, and going by the woman's tiny waist, she must have her laces tied very tightly indeed. It was so small it was a wonder she could hold up the top half of her body, particularly considering she possessed ripe melons rather than raspberries, as Stringer would say.

"Fetch luncheon for him," she ordered the men. "He may eat while you both guard the exit."

Gus shoved me in the back. I grunted and shot him a glare. He shrugged an apology, which surprised me. Seth returned up the stairs with my book.

Gus and I followed the woman into a small room off the entrance hall. I tried not to gawp at the pale blue and gold wallpaper, thick rug, and spindly-legged furniture that didn't look sturdy enough to hold a man the size of Gus. It was fortunate that he remained near the door.

The woman sat on the sofa and indicated I should sit on one of the cream wingback chairs. I hesitated then sprawled like I imagined a boy would. I'd never had the opportunity to sit on such a luxurious piece of furniture while pretending to be a boy, so I hoped I did it right. Usually sitting took place on floors or low walls, not chairs.

The room was lovely with so many elegant things on the mantel, the walls, and on top of and inside the glass cabinet, but my attention was fully captured by the woman. She perched gracefully on the edge of the sofa, giving her prominent bustle space behind her. Her midnight black hair was arranged in an elaborate style at the back of her head, unhindered by the little hat perched on top. I couldn't determine her age. There was no gray in her hair, no lines marring her smooth, pale skin, and yet her bearing was that of a middle-aged woman, sure of her appeal and without the arrogance of a pretty, pampered girl.

She oozed authority, from the tips of her manicured fingernails to her tilted chin. Coupled with the striking aristocratic bones of her face, her confident air would have intimidated most men; yet her appearance was softened by full lips that curved into a warm smile as she regarded me.

"Do you know who I am?"

"Fat Gut called you 'my lady,'" I said.

"Oi," Gus growled from the doorway. "I ain't fat." He sucked in his stomach and puffed out his chest.

"So I'm guessing you're Lady Harcourt," I finished. I almost added "Fitzroy's lover" just to see what her reaction would be, but held back. I didn't want to be beaten up by yet another member of the aristocracy.

"I am," she said in a lilting voice that held none of the harsh command of earlier. "Your name is Charlie, is it not?"

"T'is, my lady."

"Have they been treating you well?" she asked.

"I'm being held against my will. As if that ain't bad enough, a mad toff beat me black and blue yesterday."

The hint of a smile vanished altogether and she folded her gloved hands one over the other on her lap. "I heard that Lord Gillingham was too heavy handed. It is regrettable."

I snorted. "I'll say it is."

"Have your wounds been tended to?"

"Yes."

"Has Lincoln—Mr. Fitzroy—harmed you in any way?"

"He almost killed me when he kidnapped me." At her surprised look, I added, "I stopped breathing."

Her slender eyebrows lowered. "I dare say he knew what he was doing. He's not in the habit of hurting children, and I'm sure whatever methods he employed were necessary."

She said it as if it were perfectly normal for a man to kidnap a child and render him unconscious in the process. I was beginning to think I'd stepped into another world where such behavior was acceptable. Perhaps it *was* in the upper classes. Or perhaps Lady Harcourt was as mad and dangerous as Fitzroy and Lord Gillingham. I wasn't yet sure what to make of her.

"Do you have comforts in your room?" she asked.

I shrugged one shoulder.

"Ask Lincoln for whatever you desire and he'll do his best to give it to you." Lincoln, not Mr. Fitzroy. Interesting. She blinked wide brown eyes at me. "Tell me about yourself, Charlie."

She was a better interrogator than Fitzroy, I'd give her that. She'd tried to disarm me by asking after my comfort, and offering friendly smiles, then asked an innocuously broad question about myself, rather than one specific to the necromancy incident.

A naive child would have fallen under her spell, but I was no longer naive or a child. "I'm thirteen. I live in Clerkenwell, with Stringer and his gang. I steal to eat and keep warm in winter. I'm good at thieving, that's why they call me Fleet-foot Charlie. I've been told I'm too skinny, but seems to me everyone in the gang is skinny. I thought my hair was dark brown until I washed it yesterday and saw it in the mirror. Turns out it's light brown. My nose has a dint on the tip, which I hate but had forgotten about until yesterday, and my eyes are blue. There ain't no more to tell."

The curve of her lips widened a little more. "What shade of blue?"

"Just blue."

"May I see?"

"No."

"I'd call your hair honey colored, not light brown." She gave a low, throaty chuckle. "We women enjoy these little distinctions."

"I don't care. It's brown."

"Why do you cover your face?"

"I'm ugly."

"Why not allow me to judge?"

I glared at her but it was difficult to know if she noticed through my hair. Fortunately, she didn't ask Gus to pin me down while she pulled the hair off my face.

Seth arrived and deposited the tray with my luncheon on the table next to me. He backed away and joined Gus near the door. I eyed the plate of salad greens, tomato and a wing of poultry.

"You speak well," Lady Harcourt went on. "You've had an education?"

"No," I lied.

"But you can read."

I shook my head. "I was stealing the book, not reading it. I thought it might be worth something."

"I see." She indicated the tray of food. "Don't let me keep you."

"I just ate breakfast." Actually breakfast had been the cold supper from the previous night, but it was more than I usually ate in two days. "I'm not hungry."

Her smile turned a little sad, but I couldn't think why. If she felt sorry for me, it was an odd time to show sympathy for my plight. She'd made sure I wasn't going to leave. If I darted for the window now, would she pull out her pistol again?

"Do you have any questions for me, Charlie?"

I knew everything I needed to know already—these people wanted me because I'd made a dead man walk. The sort of people who knew that yet showed no fear around me weren't ordinary, moral people. There was something as diabolical about them as there was about me.

"Only one question," I said. "Where is Mr. Fitzroy?"

Her rapid blinks were the only sign that my question had taken her by surprise. "He'll be back later this afternoon." It wasn't a direct answer, but I didn't ask again.

The clock on the mantel chimed one and Lady Harcourt stood. "I have an appointment. Seth, please inform Mr. Fitzroy that I'm sorry to have missed him. If he could spare a few moments to visit me, I would be most grateful."

So it seemed she didn't live at Lichfield Towers, although she treated Seth and Gus as her servants and they did her bidding without question.

"Good day, Charlie," Lady Harcourt said. "It was a pleasure to meet you."

She walked off and I saw my chance slipping away from me. I'd taken too long to act. I blamed her lovely, mesmerizing presence. "Wait!" I leapt up and ran after her.

Seth and Gus stepped between us, protecting her, but she didn't seem as worried by my approach as them. "What is it, Charlie? Is there something you'd like to tell me?"

"I...I'd like to kiss your hand, m'lady." It seemed like such a ridiculous thing to request that I blushed. I hoped it made me look innocent and endearing.

It must have worked because she ordered the men to move aside. She extended her gloved hand and I stepped forward, close enough that I brushed against her full skirts. I took the hand and pecked it. The lace of her glove felt scratchy against my lips and her exotic floral scent filled my nostrils. I breathed deeply, committing the smell to memory. I didn't know the names of the different scents that made up her perfume, but I vowed that one day I would learn them.

"Thank you, m'lady," I said, stepping back. "You are very kind and lovely. I wish you only good things."

She laughed softly. "You are quite the flatterer. Be sure to use such sweet words on your lady love."

I dipped my head in a bow, my hands at my back, and watched as she left. Both Gus and Seth's gazes followed her, even though they didn't escort her, and I used their distraction to quickly tuck the little pistol into the waistband of my trousers. I adjusted my shirt to hide it and prayed Lady Harcourt didn't notice it missing from her skirt pocket until she was far from Lichfield Towers.

"Upstairs again with you, Half Pint," Gus said cheerfully.

I walked ahead of them out of the parlor. As we passed the front door, I heard the wheels of a carriage roll away and breathed a sigh.

"You like our Lady Harcourt, eh?" Gus chuckled as we headed up the stairs. "She ain't for the likes of you. Not even if you were ten years older."

"Is she married?" I didn't know why I wanted to know more about the woman. It wasn't like I would see her again. But I found her intriguing. I supposed it was because I'd never met anyone like her before, and it was unlikely I ever would again.

"Widowed," Seth said. "Her husband was Lord Harcourt, from a very ancient and noble line. He was much older than her, and some say she married him for his money and title."

"But you don't?"

"There's never been a whiff of scandal associated with her."

"Why would there be?" Gus said. "She knew which side her bread were buttered on. She'd be a fool to give it all up for a bit of prigging."

Seth rolled his eyes. "Don't be so vulgar, particularly when speaking about Lady Harcourt. She's a true lady, in every sense of the word."

"Except by birth."

"She wasn't noble born?" I asked.

"Nah," Gus said. "School master's daughter. Caught the eye of old Lord Harcourt and got him to the church quick, before his grown children knew what was happening."

"They never said a word against her, though," Seth protested.

"That we know."

"By all accounts, they liked her instantly. One can see why."

"'One can see why,'" Gus mimicked. "One is in love with her, isn't one?"

I saw Seth punch Gus in the shoulder out of the corner of my eye. "You can't know what his family thought of her," I said.

Seth squared his shoulders. "I can and I do. My mother moves in the same circles as the Harcourts." He sighed. "Or used to."

Gus groaned. "Seth's been dying for you to ask about him. Likes to make sure even the prisoners know he's from toff stock."

"There have been other prisoners besides me?"

"Nah. Matter of speech. You're our first."

"That explains why you're not very good jailors," I muttered.

I expected a thump on my arm for my insolence, but Gus only snorted a laugh. Seth didn't seem to have heard me. Although I was curious about his background, and why his circumstances had become so reduced that he'd wound up working as a thug for Fitzroy, I decided not to ask. It was better not to get too friendly with my captors, since I might have to hurt them.

I entered the tower room with a loud sigh, although I was pleased to see *A Study In Scarlet* on the dressing table near the other books. It wouldn't hurt to while away the afternoon reading it. I couldn't use the pistol and attempt an escape with both Seth and Gus in the room. The barrel was single shot. I would have to wait until there was only one of them.

"Don't think about running off this time," Gus warned. "Death ain't going to be happy when he hears of it."

I shrugged. "I don't care."

"You should. He's dangerous when he's in a rage."

"I'm sure he is, but it's not me he'll be angry with. As a prisoner, my duty is to escape. As my jailors, it's your duty to keep me in here. Which one of us failed?"

Gus swallowed. "What d'you think he'll do to us?" he said to Seth.

Seth gave him a smug smile and patted his shoulder. "He won't do anything to me. *I* was holding the tray and didn't have my hands free. You were the one supposedly on guard."

"That ain't fair."

"Life isn't fair. If it were, I'd be spending my evenings deflowering virgins instead of cleaning up the sick of a gutter snipe."

"Ha! You couldn't deflower a flower."

"That doesn't make sense. And I'll have you know, the ladies fell over themselves to get to me when I used to attend balls."

"You had money and a good name, then," Gus said, striding for the door. "Course they're going to throw themselves at you. Weren't nothing to do with that ugly face of yours."

Seth looked offended, and I couldn't blame him. He wasn't ugly in the least. He trailed after Gus. "I'll have you know I had an indecent encounter with a lady three nights ago. And no, I didn't pay her a penny. She gave herself freely to me."

"Gave you the French disease for free, more like." Gus's chuckles faded as he closed the door.

Finally I was alone again. I settled on the bed with the book and removed the pistol from the waistband at my back. I checked the barrel to see if it was loaded—it was—then slid it beneath the pillow beside me. I tried not to think about it and concentrated on the book instead, but it wasn't easy. I'd never shot anyone before.

Despite the apprehension curdling in the pit of my stomach, the afternoon didn't drag. The book was riveting, and I found myself reading as quickly as possible.

The clicking of the key in the lock startled me. How much time had passed? I took note of my page then closed the book and slipped my hand beneath the pillow. The metal of the pistol felt cool in my fingers. My pulse quickened.

Death walked in. His assessing gaze took in the book and my relaxed repose. "You met Lady Harcourt." He did not mention my attempted escape.

"She's very nice."

Behind him, Seth and Gus crowded in the doorway.

"I'm hungry," I said.

"I'll fetch you something from the kitchen." Seth trotted off.

"My chamber pot needs emptying," I told Gus.

He screwed up his nose. "Should've offered to get the food." He slid the pan out from beneath the bed and left the room in much less of a hurry than Gus. I was alone with Fitzroy. With Death.

He moved toward the bed, his long, easy strides bringing him close to me much faster than I anticipated. With my heart in my throat, I pulled the pistol out from under the pillow, aimed at his shoulder and fired.

Next thing I knew, he was sitting on top of my thighs, pinning my wrists to the headboard. I bucked but couldn't dislodge him. I went to butt my forehead into his nose, but he dodged the blow. I hawked up a glob of saliva, but before I could spit it into his face, he'd shifted his weight, lifted me, and threw me face down onto the mattress. He resettled his weight on my legs and pressed a hand into my back. He took the pistol off me. Just like that, I was rendered immobile and defenseless. It had been far too easy for him.

"Lady Harcourt will be pleased to have this returned," he drawled.

A grunt was all I could manage.

Footsteps pounded along the corridor and stopped at the door. Gus and Seth's faces peeped around the corner and, seeing their leader in control, they entered the room.

"We heard a gunshot," Gus said, his eyes huge.

"Sir!" Seth cried. "You're bleeding!"

I'd shot him? He'd not shown any signs of pain or even a little discomfort, nor were his movements hindered. He'd attacked me so fast that I'd not seen him coming. I tried to look back at him to see how badly he was hurt, but the angle was too awkward and he pressed his knee into my lower back, locking me in position.

I sucked air through my teeth as the bruises inflicted by Lord Gillingham flared with pain.

"You should tend to it," Seth went on.

"It's nothing." Fitzroy let me go and climbed off the bed. A patch of blood bloomed on his shoulder, but it was hardly a significant amount. "Go." He spoke to the men but didn't take his gaze off me. His eyes were like two pools of black ice.

Gus and Seth exchanged glances then left the room again. They shut the door.

I scooted back up the bed, as far away from him as possible. When it came, his retaliation would be swift and brutal. I braced myself.

"Your hands shook."

I blinked slowly. "Wh-what d'you mean?"

He balanced the weapon on the flat of his palm. "You didn't hesitate and your gaze was focused, but your hands shook. If they'd been steady the bullet would have hit my throat."

I hadn't been aiming for his throat, but his shoulder. My aim had been better than he thought, but not good enough. The bullet must be lodged somewhere in the wall. "You moved. If I didn't hesitate, how did you know I was going to shoot?"

"I can't give away all my secrets."

All? So far, he'd given away nothing. "So I am to remain your prisoner. I have tried escaping, twice today, and yet here I am. What will you do to me?"

Despite his bleeding shoulder, he remained standing. Perhaps he thought sitting was a sign of weakness. "I will not *do* anything to you, child."

I was beginning to hate it when he called me that. Nobody called me "child" anymore. Not since I was a thirteen year-old girl. "Then you will let me go?"

"No."

"Then what?"

"I will wait."

"For what? For Hell to freeze over? Because that's when I'll give you answers, and not before."

"I'm a patient man, Charlie, but the situation requires some urgency. The lives of British citizens are in danger, perhaps the life of the queen herself."

I snorted. "You think that ridiculous fairytale will have me telling you anything?"

"I thought you said you had nothing more to tell me."

Damn. "I don't. You're wasting your time and mine."

"Have an appointment to keep?"

I gave him a withering glare. His expression didn't change from his usual bland one.

"I returned to Clerkenwell today," he said. "I spoke to your friends."

"They're not my friends."

After a moment he said, "I'm glad you realize that. They were quick to tell me what I wanted to know."

"You gave them money."

"Not much."

I folded the book in my arms against my chest. "And what did they tell you?"

"They told me where they think you came from before they met you mere months ago."

"How can they know where I came from?"

Again he hesitated, as if weighing up how much to tell me. "Your accent and a few words you used were more common in the Whitehall area."

"I don't have no accent." So I'd thought. Yet he'd been correct. I'd lived in Whitehall before Clerkenwell.

"I traveled to Whitehall and asked around. A boy matching your description lived there for six months or so. They thought he'd come from Finsbury. Tomorrow I'll send Gus and Seth there to find out about a child who kept his brown hair over his face to hide it." He took a step toward me and lowered his voice. "I *will* find out where you came from, Charlie, and I when I do, I'll discover how it is you can bring the dead back to life."

I swallowed past the lump in my throat. I couldn't look away. His gaze held me, pinning me as thoroughly as his body had done moments ago on the bed.

"Here you go," Seth said, carrying a plate of food in. Gus entered behind him.

Fitzroy stepped back and marched out the door. "Follow me. Bring the boy and his books. I see he's already in possession of the spare shirt."

I was too stunned to do anything but follow meekly. Fitzroy had not only dodged the bullet intended for him, but he'd learned more about my past than I'd have liked. And his methods were going to lead him to discover the truth. My only hope was that the further back in time he went, the slower his investigation would become. Gangs broke up, and children died or moved on. And then, of course, he would hit a wall altogether. He would be asking about a boy with hair covering his face, not a girl. My secrets were safe until I chose to reveal them.

If I chose to do so. I didn't believe his silly story about the queen's life being in danger. I certainly didn't want to reanimate the dead for him or his cause, no matter what it was. On the other hand, Lady Harcourt was his ally, in whatever scheme they had in mind, and surely such a fine noblewoman wouldn't want me to do anything wrong.

"Where are we taking him, sir?" Seth's question might as well have fallen on deaf ears. Fitzroy strode ahead, heading down two flights of stairs then swiftly along the corridor that housed the bathroom.

Gus prodded me in the back with the clean chamber pot he still held and I had to trot to keep up with Fitzroy. Finally we reached the end of the long corridor and stopped at a door.

"He's to stay in here until I give further word," Fitzroy said, opening the door.

Seth gasped. "But these are *your* chambers?"

I was as confused as he and Gus. Why did Fitzroy want me in there instead of the tower room?

"It's larger and more comfortable for two."

"Two, sir? Are you going to remain here?"

"He seems to be able to outwit you both too easily. I'll guard him, from now on."

Seth shuffled his feet and Gus's cheeks colored. I wondered if they would be in more trouble later or if that was the extent of it.

I hugged the book to my chest. He was right. I could trick Seth and Gus, but Fitzroy was too clever to fall for my ruses. On the other hand, he was only one man, and even he needed to sleep. He was *not* a machine.

He stepped aside and motioned me through the door. I entered and took in my surroundings. It was a large room with a sofa and leather armchairs at one end gathered around a fireplace, and a solid desk at the other. Paintings of country scenes hung on the dark green papered walls. A large freestanding iron candelabra was tucked into the far corner beside a bookshelf that took up almost the entire wall. It reached to the ceiling, and a ladder leaned against it. I stared at it in wonder, amazed at so many books under one roof. I hadn't realized Seth and Gus had left until the door clicked closed.

Fitzroy locked it with a key that he tucked into his waistcoat pocket. "We sleep in there." He indicated a closed door.

"We?" I said on a breath.

"I'll have a trundle brought up for you. Unless you prefer the bed. It doesn't matter to me."

I blinked at him. "I...I am to be held prisoner in here now? With you?"

"I know it's not ideal, but you're too quick-witted for them."

"You were present when I sent them away to shoot you. You fell for my ruse too."

The corner of his mouth twitched, and I suspected he'd known that I was sending Gus and Seth away in order to escape. I suddenly realized how difficult it would be to get out of Lichfield Towers. He may be only one man, but he was efficient, clever and ruthless. I had no doubt he played jailor better than his men, and even better than those at Highgate Police Station. My escape attempts would need to become more sophisticated.

I sat on the armchair near the window and opened my book. Instead of reading, I thought of ways to outwit Death himself.

CHAPTER 5

"You are quite the little thief." Lady Harcourt's wink softened her accusation, but the sting of her words pricked me nevertheless. Or perhaps that was my guilt. I felt horrid that I'd dragged her into my scheme. She'd already received a sharp glare from Fitzroy as he'd handed the pistol back to her.

She checked the barrel then placed the gun inside her reticule. The evening gown she wore probably didn't have pockets. It was an exquisite outfit of mourning black satin and lace, with gold beads arranged in leaves on the bodice and down the length of skirt in two panels. A black silk ribbon choker set off the white of her throat and the lustrous sheen of the pearl at the center. It was difficult to tear my gaze away from the gown and her jewelry, but I managed it. It wouldn't do to show too much interest in feminine things.

"The pocket in your skirt wasn't deep," I told her as she sat on a chair in the parlor. Fitzroy and I remained standing, he with his hands casually at his sides, me with mine behind my back. "It's too easy to steal things from shallow pockets."

"I'll have it deepened. Thank you for your advice, Charlie." She bestowed a smile on me that had me blushing. It was more than I deserved. "I see the bullet is missing."

"It's in the wall of the tower room."

Her eyebrows arched. "Was anyone injured?"

"Only Mr. Fitzroy."

She leapt up from the chair. "Lincoln!" She crossed the floor to him, sweeping past me as if I weren't there. I could have easily snatched the reticule from her and she wouldn't have noticed in her agitated state. "Where? Where are you hurt?"

"I am unharmed, Julia." Fitzroy looked uncomfortable as she searched his face in earnest.

"I asked where?" she said with quiet steel.

His lips thinned. "The left shoulder. A graze only. It doesn't hurt."

"Of course it must." She clicked her tongue. "It's typical of you to downplay your injuries. You are fallible, Lincoln, even though you like to think you are not."

Several beats passed, during which they stared at one another in a kind of silent battle of wills. It was almost as if words were exchanged between them and yet none passed their lips. I wasn't sure who'd won, but Lady Harcourt was the first to break the silence.

"May I see your shoulder?"

"There's no point. I've already had it seen to."

"Nevertheless, I would like to assess it for myself."

He turned away from her to tug the bell pull. Her back straightened in offense. "Lincoln, stop being such a child and let me see it."

"I am not the one acting like a child, Julia. We have company."

"Your point?"

"I suggest you don't ignore him. He has been eyeing off your reticule."

She swung round to face me. I could see her temper flaring, but I didn't think she was angry with me. Fitzroy was being terribly rude toward her. It was one thing to speak abrasively to someone who'd ended their prior liaison—surely *she* must have been the one to end it—but it was quite another to call a lady a child. I wouldn't have stood for it if I were her.

"I won't steal from you again," I said quickly. "Mr. Fitzroy is cruel to blame me."

Her face softened. "He is, isn't he?"

Fitzroy didn't seem to care that I'd called him cruel. No doubt he'd been labeled worse.

Gus arrived, sporting crumbs down the front of his waistcoat. "Boy giving you trouble, sir? Want me to take him away?"

"No. How long until dinner?"

"It's just about ready. Might as well go and sit down. Save me coming back to call you." He trudged off as I heard Lady Harcourt quietly lament the lack of proper servants.

"Shall we?" Fitzroy offered her his arm.

She took it and bestowed a too-sweet smile on him. "Hungry, my dear? Or do you wish to get rid of me?"

"If I wanted to be rid of you, I wouldn't be dining with you."

Her smile faltered and she allowed him to lead her out.

"Come, Charlie," he said. "You need to eat too."

I trailed behind, somewhat stupefied by the invitation to dinner. It seemed silly to worry that I wasn't dressed for the occasion, since it was just the three of us, but they were a beautiful and elegant couple in their eveningwear, and I was disheveled by comparison. The dining room wasn't meant for the likes of me either. It was sized for large parties, with the long mahogany table seating twenty, although it was only set for three tonight. The chandelier suspended above it blazed, catching the facets of the crystal glasses and the diamond earrings dangling from Lady Harcourt's ears. I hunched my shoulders and kept my head low, not wanting them to change their minds and send the scruffy gutter rat from the room.

We sat and Fitzroy poured the wine himself. There was no sign of footmen or a butler, and moments later, Seth and Gus brought in the food. I stared at the platters piled with roast beef and poultry, lobster salad and vegetables. There was so much of it!

"You must serve yourself," Seth whispered in my ear. "Be sure to use the utensils provided and not your hands."

"I am not a Barbarian."

Behind him, Gus snorted a laugh. "Sewer rats are refined fellows now, eh?"

"Cut up his food," Fitzroy told the men, "then remove his knife."

After Seth finished cutting my food, Lady Harcourt arched her brows at Fitzroy, who dismissed the men with a nod. She served herself, placing only a minute portion of each dish on her plate. No wonder her waist was so tiny. I may eat just as little, but only because I wasn't used to so much food and I didn't want to throw it all up later. For one thing, it would be a waste, and for another, Fitzroy's rugs looked expensive.

"You could have returned the pistol to me tomorrow," Lady Harcourt said, passing the peas to Fitzroy. "Why the invitation to dinner?"

"I want you to tell the boy what it is we do here at Lichfield Towers, and why we need him."

"You haven't informed him yet?"

"I tried. He doesn't believe me."

She laughed until her eyes watered. "Why am I not surprised? Lincoln, you aren't very good when it comes to convincing people."

"I had some success in Paris," he said mildly.

"And nobody is more surprised than me. Ordinarily people run from you when you become intense. Which, I might add, is all the time."

I held my breath. I wasn't sure if she were teasing him or accusing him. Nor was I sure how he would take it. He didn't seem like the sort of man just anyone could tease. The pent in their company, the more certain I became nd Seth were right. Fitzroy and Lady Harcourt had been lovers. It wasn't clear if they still were.

"Well, now I know why I was invited to dinner," she said with a smile for Fitzroy. "I thought there had to be another reason."

He said nothing, and I wondered if it was true and he didn't particularly desire her company. It was strange that he could be so cool toward her, whereas her emotions had seemed in danger of boiling over ever since her arrival. I was beginning to think I'd been wrong and *he* had been the one to end their relationship.

"I explained about the queen's life being in danger," Fitzroy said. "Charlie didn't believe me."

"I see. Well then, after we finish the main course, I'll tell him what he needs to know."

After a few minutes, in which the only sounds were that of chewing, Lady Harcourt asked me some questions. They were innocuous enough, and I answered in a way that gave nothing away. I wanted to know more about her too, but refrained. Boys like me didn't ask impertinent questions of ladies like her, and I was afraid the only questions I could think of were impertinent.

"The boy is positively a chatterbox compared to you, Lincoln," she said as Gus cleared away the dishes.

It was true that he'd not spoken the entire time, but he'd not been addressed either. He took her teasing well enough, by showing no emotion whatsoever.

"Dessert, sir?" Seth asked. "Cook tells me he's made jellies and a trifle."

Jelly! I hadn't had jelly in an age.

I caught Lady Harcourt smiling gently at me out of the rner of my eye and quickly schooled my features. I didn't nt to seem as if I could be bought with a bowl of jelly.

"Thank you, Seth," Fitzroy said. Before the two men left, sked Lady Harcourt to begin.

ministry and its role?" she

"Not really."

She shook her head at him but he merely sat in his seat at the top of the table and waited. "He is the head of the Ministry of Curiosities. It's a government organization but operates somewhat outside the official boundaries of parliament. Lincoln makes all the day to day decisions, but the ministry is overseen by a committee. The committee decides what curiosities require investigation, but always on Lincoln's advice. He is the heart and soul of this organization. The brains, too."

Her praise of him surprised me after her teasing. If Fitzroy was embarrassed or pleased, he didn't show it.

"The committee also provide the necessary funds," she went on. "I am on the committee, as is Lord Gillingham, whom you've met."

"What are 'curiosities?'"

"Unexplained events. Phenomena that seem to happen for no *Earthly* rhyme or reason."

"Like ghosts? Angels?"

"Do you believe in ghosts and angels?"

I shrugged one shoulder.

"You are correct. But not only ghosts and angels. Raising the dead is another phenomena that most people would consider an impossibility. The ministry, however, thinks these curiosities—and more—are entirely possible. We seek to understand them better, but also to make sure they cannot harm us. It began as a group of like-minded individuals, with an interest in the supernatural, but has recently been given a more official role. The ministry investigates situations that the police and Home Office cannot get involved in because of their public role. The Ministry of Curiosities is more secretive."

outsi...

"Noboay...
put you in an asylum.

Seth jabbed him in the rib...

"The queen and prime minister ap...
I asked.

"They would if they knew we existed," Lady ...
said.

Gus grunted. "Either that or burn us at the stake for believing in all this magic talk."

"The ministry's existence has been kept secret from them for their own good," Lady Harcourt went on. "Governments come and go. The committee members are involved for life. We all have prominent positions, either at court or in parliament. Our sole purpose is to serve the British Empire and keep queen and country safe—from paranormal forces, rather than military ones."

"Think of us as the sword of the empire," Seth said, puffing out his chest. "And Mr. Fitzroy is the pointy end."

Fitzroy sat listening without saying a word. I'd felt him watching me the entire time, and I wished I knew how to react. I wasn't sure whether to show surprise or fear, or whether I should pretend they were all mad.

"Why him?" I asked. "Why is he the leader?" He was, after all, young for such responsibility. I imagined someone of Gillingham's advanced years would be more suited to a leadership role.

"He was chosen at birth," Lady Harcourt said.

"Chosen at *birth*?"

"His entire life has been dedicated to becoming the ministry's leader. His education and training were specifically designed to make him the best. There is no one better suited to the position." She shrugged thin, bare shoulders. "No one more capable."

Clearly she *hadn't* ended the relationship then. I needed no further proof than her effusive admiration and the stony expression on his face.

Chosen. Best. Capable. It all sounded so cold and calculating, yet I supposed it was no different to many gentlemen born into the nobility, raised knowing he would take over from their fathers one day. Even so, it sounded like a dull life. The old me, the dutiful daughter, probably wouldn't have thought so, but the new me did. The thought of being destined to be someone since the day I was born, and never having the opportunity to deviate from that path, sounded like a prison sentence.

"Was your father the ministry's leader before you?" I asked him. Although Lady Harcourt had told me the story, it didn't seem right to ask her the question. "Is that why you were chosen?"

"No."

I waited for further explanation but none came. Yet the air in the room tightened. It took me a moment to realize that the other three people there had gone quite still. Had they also been waiting for an answer? Or did they already know it, and I'd stumbled onto a sensitive topic?

"You are investigating paranormal curiosities," I said to him. "And you want the necromancer girl to help you. Does that mean *you* are paranormal, sir?"

For a long moment I thought I'd overstepped the line; that I'd gone too far. He simply stared at me, unblinking. What was he waiting for? "No," he eventually said.

"But you got out of the bullet's way. How, if not with an unnatural speed?"

"I'm observant and quite quick."

Quite! He was also the master of understatement.

"No one in the ministry or on the committee has any true paranormal abilities," Lady Harcourt said. "You're our first such employee."

"I'm not working for you." I kept my tone light, but my tight jaw made it sound harsh.

"Why not?"

Because I can't trust you. I can't trust anyone. "I am not a necromancer."

Lady Harcourt opened her mouth to speak, but Fitzroy leaned forward and she closed it again. She seemed anxious to hear what he had to say. We all were. "We thought there was only one in the world," he said. "But it seems there are two. You and the girl."

"I am not a necromancer. How many times do I have to tell you?" I pushed my chair back and stood.

Seth and Gus crowded round me, waiting for an order from their master to grab me and remove me from the room.

"Sit down," Fitzroy snapped.

"You have not eaten your jelly." Lady Harcourt indicated the bowl that Seth had set before me. She smiled. "Stay with us. There's more you need to know."

I picked up my spoon, wishing it were a knife I could throw at Fitzroy. I sat again. "If I must."

She scooped out some jelly but didn't eat it. It wobbled in her spoon as she regarded me. "Someone wishes to use your—a necromancer's—power to harm the queen."

"Who?"

"We don't know. Mr. Fitzroy intercepted a letter from someone in Paris we had been watching. It only bore the man's—or woman's—initials and was addressed to an abandoned house, however we think the letter reached him."

"It did," Fitzroy intoned. "I made sure of it."

"The letter mentioned that a particular girl he'd been seeking—"

"The necromancer?" I asked.

She nodded. "The necromancer he'd been searching so long for had been traced to the house of a London vicar."

I shoveled jelly into my mouth, but it tasted like ashes and was difficult to swallow. I forced it down with a gulp as I tried to digest the news too. The London vicar was my father. "There must be dozens of vicars in London."

"There are. We have not been able to pinpoint which one the letter referred to. We hope he hasn't, either."

He had. It must be the doctor I'd seen leaving Father's house. I was even more glad that I'd not revealed myself to him now. "What does he want with this necromancer girl?"

"To use her power to reanimate his...creations."

I paused, the full spoon at my mouth. "Creations?"

Her already pale face grew paler. She glanced at Fitzroy and he took over the explanation. "He takes pieces off different corpses and binds them together to make new, more superior ones. All they lack is a spirit that will bring them to life and do his bidding."

My stomach rolled. Bile and jelly rose to my throat. "Why would he do such a thing?"

"To build himself an elite force," Lady Harcourt said. "He takes the long, powerful legs of a fast runner, for example; the strong arms of a laborer or pugilist; the heart and lungs of a good swimmer. And the brain of an intelligent man, or one with knowledge he seeks to use to his advantage."

What kind of monster wanted to do such a thing? The very notion was sickening, but to actually cut up bodies and sew pieces of them together to form a new man... His surgery must be covered in blood and gore...his arms and body too. The very notion was unfathomable.

"Charlie?" Lady Harcourt rose and came round the table. She placed her cool hand on the back of my neck. "You've gone quite ashen."

"It's no wonder," Seth said quietly.

Gus murmured his agreement. "Makes my belly ache, too."

Fitzroy poured me more wine and handed me the glass. He watched as I drank. "Have you ever heard of such a man?"

"Why would I?"

"Street children hear all sorts of things. Perhaps the body of a homeless man has inexplicably disappeared, or someone saw a fellow acting mysteriously near the cemetery. You spend a lot of time at Highgate Cemetery."

So he'd learned that about me too. "I haven't seen or heard anything. If the man looks like a regular gentleman, he could be anyone."

It *must* have been the doctor I'd seen at Father's house. Only a man with medical knowledge could piece bodies back together. But I didn't know his name. I didn't know where he lived. I couldn't help Fitzroy and Lady Harcourt find him, even if I'd wanted to.

Fitzroy returned to his seat, but Lady Harcourt remained at my side, stroking my hair. "My spies told me what happened at the police station," he said. "Word gets around quickly, particularly when something sensational occurs. I suspect this man's spies also informed him. He will be looking for you now."

"You've got it wrong, Mr. Fitzroy. It weren't me that did that."

"We will keep you safe, here, away from him. He can't get you while you are under my protection."

I snorted. "You don't even know what he looks like." Lady Harcourt's hand drew too close to my fringe and I pulled away. "I ain't a necromancer. I can't help you."

She returned to her chair. "Not even for a soft bed, food and clean clothes?"

"I ain't the necromancer," I said again. I hadn't spent five years surviving on the street, doing everything possible to hide my identity and keep safe, to throw it away for a queen who meant nothing to me. "I wish I could help you but I can't. Seems to me you need the girl. Better find her before he does."

"We will. Now that we know there are two of you—"

I slammed my palms down on the table, sending the jelly into a jiggling frenzy. "I ain't a necromancer!" I pushed up from the chair, but my passage was blocked by Gus and Seth. Arms crossed, scowls on their faces, they presented an impassible wall. There would be no distracting them tonight. Besides, I had no doubt if I did that Fitzroy would catch me.

"I think that's enough for tonight," Lady Harcourt said. "A good rest is in order. Take him to his room."

"Sir?" Seth asked.

Fitzroy nodded. "I'll follow shortly."

"Lincoln?" Lady Harcourt arched her perfectly drawn eyebrows at him. "Why do you need to go too?"

"I've decided he is less likely to escape from me. I've moved him into my rooms."

"Your rooms? Permanently?"

"Yes."

"I don't think that's a good idea."

"Why not?"

A little color infused her cheeks and for one awful moment I thought she knew. She must have seen through my disguise and known I wasn't a boy, and that allowing me to stay in his rooms would be inappropriate. "Who will trace his origins tomorrow if you are watching him?"

I let out a long breath.

"Seth and Gus will be given full instructions."

"Is it wise to give them such an important task?"

Gus's mouth flattened, and he looked as if he wanted to challenge her. Seth merely flushed and stared down at his boots.

"They're capable enough, and they need the practice. Besides, I have a better idea of where they should concentrate on their search now." This last he said to me, and somewhat smugly, if I wasn't mistaken.

Lady Harcourt frowned. "I still don't think—"

"I have decided."

She bristled and glared at him. He glared back at her, their silent battle of wills once more making the air in the room feel tense and tight.

"Send for my carriage," she said to Seth.

He seemed relieved to be dismissed and disappeared from the room. Lady Harcourt marched out of the dining room and into the hall. She gathered her hat and gloves, and Fitzroy helped her on with her coat. They didn't speak. Neither his hands nor his gaze lingered at her bare shoulders or neck. It was as if he didn't even notice the silky white skin, or care that she had moved closer to him than mere friends ought. There was nothing of the lover about the way he treated her. I wasn't surprised. I couldn't imagine him consumed with passion for her—or for anyone, for that matter.

Seth returned and the carriage wheels soon crunched on the gravel outside. He opened the front door for her and bowed. Lady Harcourt offered him her hand and he kissed it. Gus didn't receive the same privilege and he didn't look like he expected to.

"Walk me out, Lincoln," she said in a mild voice.

Fitzroy's gaze slid to me.

"I won't try to escape," I told him.

"Take him to the library and wait for me there." He followed Lady Harcourt outside.

Gus nodded at a door leading off from the entrance. "Library's in there."

Seth led the way and Gus followed behind me. I thought there'd been a great many books in Fitzroy's rooms, but the library held triple. Bookshelves reached to the ceiling on all the walls, leaving some gaps between them for lamps, windows and framed pictures. A circular iron chandelier, sporting dozens of candles, plunged from the ceiling rose, stopping just above the round table. Seth lit some in candlesticks and handed one to Gus.

"Over here," I told them. "I want to see the books."

"We ain't at your beck and call," Gus growled.

I ignored him and strolled around the room, brushing my fingers along the spines of the leather bound tomes, breathing their earthy scent into my lungs.

"Don't think about throwing them," Seth said, trailing behind me with a candle.

I paused at the window. Fitzroy and Lady Harcourt stood at the carriage door, talking. Or, rather, arguing, if her expression was anything to go by. His back was to me, but in the light cast by the moon and the coach lamps, her face looked stern, her body rigid.

"What do you think they're arguing about?" I asked.

Seth peered over my shoulder. "It's hard to say. You, perhaps, and Death's decision to keep you close. His decision to give Gus and me more responsibility."

"Or his decision not to take her to his bed," Gus said, coming up behind me on my other side and watching through the window too.

"You think it was his choice to end their...liaison?" I asked.

"Maybe."

Lady Harcourt spun round and climbed into the coach, ignoring Fitzroy's outstretched hand. He pulled it back as she slammed the door closed.

"If it were," Seth said, as the coach drove off, "he probably didn't end it the way a gentleman should."

"Why do you say that?"

"You may not have noticed, but he's not good with people."

I snorted. "I noticed."

"I'm not sure he knows how to treat a lady properly. I certainly don't think he understands the fair sex."

"That don't stop Lady H from throwing herself at him," Gus said. "Other women, too."

Seth rounded on him. "Lady Harcourt does not *throw* herself at anyone. She's much too—" He broke off when Fitzroy appeared at the door.

"Upstairs," Fitzroy said, turning away. "Now."

Gus and Seth gripped one arm each and led me out of the library. We followed Fitzroy up the stairs and along the corridor, then they shoved me into the room after him and shut the door. He locked it and pocketed the key. I swallowed hard as Fitzroy faced me. It was one thing to pretend to be a boy in his presence during the day, but now I had to spend an entire night with a man who made my blood alternately run hot and cold. A man whose gaze seemed to see everything.

CHAPTER 6

Someone had set up a truckle bed in the master bedroom suite, much too close to the main bed for my liking. I usually slept as far away from the boys in our den as possible, while remaining close enough for safety. It wasn't as close as this.

I didn't complain. I didn't want Fitzroy's suspicions raised. But there were some things that needed to be made clear from the beginning. Best to get them out now.

"You have to leave when I use the chamber pot," I told him.

He shot me a flinty glare from the clothes stand, where he stood removing his dinner jacket. I suspected that meant he agreed.

"And when I wash and change."

"As you wish." He hung the jacket on the stand and began unbuttoning his waistcoat.

I didn't look away, but I didn't stare either. Neither would be the sort of thing a boy would do. Besides, I'd seen men before. Or, more specifically, boys and youths. While I never undressed in front of them, they were not so inhibited. They even pissed in front of me, and Stringer had once bedded a whore where the entire gang could see. I was no stranger to a man's parts or their function. Fitzroy's nakedness wouldn't concern me.

"You have the run of these rooms," he told me, bowtie in hand. "The book is on my desk, spare candles and matches are in the top drawer. Don't burn the house down."

I blinked. Had he just told a joke? His mouth didn't twitch, so I suspected he was serious and did indeed suspect that I would try and start a fire.

I left him to his undressing, somewhat disappointed that I wouldn't get to see if the magnificent face was accompanied by a magnificent figure, and found the book. There was no point pretending I couldn't read anymore, so I tried to think of a reasonable explanation for my education as I searched in the top drawer for the matches.

As my hand closed around the box, a thought struck me. My father used to keep a small knife inside his middle desk drawer. I felt all around, but there seemed to be none in the top drawer. I tried the others, and still nothing. I sat on the chair and checked the desk surface and inside an unlocked coffer. It contained only papers. I groped beneath the desk and my fingers found a small, narrow shelf at the right. It contained one item—a knife.

I slipped it from the shelf and pressed it to my thigh. I stood and carried the book and knife to the other side of the room where I lounged on the sofa. As interesting as the book was, I didn't even read one sentence as I waited for Fitzroy to emerge from the bedroom.

He seemed to take forever, and when he finally came out, barefoot and dressed in loose white trousers and an Oriental style shirt, I was already having second thoughts. Not about using the knife, but about my ability to succeed. He was stronger and faster than me. In a close combat situation, I would lose. I had to throw it at him when his back was turned, or not bother.

The thought of knifing someone in the back didn't sit well. Even more so because Fitzroy had not harmed me, except to save himself. I slid the knife beneath my thigh then openly watched him.

He stood in the open space between the two different sections of the room and began jumping up and down on the spot, drawing his knees up high to chest. It was such an odd thing to do that I couldn't tear my gaze away. Then suddenly he dropped into a squat, spun round on the ball of one foot, and lashed out with the other at an imaginary foe. I set the book aside and continued to watch as he performed more maneuvers, sometimes kicking, sometimes thrusting with closed fist or open hand. His face was set with concentration and he did not once glance at me. He wasn't wearing trousers and a shirt, I realized, or not any that I'd seen before. The clothes were loose, the fabric flowing, ensuring his limbs weren't hindered.

After several minutes of repeating the moves, he opened a casket on the bookshelf and removed an object. Or was it two? It appeared to be two handles as long as his hands with the end of one connected by a chain to the end of the other. He returned to the clearing and began his moves again, this time incorporating the contraption by flicking it out and back, up and down. Blows from the metal device would cause a lot of damage to exposed flesh. It was something to remember, as was the place where he kept it.

I continued to watch, fascinated by his smoothness and speed. He exercised for an hour, not once stopping or looking my way. It didn't seem to bother him that he had an audience. Perhaps he liked it. When he finally finished, after almost two hours, his face was a little flushed and the hair at his temple damp, but he otherwise seemed unflustered. I would have been flat on the floor panting.

Without a word, he padded back to the casket and placed the weapon inside, then returned to the bedroom. He re-emerged after ten minutes wearing nothing but a towel around his hips and carrying another that he used to dry his hair.

His lack of attention to me allowed me to take in the sight of his chest and shoulders, the left one with a bandage covering it where I'd shot him. The youths in the gangs I'd been in had never had bodies like that. Fitzroy's shoulders were broad, with bulges of muscle rippling down his arms and across his chest. The sprinkle of dark chest hair tapered off before reaching his ridged stomach. From a distance, it was difficult to tell if it was curly like the hair on his head. I found myself wanting to find out.

Not really aware of what I was doing, I untucked my feet from beneath me and set them on the floor. He looked up and a small furrow connected his brows. I swallowed and reopened my book. I hoped my fringe covered the blush burning my face. Beneath my thigh, the knife point dug into me. I'd forgotten about it. I probably should have used his inattention during exercise to throw it at him.

Fool. Foolish *girl*. Surely he must know my secret now. Surely he could *see* my interest in him. No boy would stare like that. Good lord, I hoped I hadn't drooled. I wiped the corner of my mouth on my shoulder, just to be sure.

"It's late," he said, tossing the towel he'd used on his hair over the back of one of the chairs. He dragged his damp, tousled locks off his face, and my heart kicked in my chest at the way it somehow made him more handsome.

"And?" I prompted.

"Aren't you tired?"

"Aren't you?"

"I don't need much sleep." He sat at his desk. Wasn't he going to dress? His semi-nakedness was a distraction.

I rearranged myself on the sofa so that I faced away from him. "Nor do I." It was the truth. Staying awake and alert was just one way I'd kept alive and safe for years.

He emitted a soft sound, but I wasn't sure if it was in humor or derision. I refused to glance at him, and instead slumped down into the sofa, placing my head on the armrest and stretching my legs out. I held the book close, to see the words in the poor light, and I was soon lost in the story, swept into the world of Sherlock Holmes and his puzzling mystery.

Some time later, Fitzroy deposited a candelabra on the table behind my head. My breath caught as I waited for him to say something, do something. When nothing happened, I turned my head. He was once again at his desk. He still only wore the towel and he seemed lost in the paperwork spread out before him.

I fell asleep at some point and awoke in the morning in the same position, the book splayed across my chest and Fitzroy looking down on me. The nightmare that had woken me drifted away as we regarded one another. Had I said something in my sleep? Cried out? It was difficult to tell from his blank face.

I sat up and received a sharp reminder that the knife was still under my thigh. "What do you want?" I snapped.

"Breakfast will arrive shortly." He moved away and sat at his desk. The man liked to work.

I tucked the knife up my sleeve and headed into the bedroom. With one eye on the closed door, I slipped the knife under the truckle bed's mattress, then I quickly washed and changed into the clean shirt. With my hair once more covering my face, I returned to the sitting room.

"Good morning, lad," Seth said cheerfully from the small table where he was setting down a tray. "Sleep well?"

"Well enough."

Gus moved past me into the bedroom and re-emerged a few minutes later with the bowls of washing water. "When are we going to get proper maids, sir?"

Fitzroy didn't look up from his paperwork. "When we find some that won't tattle."

"Girls who don't tattle?" Gus grunted. "Ain't no such creature."

Seth patted the chair near the table. "Sit down and eat, Charlie."

I sat and noticed that Fitzroy had his own tray laden with bacon, sausages and eggs. "I can't eat all this," I said.

"Try. You need fattening up." Seth ruffled my hair as he passed and I slapped his hand away. He chuckled and I found I couldn't be mad at him. He wasn't a bad sort, despite his participation in my kidnapping. He was only following orders.

Gus handed me a steaming cup of tea and bent his head close to mine. "Does he snore?" he whispered.

Despite everything, I laughed. "Like a trumpet," I whispered back, keeping Fitzroy in my line of sight.

Gus grinned, revealing a patchwork of broken and crooked teeth. "I knew there had to be *something* human about him."

"Or maybe his gears get jammed when he lies down."

Gus roared with laughter. Fitzroy glanced over his shoulder, catching us both watching him. Gus choked on his laugh and turned it into a cough.

"Eat, Half Pint," he commanded. "Growing boy like you should eat every crumb."

Seth emerged from the bedroom carrying jugs and bowls. He mouthed, "What's so amusing?" at Gus, but Gus merely shrugged.

"You know what you must do," Fitzroy told them.

"Yes, sir," Seth said. "We'll head out now."

Fitzroy locked the door after they left then settled back at his desk. He read the newspaper flattened out before him and absently ate his breakfast. I ate all of the bacon on my plate. It was one of the foods I'd missed in the last five years, and I savored every bite. I didn't touch the rest. The bacon had filled me up.

"You do not eat," Fitzroy said, some time later when he approached.

"I'm not hungry."

"If you don't eat, you won't grow."

"Perhaps I like being short and thin."

"No boy likes being short and thin."

I watched him for signs that he suspected, but he was already turning away from me. He paced the room, covering the entire length quickly with his long strides. He seemed agitated or frustrated.

"I'm sure they're doing as you asked," I said.

He stopped and looked at me. Then he began pacing again. Back and forth, back and forth for an eternity, it seemed. I turned my back to him and read, but the rhythm of his footsteps distracted me. I plugged my ears with my fingers but the rhythm continued to tread through my head and it was difficult to keep the book open with my elbows.

With a sigh, I withdrew my fingers and closed the book. "Are you worried about them?"

"No." He almost sounded amused at the idea. Almost.

"Are you concerned they'll fail?"

"Somewhat."

But not enough to warrant the pacing, I thought. "Are you concerned they'll give away too much about you and the ministry?"

"They're not that incompetent."

Perhaps he was disappointed with the way the dinner with Lady Harcourt had ended the night before. Perhaps he didn't like her leaving on a sour note. Yet he'd shown no such qualms upon her departure. Curious.

He finally stopped pacing long enough to glance out the window. He looked to the bright blue sky, to left then right, and up at the sky again. Then he continued pacing.

I got up and padded barefoot to the window to see what he was looking at. There was nothing but gravel drive, garden, trees and sky. The roses were like jewels dropped on a carpet of green, and the sky was bluer than I'd seen it in an age. There must be a northerly breeze blowing the factory smog away, and most homes wouldn't light fires in summer except in the kitchen. I was so used to being surrounded by gray and brown that my eyes hurt from the dazzling sunshine and bright colors. It was a perfect day and I ached to be outside.

Now I understood Fitzroy's frustration. He didn't like being shut inside his rooms any more than I did—perhaps less so. While I was content with the books, he seemed to need to move and there simply wasn't enough space.

"Put on your shoes." His voice came from closer behind me than I realized and I jumped.

"Where are we going?"

"Outside."

I rolled my eyes at his back as I followed him into the bedroom. "Anywhere specific?"

"No."

A few minutes later we were walking across the lawn. I had to take twice as many steps to keep up with his long strides but I didn't mind. I liked stretching my limbs and feeling the blood pump through my veins. If I'd been a lady, we would have slowed to an amble, but I didn't want to amble. I wanted to run. I wondered what he'd do if I took off. Tackle me to the ground? Jerk me to a stop by my hair? Or race me?

I settled for the brisk walk. We didn't speak as we passed the rose garden and the lily pond, where a frog croaked a greeting. We headed toward the stand of trees at the edge of the property then abruptly changed direction and headed back toward the house. I wasn't ready to return inside, even though I was hot under my layers of shirt and jacket.

"What's around the back of the house?" I asked.

"Outbuildings, orchard, walled garden and tennis court."

"Tennis! Do you play?"

"Play?"

"Yes. Tennis. Do you play?"

"No."

"You've never challenged Seth or Gus to a game?"

"There is no time for games at Lichfield Towers."

"How dull. I'm sure the men would appreciate a little time to play games like tennis or cards."

"I've seen them play cards after dinner."

"You've never joined them?"

"Rarely."

"Is that because they don't ask or because you don't want to play?"

His only answer was to increase his speed. I had to trot to remain alongside him.

"You don't talk much," I said. If he wanted to keep a close eye on me, I might as well annoy him. It was my duty as his prisoner.

"You ask too many questions."

"Ha! That's rich coming from you. You *only* ever ask questions."

"I haven't asked you any today."

"It is only mid-morning. I expect them to come after Seth and Gus return."

"You are probably right."

I glanced sideways at him, but he kept his gaze directly ahead. He did slow down somewhat, which was just as well since I was starting to get a little breathless.

"You've almost finished the book." His attempt at starting a new conversation that had nothing to do with my background surprised me. I was growing used to his silences.

"It's a good book."

"Nor have you asked me the meaning of any of the words."

"So?"

"You're educated."

Ah, there it was. His attempt at digging into my past had begun more subtly this time, but he'd ruined it with that comment. "Very observant, Sherlock."

He said nothing.

"Sherlock is the character in the book I'm reading," I explained. "He's very observant."

"I've read it."

"Oh. So you didn't find my reference clever or amusing enough to bother replying, or even smirking."

"I didn't say that."

"I see. You only *thought* me clever and amusing. Be careful, Mr. Fitzroy, I've heard that keeping your emotions bottled up will rot your insides."

"You have a dry sense of humor. I wasn't expecting that."

"And you, sir, have no sense of humor whatsoever."

When he didn't answer, I worried that I'd offended him. Then I told myself to stop worrying. He was my jailor; his feelings were of no concern to me. Besides, I doubted he had feelings.

"Why do Gus and Seth call you Death?"

"Because I've killed people."

My step faltered. I'd been trying to goad him again, and wasn't expecting his frankness. "How many?"

"Enough."

"Why did you kill them?"

"They talked too much."

I stopped altogether, but he continued on, not caring that he was leaving me behind. I blinked rapidly, then realized he was teasing me.

"And you call my sense of humor dry," I muttered when I caught up to him near the stables. "Yours is positively parched."

We walked past the stables and other outbuildings, then crossed the courtyard and headed up the back steps. He opened the door for me and I went inside. We were in the service area, near the kitchens if the delicious smell of baking bread was an indication.

We passed the servants' dining room, the butler and housekeeper's offices, scullery, and the bells labeled with the names of the rooms they serviced. They were eerily silent, as was the entire house, until we came to the kitchen. A large man hummed as he kneaded dough, his attention focused entirely on his work.

"Cook," Fitzroy barked.

The cook looked up and his eyes widened. He had no hair on his head or face, not even eyebrows, and the lack of it made his cleft chin and red cheeks more obvious. I couldn't be sure if he had a naturally rosy complexion or he was simply hot. The kitchen was terribly warm.

"Mr. Fitzroy, sir! I weren't expecting you." He screwed his hands into his apron to wipe them, but they still came away doughy. "You be hungry, sir?"

"No," Fitzroy said. "This is Charlie. Charlie, this is Cook."

"You don't eat much," Cook said to me.

"No."

He frowned. "Can't be the food. I'm a great cook."

"Yes, you are. I just don't get hungry."

"Growin' lad like you should be."

I shrugged. "Maybe I'm not used to eating."

Fitzroy continued along the corridor, leaving the cook and me staring at one another. The cook jerked his head in the direction Fitzroy had gone. "Don't keep him waitin'," he whispered. I was about to head off when he added, "You can't live on bacon and jelly alone, boy."

"Just put less on my tray next time and I'll eat it all."

He winked and jerked his head again. I nodded thanks and hurried after Fitzroy. He waited at the base of the service stairs and stepped aside to allow me to go ahead of him. I was very aware of him behind me as we ascended. I wasn't a curvy woman in front, but I wasn't sure what I looked like back there. Certainly not too round, or the boys in the gangs would have teased me for having a feminine arse. Yet they weren't as observant as Fitzroy, and had no reason to suspect me of being a woman. I wasn't sure if he did suspect, but I felt his gaze on my rear nevertheless.

We emerged from the service stairwell onto the second floor corridor, not far from his rooms. I wasn't ready to be cooped up again. There was still so much I hadn't seen. "May I look around the rest of the house, with you as my tour guide?"

He paused. "Are you trying to find out where I hide the weapons?"

"Of course not."

"Good. You will not be given the chance to escape and I wouldn't want your hopes to be raised falsely."

"How considerate," I sneered.

"Except for the attic, this is the highest level in the east and west wings. The tower goes two levels higher."

"I know that already."

"You've seen the bathroom." He indicated the other doors up and down the corridor. "These are bedrooms. They're unfurnished." He did not open the doors but strode past them and the main central staircase too then opened another door on the right. The room beyond was large but clearly unused. Dustsheets covered the furniture and it was just as well, as there was dust everywhere. I wrinkled my nose at the musty smell, even as I admired the large windows, the giant marble fireplace, and the multi-tiered chandelier.

"This is the drawing room," he said.

"Such a shame to see it in this state," I whispered. Imagine the conversations those walls had been privy to over the years.

We headed past the ghostly furniture and through another door on the other side. It was empty. "This is the ballroom."

"It's magnificent." It was very long, but the dark wood paneling made it feel cozy. I could imagine elegantly dressed ladies and gentlemen dancing and chatting beneath the three enormous chandeliers, their jewels sparkling in the light.

"Have you ever held a ball here?"

"No."

"You should, if only to enjoy such a lovely room."

"I'll keep that in mind for when enjoying ballrooms becomes one of the ministry's primary aims."

We rejoined the corridor. It bent suddenly to the left then stopped at another, narrow staircase. "That leads to the attic and the servants' rooms," he said.

"Is that where Gus, Seth and Cook sleep?"

"Yes."

"Are they the only servants here?"

"Yes."

"But Seth and Gus are more guards than footmen."

He didn't say anything, and I suspected it was because I hadn't posed it as a question.

"You've not thought about employing some maids or a butler? Someone discreet?"

"No." He returned back the way we came and headed down the grand stairs to the ground floor. "You've already seen the dining room, library, and the parlor, which we use instead of the drawing room for visitors."

"Do you get visitors often?"

"Only committee members."

"What about your friends and family?"

He paused on the bottom step, his back to me. "You've also seen the service areas in that direction. Adjoining the dining room is the billiard room."

"Do you play?"

"There's no table."

"What an entertaining household this is. No tennis, no billiards, and no visitors."

"You're not here to be entertained."

"True. But *I* don't live here, nor am I staying long. You, Seth and Gus, however, need *something* to do in the evenings."

He indicated I should go first up the stairs. "I told you, they play cards. Most evening they spend with Cook."

"And you? How do you spend your evenings?"

"Reading. Writing correspondence and reports. Scientific experiments. Exercising. Thinking."

I stopped and he stopped beside me. "You mean all you do is work?"

"Sometimes I sleep." He continued past me.

I laughed. "That was a joke. Wasn't it?" I trotted after him. "Tell me you at least read for pleasure. You said you've read my book, so you must."

"On occasion. And yes, I have read *your* book."

My face heated. "I didn't mean it like that."

We returned to his rooms and I picked up the book. I finished it in the afternoon and spent another hour or so watching him as he mixed liquids together in little bottles and set them over a tiny gas burner. He took copious notes in a complicated scrawl that appeared to be some kind of code. It made no sense to me, but I liked watching the experiments and trying to guess what would happen. He answered my questions when I asked them, but mostly we didn't speak. It didn't feel in the least awkward or strained, and I began to like his quiet company. It made a nice change to the constant, inane chatter of the boys.

Seth and Gus brought our meals in for an early dinner, and gave Fitzroy their report. I wasn't concerned before they began and I still wasn't concerned when they finished. They'd traced my life back some three years. The following day they planned to continue.

They were about to leave when I stopped them. "You two got any cards?" I asked. "Or dice?"

"Can't gamble with what you don't have, boy," Gus said.

"I don't want to gamble, I just want to do something other than read and watch the machine work."

Gus and Seth glanced nervously at Fitzroy.

"You may play cards," Fitzroy said, turning back to the notes Seth had handed him along with his dinner tray.

"So kind," I said, bowing.

Gus suppressed a snigger and both men left. They returned after I'd finished my meal—a small portion of game pie and a salad—and deposited a deck of cards on the table. Gus arranged three chairs around it.

"What do you know how to play?" he asked me.

"Very little." Card games had been forbidden in our house by Father, but I'd seen the boys play when they could get hold of a deck. "Teach me something."

"We'll start with Loo." As Seth dealt, I surreptitiously glanced in Fitzroy's direction. He was watching us from beneath hooded lids.

"Are you joining us?" I asked him.

He turned back to the papers on his desk. "I have work to do."

"All work and no play makes Sir a very dull fellow indeed," I whispered.

Seth grinned and Gus snorted a laugh. "You better mind he don't hear you say that," Gus whispered back.

"He won't hurt me. Not while he thinks I'm a necromancer."

"And if you're not, like you say?" Seth drawled. "What do you think he'll do then? Simply allow you to walk away so you can blab about the ministry all over London? Think again, lad."

I swallowed hard. I hadn't considered that. "I ain't seen no evidence of him being cruel."

"I didn't say he was cruel. Just that he will do whatever it takes to stop you talking."

"By bribing me?"

"Or threatening you."

"And if I don't take his threats seriously?"

Seth met my gaze over the top of his cards. "Then you take your life into your own hands."

Gus leaned forward. "You see," he whispered, "telling people about the ministry and Lichfield Towers brings danger to his door. And when Death feels like he's in danger…" He sliced a finger across his throat.

I remembered how he'd rendered me unconscious to capture me, then quickly disarmed me when I'd shot him. He hadn't hurt me on either occasion, but if he no longer needed me…would he?

I lost every round and ended the evening by telling them I was too tired to play anymore. They left, taking their cards with them. I wasn't tired, however, and started a new book. At around nine, Fitzroy removed himself to the bedroom and re-emerged wearing his loose fitting exercise clothes.

He began with the same routine of jumping on the spot, drawing his knees high, then practicing kicking and punching moves. He varied it after that by grasping the top of the open bedroom door and pulling himself up to his chin then slowly lowering himself again. I lost count of how many after fifty.

Instead of using the handles connected by a chain next, he found a walking stick from somewhere in the bedroom and used it like a sword against an imaginary opponent. His actions were sleek and smooth, yet I imagined they would be lethal if he struck anyone. His face was rigid with concentration, his eyes fixed on his invisible foe with murderous intent.

I sat transfixed by the power in his graceful moves and the seriousness with which he practiced. What would distract him? A tickle? A kiss? My nakedness?

The mischief-maker in me was tempted to try, but I remained where I was, watching. When he finally finished and returned to the bedroom, I blew out a long, measured breath. It was shaky. Blood rushed through my veins and my heart pounded. The sight of him had affected me, the way a woman should be affected by a handsome, powerful man.

But not this woman, and not that man.

I tried to concentrate on my book to calm my tingling nerves and slow my heart, but I'd read barely a few lines by the time he emerged, wearing only a towel wrapped around his hips. That chest, those shoulders and arms…it was all too much, too overwhelming, too *male*. And I was weak.

I sprang up and rushed past him, catching a whiff of the spicy scent of his soap. Whether he thought my behavior strange or not, I didn't turn around to see. I shut the door with my foot and threw myself on the trundle bed. I pounded my fist into the pillow, but it did nothing to dampen the desire coiling within me. Perhaps I ought to take up exercising too and remove my frustrations that way.

Some time later, my blood had calmed but my head was still filled with images of a naked Lincoln Fitzroy, towel drying his hair, and then a naked Fitzroy exercising. Oh

Lord, this had to be punishment for my sins. My one true sin was the necromancy, the devil's work according to Father.

If I didn't get away from Lichfield Towers—from Fitzroy—I would be found out. If I were found out, I would be in danger. I'd been a fool to allow myself to succumb to the comforts. He'd deliberately lulled me with food and clothing, a soft bed, pleasant walks. It was working. All he had to do was wait for me to confess so that I could stay at Lichfield.

Stay with him.

But I hadn't lost my will to survive. It had been with me so long that it was a difficult habit to break. It overrode everything else, even my desire for comfort and for him.

I rolled onto my side and reached under the mattress. My hand closed around the knife. I drew it out and slipped it under the pillow near my head, then I closed my eyes and waited.

Some time later, Fitzroy entered. He did not carry any light and he was as silent as a mouse. He climbed into the bed, and I listened to his breathing. He didn't snore, but his breathing became more audible as he fell asleep. I continued to wait then, when I calculated that it must be the early hours of morning, I quietly got up.

With the knife in my hand, I checked the bed. He didn't stir. The bedroom door was open, but I needed the key to unlock the main door. It was dark and I was unfamiliar with the room, but I found the clothes stand where he'd draped his waistcoat. The pocket was empty.

Where was the damned key?

I searched it again, then moved onto his trousers. Perhaps he'd put it in his jacket. But he'd not worn a jacket all day. I'd seen him put the key in his waistcoat.

"It's not there." His voice startled me, even though he'd spoken softly. I felt his chest at my back, his breath in my hair, and his fingers around my hand. I couldn't move it or my arm. I was trapped.

I should have felt afraid. He was stronger than me, faster, a skillful fighter, and I didn't trust him. Yet I felt no fear. What I did feel was a thrill skipping down my spine with abandon. His scent filled my nostrils, his touch left me tingling in the places where our bare skin connected. I tried to steady my breathing, but it was impossible. It came out labored and shuddery.

The anticipation was exquisite torture. I wanted him to touch me, to hold me, to see me as a woman. Yet being discovered terrified me. The devil's daughter was only good for doing the devil's work.

Without a word, he took the knife off me. My back suddenly felt cold and I turned around. He set the knife on his bedside table then climbed into the bed. He lay on his side, but it was too dark to see if his eyes were opened or closed.

I returned to my trundle and lay down, but I didn't sleep until after dawn when he rose and left me alone in the bedroom. I checked the bedside table, but the knife was gone.

CHAPTER 7

Fitzroy didn't mention the knife incident the following day, but I was curious about something. "When did you realize I had it?" I asked as we ate breakfast.

"When I sat at the desk, I felt for it and noticed it missing."

Almost immediately then. "Why didn't you confront me at the time?"

He flattened the newspaper on the desk, his back to me. Clearly he didn't think me a threat. "I wanted to see what you would do."

"But what if I'd caught you by surprise, when your guard was lowered?"

"I never lower my guard."

"Not even when you're alone?"

He half turned so that he was in profile, and considered his answer before he said, "Sometimes."

"Which times?"

He turned a little further and regarded me through narrowed eyes. "You expect me to tell you?"

I grunted a laugh. "I suppose not."

He cracked the top of his boiled egg open with a spoon. "You won't catch me at such a moment, anyway."

"You're very arrogant, aren't you?"

"So I've been told."

After breakfast, he proposed another walk around the estate, and I readily agreed. The day was overcast and warm, with dark clouds gathering on the horizon. I got hot quickly. Sweat trickled down my spine and gathered in uncomfortable places. Fitzroy didn't look the least bit hot, but he only wore a shirt with no waistcoat or jacket, whereas I kept my jacket on. Taking it off would reveal too much now that my shirt was damp.

This time we stopped at the stables to see to the horses. Fitzroy rolled up his sleeves and mucked out their stalls, but I hung back. My father had not owned a horse, and while they were always present in the street, pulling carriages and carts, I'd never gone too close. Those hooves looked dangerous and the teeth large. I filled a pail with water from the trough and another with feed, but passed it to him instead of going in. I admired the way he walked behind them, without a care for the hooves, and rubbed their noses, getting close enough to have his own bitten off.

"Do you ride often?" I asked.

"When I have the opportunity," he said, closing the stall door and rejoining me.

"For pleasure?"

"Not anymore." He handed me an empty pail and I returned it to the back of the stables. "You don't like horses?"

"I like them well enough," I said. "As long as they are over there and I am over here."

"They frighten you?"

"I don't want to get too close to an animal that could crush me, kick me or bite me. What if it were startled? What if it didn't like the way I smelled? Or it liked my smell too much?"

"Unless you smell like an apple, there is little danger that a horse will eat you."

He led the way outside, and once again I had to trot to catch up to him. I passed a number of sharp and heavy looking tools that I could have grabbed and used on him, but he didn't seem worried. Either he knew I couldn't go through with hurting him or he had faith in his ability to stop me, even with his back to me.

"Fitzroy," I said, "slow down. I wish to ask you something."

He slowed his pace. "You should refer to me as Mr. Fitzroy."

"Or I could call you Death. Or do you prefer Mr. Death?"

He walked off. "Go on."

I blew out a breath. "What will you do when you cannot trace me as far back as you wish to go?"

"You think we'll fail?"

"Yes."

"I don't fail." He didn't look like he was joking. Not that he ever seemed anything other than deadly serious.

"Everyone fails from time to time."

He said nothing, but his strides lengthened as we crossed the courtyard. We did not go the back way into the house this time, but headed toward the side. It would seem our walk wasn't yet over.

"Let's assume you fail," I said. "Let's also assume that I continue to deny that I am a necromancer, which I will because I'm not. What will you do with me?"

He stopped and a small crease settled between his brows. He didn't look at me but at the corner of the house. "Come with me." He set off again, his strides longer and faster. Keeping up meant I had to half walk and half run. When we rounded the corner of the house I saw what he'd heard—a glossy black carriage approached.

When it pulled to a stop I saw that it was a private landau, not a hansom cab, with a gold escutcheon painted on the side.

"Is it Lord Gillingham again?" I asked. Cold sweat trickled down my spine. I shivered.

"It's not his carriage, but if he's one of the party, he won't hurt you."

"How can you be certain?"

He walked forward as a footman jumped down from the rumble seat and opened the door. Lord Gillingham emerged, a new walking stick in hand. He paused on the step when he spotted us. He nodded at Fitzroy and glared at me. Fitzroy didn't respond.

"Keep moving, Gilly," came a gruff voice from inside the cabin.

Fitzroy moved forward as Gillingham stepped onto the drive, allowing the man behind him to alight. The new fellow was very tall and strongly built, with shoulders as wide as Fitzroy's. Even at his age, which I guessed to be about sixty, he looked in good health with the figure of a much younger man. His age showed on his face, however, in the deep grooves across his forehead and around his eyes, and the full gray mutton chops.

"General Eastbrooke," Fitzroy said in greeting.

The man took Fitzroy's offered hand and shook it heartily. "Dressed for the occasion, I see, Lincoln."

"I didn't know you were coming, sir."

Their hands parted, yet Fitzroy didn't offer his to Gillingham. He didn't acknowledge the lord at all, and Gillingham grew more and more agitated as he waited. With a stomp of his walking stick into the ground, he turned to me. His cold eyes drilled into me.

I sidled closer to Fitzroy. The irony wasn't lost on me that I felt safer with my captor.

"Is this the boy?" General Eastbrooke said, in a deep, blustery voice. He placed his hands at his back and approached.

I remained where I was and tilted my head up. Fitzroy didn't seem to detest this man as he did Gillingham, so I assumed the general wasn't as willfully cruel as the lord.

"It is," Fitzory said, looking down at me. "Charlie, this is General Eastbrooke."

I crossed my arms. "Another committee member?"

Eastbrooke's thick gray brows lifted. "You're supposed to say it's nice to meet you, sir."

"But I don't know if it's nice to meet you or not." I was being deliberately irritating, but I didn't care. The more people I annoyed during my stay, the less likely they were to keep me when they realized I wouldn't help them. "You could be an arse, like him."

Gillingham raised his walking stick, but lowered it upon a glare from both Fitzroy and Eastbrooke. "I don't know why you protect him," Gillingham snapped.

"He's valuable to us," Eastbrooke said.

Fitzroy's gaze slid to the general's. Gillingham snorted. "For the time being," he muttered.

"How old is he?" Eastbrooke asked.

"Thirteen," Fitzroy said.

"Gilly tells me he's tried to escape."

"He has."

"And yet you allow him outside?"

"He needs exercise."

I needed exercise? Ha!

The general regarded me. "He'll try to escape again while he's free."

"Then I'll catch him."

"I'm sure that will not be a problem for you. He looks rather scrawny."

"Street urchins usually are."

"Hmmm." He paced around me, hands at his back, then came to a stop in front of me again. He thrust his chin forward. "Show your face, boy."

I backed away and kept my gaze down.

"You're going to defy me?" He clicked his tongue. "I don't think you're in any position to do that, do you?"

"I'm ugly," I said. "My ugliness embarrasses me."

Gillingham snorted, but the general simply continued to regard me with his cool eyes, his out-thrust chin. If he ordered Fitzroy to hold me while he swept my hair back, I would not be able to resist.

"Time is running out," Eastbrooke said. "You have this necromancer, but what of the other? If the girl is found by V.F, he will succeed. We need to win her to our side first or the battle is lost."

"We'll find her through Charlie. I'm sure of it."

Hearing Fitzroy speak about his suspicions of a link made my heart stop in my chest. How much did he know, and how much was a guess? He gave nothing away.

"And how will you do that?" Gillingham sneered. "He doesn't care what we're trying to achieve. He only cares for his own skin."

"I can't blame him for that, considering how he's lived."

"You're too soft, Fitzroy. Never thought I'd hear myself say that, but there you have it."

"Enough, Gilly!" Eastbrooke snapped. I wasn't sure if a lord outranked a general but Gillingham shut his mouth. Perhaps he was as awed by Eastbrooke's military bearing and powerful frame as I was.

"Do not forget what we're trying to achieve here," Gillingham muttered to Fitzroy.

"I haven't forgotten," Fitzroy said. "It's all I think about. It's all that matters to me."

Eastbrooke nodded. "Your loyalty and dedication to achieving the ministry's goals are not in doubt." He cut a flinty glare at Gillingham.

Gillingham bowed. "You're right, and I didn't mean to imply otherwise. It's just that your methods—"

"Are not up for discussion," Fitzroy told him.

Gillingham cleared his throat. He tapped the carriage steps with his walking stick. "Shall we leave your man to his work, Eastbrooke? It's too hot to stand around out here, and it doesn't seem as if we'll get an invitation to go inside."

His man? What an odd thing to call Fitzroy. He didn't seem like he could be anyone's anything. I would have called him his own man. Yet Fitzroy did call him "sir," while Eastbrooke called him "Lincoln" in turn. I still wasn't sure what that implied about their relationship.

"I look forward to your report, Lincoln," Eastbrooke said. "Let's hope I don't have to wait too long." The general turned to me. "If the queen or her family suffer because of your refusal to help us find the other necromancer, you will be blamed."

"And if *I* suffer because I helped? Who will be blamed then?"

"Nobody cares about you, boy," Gillingham said from inside the cabin. "Never forget that."

"How can I, with people like you to remind me?"

Eastbrooke sighed heavily. "You ought to instill some manners into him while he's here, Lincoln. You should know how to go about doing that. I seem to recall you lacked quite a few manners when you were young." He gave a wry smile as he turned away to climb the coach steps.

Because he turned away, he didn't see the muscle in Fitzroy's jaw bunch as he ground his back teeth. I wondered what methods the general had used to instill manners in him.

The coach rolled away and we returned inside before it was out of sight. "You've known those men a long time," I said as he closed the front door.

"Yes."

"How long?"

"I'm thirty. I've known Eastbrooke since birth and met Gillingham some years later."

"He was cruel to you as a child? General Eastbrooke?"

He blinked at me, and I could have sworn he was surprised. "He never touched me."

I frowned but didn't question him further. He strode away, and I suspected he wanted the conversation to end. He suddenly stopped at the foot of the stairs.

"I forgot to show you something yesterday, on our tour," he said.

"I would hardly call it a tour. You were the worst guide."

"I showed you every room worth seeing."

"With the blandness of an automaton. There was no vivid description, and no stories about the previous occupants or the rooms themselves."

"You didn't need a description since you could see the room for yourself, and I'm not a storyteller."

"So I see. So what room did you forget to show me?"

"The dungeon."

I gasped. "There's a dungeon under our feet?"

"The previous house on this site was medieval. When the house was removed, the dungeon was not filled in. It still has chains hanging from the walls. Would you like to see it?"

"No! What makes you think I'd want to see a dungeon?"

"Boys like gruesome things."

I strode past him up the stairs. "Not this boy. I've seen enough gruesome things in my life without needing to see more."

He followed me up in silence and together we headed back to his rooms. Once inside, he locked the door and pocketed the key in his trouser pocket.

"So what happens now?" I asked, throwing myself on the sofa. "Are you going to question me again? Has the visit from the committee members rattled you enough that you want to throw me in the dungeon and apply the thumb screws?"

"No."

"Then we have hit a wall. Your men will learn nothing of use by roaming around London, and you have learned nothing of use by roaming around the grounds with me."

"You're mistaken." He touched a teapot sitting on a tray on his desk to test its temperature then poured two cups. He handed one to me then sat on the chair opposite. "I've learned a great deal from our conversation."

He couldn't have. I'd not said a thing about my gender, my necromancing, or my home. I'd been very careful. I sipped, watching him through my hair.

He sat back and sipped too, never taking his gaze off me. He seemed to enjoy drawing out the moment, teasing my frayed nerves to breaking point. Finally, he placed the cup in the saucer. "You're witty and observant," he said, "and educated."

"That's not very useful."

"And your accent changes when you're not thinking about it."

I lowered my cup. Had my accent changed or was he bluffing? None of the boys ever commented on the way I spoke. I was always careful to sound like one of them.

"When you feel comfortable, it becomes more refined. It's a north London accent, middle class, perhaps originating not far from here. You only resort to gutter language when you think it will make an impact and drive home the disguise you've built for yourself. When you're having a conversation with me alone, it changes. My guess is that you haven't lived on the street all your life, but came from a good home before your circumstances changed."

A good home. That's what everyone called middle class households like mine. A good home inhabited by a good man who'd sadly lost his cherished daughter the same night his wife died. Yes, that summed it up nicely.

Fitzroy watched me, and I watched him in return; my heart had sunk to my stomach. So he'd been kind to me only to get me to relax in his presence and extract information from me. I should have known and been more alert. I should not have lowered my defenses for a moment. I should not have allowed myself to be coaxed into submission like a dog.

I tossed the cup and its contents on the beautiful thick rug and marched toward the bedroom. I slammed the door and looked around for something to throw. I picked up the bowl of water from the washstand but lowered it again.

I'd been around boys for so long I'd forgotten how not to behave like them.

With a sigh, I lay on the truckle bed. After an hour or so, Fitzroy entered. He didn't speak; he just set my book down on the bedside table and left again.

I warred with myself. I wanted to read, but he was so smug—so arrogant—that I didn't want to give him the satisfaction of letting him know that he'd understood my needs. It felt like letting him win.

When I could stand the boredom no longer, however, I retrieved the book and flipped to the page I had read up to. My temper was only harming me, not him, after all. With that in mind, I returned to the parlor and passed by his desk, where he sat conducting his scientific experiments. I would have preferred to watch him but I was determined not to show any interest.

"There's cake," he said without looking up.

A slice had been set down on the table near my cup, which had been retrieved from the floor. It was empty and the rug damp where I'd spilled the tea. I padded back to his desk and the teapot and refilled my cup. I had the sudden urge to spill it over his experiments and ruin them.

As if he knew what I was thinking, his hand darted out and caught my wrist. The brown liquid in the dish in his other hand didn't so much as splash a drop over the side.

"I wasn't going to do it," I said.

He paused then let me go. I returned to the sofa and continued reading from where I'd left off. It was another mystery book. Perhaps that was the only type of fiction he read.

Fitzroy was packing up his experiments when there was a knock at the door. "Sir!" called Seth. "We have news."

They couldn't have found out about me. Surely not. I tucked my legs up beneath me and gripped the book harder.

Fitzroy let Seth and Gus in. Their hair was damp with sweat, and dust smudged their clothing, hands and faces. Their gazes flew to me.

I swallowed heavily.

Fitzroy waited patiently for them to begin. I didn't know how he could remain so calm and not pester them to speak. I was coiled tight and felt sick to my stomach. I pretended to read.

"We did as you said, and asked some questions of the little gutter snipes," Gus said. "Cost us a bleeding fortune."

"But we found out much," Seth went on. "Something very curious is going on, sir."

I felt their gazes on me again and glanced up. I closed the book. There was no point trying to fool anyone.

"Curious how?" Fitzroy asked. He stood with his arms crossed over his chest. Although the men looked exhausted, he didn't offer them a seat or refreshments.

"We traced him from district to district, just as you told us to," Seth said. "He was remembered, and it wasn't hard. In fact, it was too easy. They recognized him from our description immediately."

"We found out where he were three years ago, then four and five," Gus said, staring at me. He had an odd expression on his face. It took me a moment to realize he was wary, perhaps even scared.

"It was then that we understood why it had been so easy to trace him," Seth said. "He was always the same as the way we described him—a young lad of thirteen with a pointed chin and with brown hair hanging over his face, only staying for six months or so then moving on. A lad who never told anyone where he was from. Exactly the same, sir. He never aged."

They weren't the smartest fellows. Fitzroy wouldn't have needed to go back all five years to realize something was amiss. He was looking at me now too, but it wasn't clear what he thought of my supposed agelessness.

"Is it magic?" Gus whispered, still staring at me.

I wasn't clear if he was addressing me so I refrained from answering.

"Perhaps he's actually an elderly man," Seth suggested.

I smiled. They couldn't be further from the truth.

"You said you traced him as far back as five years ago," Fitzroy said. "No further?"

"We hit a dead end, sir," Seth said. "Five years ago, he just seemed to suddenly appear from nowhere. The gang he joined doesn't know where he came from before that. The trail went cold in Tufnell Park. We're sorry, sir."

I was giddy with relief and gripped the book harder to anchor myself. My cheeks warmed again, and I hadn't realized I'd gone cold until that moment.

Fitzroy dismissed his men.

Seth and Gus left, their gazes upon me as they backed out of the room. The poor men looked terribly confused, although less worried since I hadn't shriveled them with my "magic."

Fitzroy came to my side and calmly squatted down. His face was only inches from mine, but I didn't dip my head. I watched him through the strands of my hair, daring him to see the woman behind the veil. Did he realize what Seth and Gus's findings meant? The man's pitch black eyes gave nothing away.

"Tell me your secret, Charlie." His deep voice rumbled from his chest and vibrated over my skin. The undercurrent raised the hairs on the back of my neck.

"Or what?"

"Or I will need to employ more…drastic measures."

I huffed out a humorless laugh, flipping out the hair at my nose. "I have nearly starved to death, almost frozen to death, been beaten to near death, left to rot in jail with men who wanted to do things to me that made me want to die. Unless you plan on killing me, your drastic measures will be a gift by comparison."

I stood, and he stood too, blocking me. He towered above me, and I was more aware of the difference in our sizes than ever. But he didn't touch me. He simply eyed the book clutched in my arms then walked to his desk.

Did he mean to deny me the books? Perhaps other entertainments too, or even his company? I would regret that most of all—and I wished I wouldn't.

"Boring me to death is something new, at least."

***

I slept fitfully that night. My nightmares kept waking me. I wondered if I'd made any sounds and woken Fitzroy too. The devil in me hoped so.

He was gone before I got out of bed in the morning. When I tried the door to see if he'd forgotten to lock it, Gus spoke from the corridor outside.

"Don't try escaping, lad. You won't trick me today."

"Where's Death?" I asked.

"Out."

"How long will he be?"

"Depends."

"On what?"

"On how quick he'll be."

Breakfast must have been sitting on the tray for some time. The bacon was cold and the toast limp. I nibbled the bacon before returning to the bedroom and washing.

I read all morning. Fitzroy had not removed the books, thank goodness, and he'd even left the newspaper. I read it too, for variety. His threat of "drastic measures" had come to nothing, it seemed. So much for my fears.

Gus and Seth took turns at bringing in tea and then luncheon, and finally dinner arrived as dusk settled on the horizon. Fitzroy was still out, they said. His long absence stretched my nerves, and I couldn't concentrate on reading anymore. I knocked on the door.

"I want to go for a walk," I told whoever was on the other side.

"No," Gus called back. "You're not allowed out today. Death's orders."

I sighed. "Come inside and play cards with me then."

"Can't do that neither. Death said we're only to come in to bring you food."

"So I can't even have a bath in the bathroom?"

"Why do you want another bath? You had one two days ago."

I kicked the door. "I hate you!"

"Because you can't have a bath?" He grunted. "Don't see how that's my fault."

"What about warm water? Can I have some delivered to the bedroom?"

"S'pose so."

I heard his heavy footsteps disappear, but they returned almost immediately. Seth mustn't be too far away.

Several minutes later, Seth delivered a jug of hot water. I added it to the cold water in the basin and dipped my fingers in. Perfect. Perhaps I'd wash my hair again. It still smelled faintly of kerosene.

"Civilization agrees with you," Seth said with a nod at the water.

"What do you mean?"

"You were filthy when you first came here, and now you want baths all the time, and warm water for washing. There were no baths or warm water where you came from. It'll be hard to give it up and go back to that life."

Yes, it would be hard. I'd settled into the easy life at Lichfield Towers much too readily, and the thought of walking away from it was becoming less and less appealing with every passing day.

What would happen if I gave in and told Fitzroy everything? Would it really be so bad?

Seth left and the lock on the main door clicked. I shut the bedroom door too, just to be safe, and removed my clothes. I washed my body first and dried off with the towel, then tipped my head forward into the basin and rinsed my hair. I closed my eyes as water cascaded down my neck, over my ears, my face. Its warmth was heavenly. I sighed.

"You lied to me." The familiar, deep voice sent my heart plunging to my toes. I opened my eyes to see Fitzroy standing beside me, his fists clenched into tight balls at his sides. From the angle of my position, I could not see his face, yet I knew he could see me. All of me. There was no hiding my nakedness now, or my womanliness.

CHAPTER 8

Slowly, slowly, I straightened, turning away from him and covering my chest and nether regions as I did so. Nobody had seen me naked since I was a little girl, and my humiliation was absolute. My face and neck burned. My heart smashed into my ribs. I wanted to run. I wanted to curl into a ball and hide under the blankets. Hot tears stung my eyes and my lower lip wobbled. I bit it hard.

A towel came around my shoulders. I grasped the edges and pulled it tight around my body. It provided enough modesty to allow me to turn around and meet Fitzroy's gaze. A gaze that quickly flew to my face. Had he been staring at my legs? If so, there was no heat in *his* cheeks, nor his eyes. They grew blacker as they drilled into me.

"You should have told me," he snarled.

"Should I?" I shot back. "You kidnapped me, held me prisoner, and want my necromancy magic for reasons I can't yet fathom, and yet I should have trusted you enough to tell you my greatest secret?" The moment I'd said it, I regretted it. I'd just admitted to being a necromancer.

It probably didn't matter now. He showed no surprise. I suspected he'd discovered more than my gender today.

He lowered his head but continued to watch me through those midnight black eyes of his. His chest and shoulders heaved with his deep breaths, and his jaw was set like iron. His unbound hair tumbled forward. He couldn't have looked more like the devil if he'd worn horns and carried a pitchfork.

I tossed my head, flicking my wet hair back. I no longer needed to hide behind it. His eyes roamed over my face, slowly taking in the parts of me he'd not seen until now. I felt my blood heat again and I prayed I could control the blush. Fortunately, his gaze met mine once more, and his fury returned. Indeed, he seemed angrier than ever.

As was I. He may have discovered my gender, but he hadn't switched to acting the gentleman. He hadn't left me alone to dress. Did he expect me to do it in front of him? I couldn't guess what he wanted. All I knew was that he was furious with me.

"Are you mad at me because you didn't realize sooner?" I smiled, but it was all teeth and no humor. "The clever Lincoln Fitzroy failed to notice that I was a girl. How disappointed in yourself you must be."

He shifted his weight, and the movement had me stepping back, away from him, out of his reach. I'd said too much. He would surely force me to stop talking somehow.

Yet he didn't come closer. To my surprise, the fury in his gaze dampened a little. His body was still rigid, however, and his hands balled into fists.

"You're right. I should have noticed. But to be fair, you were very good, Charlie. Or should I say, Charlotte."

I jerked my head to the side. Being called by that name brought back memories; some good, some horrible and sad. But it also felt wrong. I wasn't Charlotte anymore. She was gone. "My name is Charlie and that's what you will call me."

"I'm not angry because I didn't see what you truly were," he said. "I'm angry because you lied to me about it."

"Of course I bloody lied! Do you know what it's like for girls living on the streets? It has been…difficult as a boy. As a girl…" I shook my head. I couldn't finish the sentence. I didn't want to think about the horrors that would have befallen me if people had known I was a girl—and a virgin from a good family at that.

His fingers uncurled at his sides. He crossed his arms. "You think I would have taken advantage of you?"

"I don't know. You did kidnap me and were rather rough in the process."

"That's because I thought you were a boy."

"You think it's acceptable to be rough while kidnapping a boy?"

"I kept you in *here*. In my private chambers."

"What was so improper about that? You didn't see anything until today. And you already knew I was a woman when you marched in here," I added with a sniff. "If impropriety bothered you, you would have knocked first."

"I could have hurt you. You resisted me in the street, you tried to escape and kill me in the process. I could have hurt you at any of those times to stop you." He lowered his face to mine. "I do not like to hurt women."

"So my lie upsets your moral code? Ha! Forgive me for thinking you a hypocrite, Mr. *Death*."

His lips tightened. His nostrils flared. I feared I'd gone too far, but it would seem his moral code was strong—at least where the harming of women was concerned.

"You didn't hurt me much," I told him. "Even though you probably wanted to, after I shot you." As soon as I said it, I wished I hadn't. I didn't want to soften. I wanted to remain mad at him for walking in on me. Anger was better than humiliation. I still felt sick, knowing that he'd seen everything. He couldn't fail to measure me against Lady Harcourt and other beautiful women he must have bedded. My body was skeletal compared to her lushness. How he must find the comparison amusing.

"Get dressed." He stalked to the door, his strides long and purposeful. "This conversation isn't finished."

I glared at the closed door, anger and humiliation swirling inside me because of that man. That insufferable *bully*. I hated him. Hated his smugness and arrogance, hated the way he stomped over my pride. I was caught between wanting to slap his cheek and never seeing him again. One would satisfy the furious woman in me, the other the embarrassed one. I would both slap him and leave if I thought I had a chance of success. But I wasn't fast enough to hit him and he'd proven too difficult to escape from so far.

I took my time dressing. I sat on the bed for an age, the towel wrapped around me, and thought of all the tricks and horrid things he'd done to me in the last few days to fuel my anger and dampen the embarrassment. But there were so few instances. He'd even shown kindness, on occasion. Whenever I thought of those times, and how I'd wanted more of them, I felt even sicker at what he'd seen and what he must think of me now.

The best way to remain angry was to face him, so I dressed. Instead of dragging my damp hair over my face, I decided to sweep it back. Let him look me in the eyes as he gloated.

He was sipping whiskey by the unlit fireplace when I entered his sitting room from the bedroom. He paused, the glass at his lips. A beat passed. Two. I gave him a defiant glare and he downed the remaining contents.

He crossed to the sideboard and poured another. A bottle of wine was open on a tray and a glass sat with it. Either Seth or Gus must have brought it up, along with the selection of cheeses. I wondered if they knew about my being a woman yet. I wondered what their reactions would be.

Fitzroy held out the wine glass to me. "If I give you this, will you throw it in my face?"

"Let's find out, shall we?" I accepted the glass. My fingers brushed against his and something inside me jolted at the touch. Despite everything, I had a strong urge to linger.

He let go of the glass and indicated I should sit on the sofa. He occupied one of the armchairs, looking every bit a king on his throne. I lowered myself to the sofa, but no longer felt sure how to sit. Legs slightly apart like a boy didn't seem appropriate, nor did lounging. But without a woman's bustle to get in the way, I didn't need to perch. I sat back and kept my knees together. It felt far too prim and unnatural.

"I didn't know you were in a state of undress," he said. "I apologize for walking in on you."

"And for not turning around and walking out again immediately? You could have left, Fitzroy, yet you didn't. Did you enjoy witnessing my humiliation? Will you enjoy telling Seth and Gus what I look like without clothes?"

His glare turned chilly. "Is that what you think of me?"

I sipped my wine.

After a moment, he finished the rest of his whiskey and set the glass down on the table beside him. "Remind me to thank Lady Harcourt when next I see her."

"What has she to do with anything?"

"It was she who told me you might be a girl."

"You already knew before today?"

"Suspected."

"Then why continue to allow me in your room? Not that I cared," I added quickly, "but you are the one who seemed upset by it."

"I wasn't sure I agreed with her suspicion. I thought spending more time with you would help me decide one way or another, although she was very much against it. It didn't help, by the way. Your disguise was impeccable. I did realize you were educated and from a well-off family, but not that you were female."

"What gave me away to Lady Harcourt?"

"You took an interest in her clothes and not the woman inside them. She claims the way you looked at her was that of one woman appraising another out of curiosity, not desire."

"She thinks every male looks at her with desire?"

"She is a desirable woman."

I took a long sip of my wine. Lady Harcourt was everything I would never be. There was no point wishing it could be otherwise, but his words stung nevertheless.

"She confided her suspicions to me the night she returned for dinner," he said. "I didn't believe her until last night. When Seth and Gus returned with the tale of the ageless boy, it began to make sense. As a thirteen year-old girl, you had done most of your growing, although perhaps your lack of nourishing food has kept you on the small side. Thirteen year-old boys still have some growing to go, but *you* never changed. That's why you had to move on every few months. With Lady Harcourt's suspicions in mind, I returned to Tufnell Park today to follow a different line of inquiry to Seth and Gus. I asked about a *girl* who arrived in their midst five years ago. There was one who stood out, but she appeared only briefly. The boys remembered her as being a miserable, frightened thing with beautiful golden brown hair. That hair and her pretty face—and innocence—made her a target for every whore's minder in the district. When you suddenly disappeared, they assumed you'd been taken and put to work. Or died."

"Clearly I didn't die." I hated how my voice sounded weak. I cleared my throat and sipped my wine.

He picked up his glass, but seeing it empty, set it down again. He didn't let it go, and the fingers gripping it turned white. "How did you escape?"

"The man who caught me planned on selling me to the highest bidder, that first night. He dragged me into every gambling den and disreputable tavern in the north of the city, making sure everyone got a good look. Men, including so-called gentlemen, placed bids on me. Some bought my abductor drinks. By midnight, he was so drunk he couldn't stand. I slipped away while he was pissing in an alley behind a tavern. He was too slow and slipped over in his attempt to come after me. When I was far enough away, I hid until morning. I didn't know where I was, but the area was poor. At around dawn, a door to one of the nearby houses opened and a woman emerged with some clothes to hang out to dry. When she returned inside, I stole some boys' clothing from the line. I peeped through the window into her kitchen and waited until she left, then I snuck in and stole a knife. I cut my hair and sold it to a man who paid me a shilling for it. I bought a loaf of bread, but instead of eating it, I found a gang of boys living nearby. I offered it to them in exchange for joining them. They thought I'd stolen it, and since they were always looking for good thieves, they included me immediately. None of them ever thought I was anything other than a boy."

"It's been hard for you," he said quietly.

"Not as hard as it has been for some." Or as hard as it could have been, if I hadn't disguised myself. "What I told you does not leave this room. You do not tell Seth or Gus, Lady Harcourt or any of the other committee members. Do you understand?"

"I won't betray your trust."

I wasn't sure whether to believe him, but I had no choice. "So you know that I'm a woman," I said. "What else?"

He drew in a long, measured breath. "After I learned about the girl with the golden hair in Tufnell Park, I changed tactic. I visited the local police station and asked about any girls that had been reported missing five years ago."

"They didn't think that odd?"

"Probably. I claimed I was a private enquiry agent, employed to find missing girls by a good Samaritan."

I snorted. "Only an idiot would fall for that."

"They fell for it."

"Just proves the constabulary are dolts."

"The detective inspector remembered a local girl going missing from her home at about that time. Her name was Charlotte Holloway and her father was a vicar."

"And you just happened to be searching for a girl who was known to live with a vicar, and my name just happened to be Charlie, so similar to Charlotte. Were you surprised that I was *that* necromancer?"

"Not by then. When I realized you were a girl, I suspected you must be the necromancer I sought."

"It would seem I am the last necromancer after all." I raised my glass in salute and drained it. "And you have me in your clutches. You have succeeded in keeping me away from the man who wants to use me against the queen, so all is well. There is no other necromancer for him to find, now. If I promise not to fall into *his* clutches, will you let me go?"

"No."

I rubbed my forehead. I wasn't used to the wine and felt dizzy from drinking it so quickly. "Why did I suspect you would say that?"

"Go to bed, Charlie. You're tired. We'll discuss this further in the morning."

I dropped my hand and thumped it on the sofa arm. "I may be three years away from reaching the age of majority, but I am an adult in every other way. Do not treat me like a child, now that you know I am not one."

"I won't. But the truth is, I am in a difficult position. This is a household full of men and you are a young woman."

"Then lct me go."

"I can't. I cannot risk you being caught by him. Legally and morally, I should return you to your father. You belong there, but I—"

"I do not *belong* in his house," I snapped. "Not if he doesn't want me."

His eyes widened. "You did not run away?"

"No. He threw me out."

I had the great satisfaction of seeing him shocked. At least, I think he was shocked. His lips parted ever so slightly, but shut again almost immediately. Then they flattened. "I assumed he beat you," he said quietly, "and that you'd had enough. I wouldn't have returned you to him if that were the case."

"And now, when you know that he didn't beat me, that he simply doesn't want me?"

"It seems I still won't be returning you." He leaned forward and rested his elbows on his knees. It was almost a casual position, except he seemed as tightly coiled as ever. Was he expecting me to try and escape, even now? "The detective said you disappeared the night your mother died. Did you raise her spirit? Did your father see? Is that why he…?"

"Thought me abhorrent? Yes. She died. I held her in my arms and begged for her to come back and not leave me. To my utter surprise, the smoky thing that looked like her saw me. It lay on her body, and the body came to life. I was so shocked that I let her go. Father was shocked too. Horrified, in fact. He got down on his knees and prayed and cried. My mother's spirit spoke through her body and asked me to release her. She said it wasn't what she wanted. That she was sorry, and she needed to go. So I said some words to the effect that I release her. The spirit drifted away and the body collapsed, dead once more. My father stopped praying and turned on me. He never hit me, but he called me things. What I'd done was unnatural, against God, and all things holy, he said. He ordered me to leave and hustled me out the door. I haven't set foot inside the house since, nor have I spoken to him."

Fitzroy was silent for a long time. His finger brushed against his top lip as he watched me. It was unnerving. I was just about to tell him to stop staring when he said, "Now that we know you are the only necromancer, we can proceed."

"What do you mean?"

"When I assumed you were a second necromancer, I was only concerned with getting to the girl before he did, the man with the initials V.F. But now I know you are she, it's time to flush him out."

I gasped. "You mean to use me as bait!"

"Incentive."

"You are going to use an eighteen year-old woman as bait to catch a monster!"

"You prefer I use a thirteen year-old boy?"

"This is not a joke!"

"I am not joking."

I couldn't believe what I was hearing. He was as heartless as the man he was trying to catch. Perhaps I shouldn't have been surprised; Seth and Gus had warned me he was an unfeeling wretch.

"You will be safe," he said.

"You cannot guarantee that."

His jaw worked, and I wondered if I'd insulted his manliness by bringing his ability to keep a woman safe into question. Well, good. He could not guarantee such a thing, and it was arrogance to even think he could.

"I won't help you, Fitzroy, and you can't make me." I crossed my arms over my chest in a somewhat petty show of defiance.

"I understand your fear, Charlie."

"Do you? You're a necromancer wanted by a madman, are you?" I grunted. "Don't pretend to sympathize. You don't have a sympathetic bone in your body."

He snatched his glass off the table and stalked over to the sideboard. He poured himself another glass of whiskey but didn't drink it. Instead, he set it aside, very deliberately, and prowled back to me.

I swallowed heavily. *He can't force you, Charlie. He can't make you do anything you don't want to.*

Except he could. He was strong enough and, dare I say it, ruthless enough to do anything. I wondered how far he would go to get his own way.

I dug my fingernails into the armrest. "I won't work for you, but I won't give myself up to him, either."

"That's not enough."

"It has to be. I'm not offering more. Put me back on the street if you want. I don't care. I'll be safer there than if I parade myself in front of him."

His eyes narrowed and I wondered if he suspected that I'd seen the fellow. I'd yet to tell him anything about the doctor who'd visited Father. I wasn't sure whether I wanted to. He might see that as my agreement to help.

"You refuse, knowing that the queen's life may be in danger?"

"I care nothing for a queen who doesn't lift a finger to help the children starving on her city's streets."

He crossed his arms and regarded me down that straight, handsome nose of his. "I'm offering you a roof, food, clothing and comforts. It may be summer now, but winter is always around the corner."

"I've survived winters before."

"How many more years can you pass yourself off as a boy? It won't last forever."

"I know that. I'll adjust when the time comes."

"It's a lonely life, moving on every few months, never allowing yourself to have friends. Do you want to be alone forever?"

I leveled my gaze with his and tried very hard not to let him see that he'd rattled me. "Perhaps I'll offer myself to a kind man. One willing to protect me in exchange for keeping his bed warm."

He leaned forward and rested one hand on top of mine on the chair arm, trapping it. He drew so close to my face that I could have kissed him. The traitorous feminine part of me wanted to do it. The other part of me wanted to smash his nose with my forehead.

"I can protect you," he said, voice velvety thick and soft.

In that moment, with his dark eyes boring into mine, his breath on my cheek, I wanted to believe him. I wanted to stay with him. I wanted to offer myself to him and keep *his* bed warm, and I would do it without the offer of protection, too.

He suddenly let my hand go, releasing me. "You don't have to do anything in exchange except lure V.F. into the open."

My breathing sounded loud in my ears, so I concentrated on steadying it before he saw how much his presence affected me. "I want nothing to do with a scheme that puts me in danger. And don't tell me you'll protect me," I added as he opened his mouth to speak. "Because why would you? What do you care if I am alive or dead? You don't need me or my necromancy, beyond it being a lure. In fact, my presence causes you problems. With me around, I am a danger for all sorts of madmen—not just this one."

He sat down again and stretched out his long legs. His shoes almost touched my bare feet on the rug. "You're right," he said eventually. "Bad people will always want you, when they learn what you can do. All the more reason for you to remain here, under my protection. I can't send you back to your father, so it seems you are under my care now, whether we like it or not. It's my duty to see that you are safe, and I take my duty very seriously."

Duty, safe…they were just words; easily spoken and easily discarded once I'd done what he wanted me to do. "Forgive me if I don't put any faith in you doing your *duty*," I spat.

"I am not your father, Charlie," he growled. "If I promise to protect you, I will."

I pushed myself up from the sofa and strode to the bedroom door. "I've had enough talking. We're getting nowhere. I suggest you look for other options, Fitzroy, because I am not going to help you."

Before I knew what was happening, he'd grabbed my arm and spun me round. He loomed above me, his face set hard as granite, his eyes two black pits that went on forever. "You don't seem to understand, Charlie. There are no other options. Let me make two things very clear to you—you will help me, and I will keep you safe." He released me, but the heat of his fingers remained on my arm.

He strode to his desk, leaving me standing in the bedroom doorway with my insides in knots and my heart beating in my throat. With an almighty heave of breath, I turned and slammed the bedroom door closed behind me. I threw myself on the truckle bed and pulled my knees up to my chest.

"I hate you!" I shouted at the door.

He didn't answer.

CHAPTER 9

"You have to wear it." Lady Harcourt held the corset open like a trap that she would close around me as soon as I was near enough. "All ladies must wear corsets."

"I'm no lady." I stood with hands on hips and kept a wary eye on her. I could dodge her, if need be. "And I am not wearing a corset. I wore them when I was younger and discovered how unsuitable they are for someone like me."

She sighed and her shoulders lost some of their tension. "I understand, Charlie. I do. But you are not living on the street anymore. You don't need to run and hide like a lost boy. You can be yourself."

I wasn't sure who that was but I didn't say so. She seemed intent on turning me into a respectable woman. She had arrived after breakfast, summoned by Fitzroy, and hustled me into the bedroom where she proceeded to lay some women's clothing out for me on the large bed. I'd refused to change into the items, but she'd threatened to order Seth and Gus to hold me down while she stripped me. She'd been so unruffled about it that I couldn't tell if she was joking or not. I'd decided I could make a concession on most of the clothing. The corset, however, seemed a step too far.

"I'm not concerned about running and hiding," I told her. "I am concerned about breathing."

"I won't lace it too tight."

Could I believe a woman whose own corset had deformed her waist to an unnaturally tiny size?

She lowered the device and took my hand in hers. "You cannot parade yourself near the men without a corset. It's indecent."

"It wasn't a problem before."

"They didn't know you were a girl before. Now that they do, I'm afraid they will be…looking for evidence of your femininity."

I snorted. "They'll have to look very hard. My femininity is not very noticeable, even without a corset."

"My dear, we both know what men think of women who don't wear proper underwear." Her voice took on a sympathetic hush and the color rose to her cheeks. Had Fitzroy told her what had happened to me when I first found myself on the streets? Even though he'd promised not to? Or was her statement merely a general one? "I'm sure you've seen how the prostitutes dress."

"Some of them wear those contraptions."

"Loosely."

"What will you do if I continue to refuse?"

"I'll instruct Mr. Fitzroy to deliver you to my house this afternoon, where you will be safe from the roaming gazes of Seth and Gus."

The notion brought an inexplicable swell of disappointment to my chest. I'd fought tooth and nail to get free, and yet I wasn't prepared to leave Lichfield Towers for a residence I knew nothing about, with a woman who would make me wear corsets and act like a lady.

I snatched the corset off her and put it on over the new chemise. I turned my back to her and gasped as she pulled hard on the laces. "You said you wouldn't do it tight!"

"This isn't tight." She pulled again, jerking my entire body toward her. "Hold onto the bedpost."

I grumbled as she finished the lacing, then stood like a ridiculous statue with a straight back. I tried to draw in a deep breath, only to find my chest wouldn't expand enough. "This is torture."

"It gives you a fine shape." She smiled. "You almost look respectable. Now, the petticoats."

She helped me slip two petticoats over my drawers, then a black cotton gown over the top. The outfit was a spare one that had been used by a previous servant girl in her household. It was a little large, but not a bad fit. I'd hoped for something prettier when she'd announced that she would be outfitting me in women's clothing upon her arrival. If I had to wear a dress again, I'd prefer it to be something with a bustle in a brighter color. The servant's garb was drab.

I laced up the boots, but she wouldn't let me out of the bedroom until she'd fixed my hair. There was little she could do, with it being so short, but she managed to make it a little more feminine with the strategic placement of a few pins at the front and a bonnet positioned toward the back.

I admired her handiwork in the dressing table mirror and had to admit she'd done a fine job. I looked like a woman, albeit a somewhat gaunt one with owlish eyes.

"They'll wonder how they ever mistook you for a boy." Lady Harcourt touched a finger under my chin and turned my head this way and that to inspect me from all angles. "You're quite pretty, with that sweet oval face and those big blue eyes." She let me go with a sigh. "You will have to come home with me after all."

"No! I'm remaining here. Or I leave altogether," I added.

She blinked. Was she offended? "Why don't you want to live with me? My house is larger than this. I have many servants, some of them girls of your age. You'll be bound to find a friend among them."

"I do not wish to be your servant, Lady Harcourt. As kind as you have been to me, I prefer it here."

"But there are only men here!"

"Men are only large boys, and I'm used to boys."

She spluttered a laugh. "I'm afraid you can't stay. I cannot, in all conscience, leave you here. Besides, Fitzroy won't know what to do with you, now that you're a girl. He has almost admitted as much to me."

I stormed past her and opened the bedroom door. Fitzroy looked up from his desk and his eyes widened. He took in my dress and hair with a cool, sweeping gaze that finally settled on my face.

"Is there a problem?" he asked, looking past me to Lady Harcourt. Despite his casual stance and words, his mouth was set firm and his eyes were hard. From the little I'd seen of him that morning, he was still furious with me for refusing to help. Well, I was furious too, and I wasn't giving in.

"I am not going to live with her," I said, hands on hips. "Either you keep me here as your prisoner, or you let me go."

"She cannot stay here." Lady Harcourt came to stand beside me. She was taller than me, but I liked to think I presented a fiercer façade.

"If you make me go with her, I will find a way to escape," I said. "It'll be easier in a big household with more servants. Besides, won't they grow suspicious about the girl locked away in a room?"

Fitzroy lifted a brow then nodded. "I agree."

"She cannot stay here, Lincoln." Lady Harcourt's tone turned crisp. "Look at her!"

What was that supposed to mean? "This was a pointless exercise." I went to remove the bonnet and veil, but Fitzroy grasped my hand. I glared at him.

He glared back. "Leave it on."

"Why?" I spat. "I am not going to help you, which means you are going to keep me here indefinitely, locked away where no one can see me. Or you will let me go. What does it matter how I dress?"

"The ministry is not a charity," Fitzroy said in a voice that sent a chill skittering across my skin. "And I am not a kind person. You will do as I say and help us."

"Or?"

"There is no 'or.'"

"Ha!"

Lady Harcourt bustled past me and laid a hand on his arm. She searched his face, her brow deeply furrowed. "Lincoln? What are you going to do?"

He met my gaze over the top of her head. It was masked; unreadable. He pulled away from her and strode to the door. "In here," he growled at Seth and Gus.

The two guards stopped dead just inside the doorway. Neither could take their eyes off me. Their warm, lingering gazes brought heat to my cheeks and I wished I could hide beneath my hair again.

"Stop staring," I snapped. "Haven't you seen a girl before?"

"Um, I, um, didn't know you was so pretty." Gus no longer looked at me but at his feet; most of his words were mumbled into his chest.

Seth cleared his throat and sketched a short bow. "That dress is very fetching on you, Charlie. Er, Charlotte. *Miss* Charlotte."

"It's a servant's dress and plain black," I said. "It is the least fetching outfit imaginable. And you can continue to call me Charlie. Or better yet, don't speak to me at all."

Seth's face fell, and I regretted my harsh manner. It wasn't his fault that I was in this predicament. It was entirely Fitzroy's.

Out of the corner of my eye, I caught Lady Harcourt raising her brows at him. *See,* she mouthed.

"Prepare the carriage," Fitzroy ordered his men.

"Where are you taking me?" I asked as Gus and Seth left.

"Out." To Lady Harcourt, he said, "Does she have gloves?"

"I'll fetch them." She disappeared into the bedroom.

"I am not going anywhere with you," I told Fitzroy.

He said nothing, which worried me. I'd found he was far more dangerous when he didn't speak.

Lady Harcourt returned and handed me a pair of black gloves. "It's warm out and you won't require a coat." When I neither put on the gloves nor moved, she lifted her brows at Fitzroy. "Now what?"

Fitzroy put out his hand. I hesitated then placed the gloves on his palm. "What are you—?"

He picked me up and slung me over his shoulder. One arm clamped across my kicking legs like a steel barrier, the other still clutched the gloves.

"Let me go!" I tried to straighten, but the corset not only made breathing difficult, it limited my movement. I squirmed instead, intent on not making it easy for him, but it made little difference. Besides, I was very aware that my bottom was close to his face. I might not be much of a lady, or want to be one, but wriggling my rear end in his face was not something I could bring myself to do. I stilled.

He carried me out of the room. Lady Harcourt followed behind us, her steps short and quick.

"Put me down!" I shouted.

"Don't bother screaming," he said as he descended the stairs. "Cook, Seth and Gus won't help you."

I called him every crude name I could think of, loudly, and pounded his back with my fists. Nothing made him stop, but at least he would sport bruises for a week. Not only did he not stop, he didn't slow down. Indeed, his pace quickened, and his steps became jauntier as we reached the next flight of stairs. It made for a very uncomfortable ride.

"You're deliberately being rough now," I snapped.

"This is my natural way of descending stairs."

"It is not. You've got the smoothest stride of anyone I've seen. It's why you're able to sneak up on people." I tried to twist to get a better look at him, but it was impossible. I could only see the back of his head. His unruly black hair was tied up with a leather strip. Perhaps if I pulled it…

Lady Harcourt clicked her tongue. "I'll need to fix her hair in the carriage."

"You're not coming with us," he said.

"I must! She needs a chaperone!"

He reached the base of the staircase and turned toward her as she stopped alongside us. I suspected he was bestowing one of his chilling glares on her because she stepped away.

"It's a mistake, Lincoln," she said as he carried me outside. I took that to mean she'd given in.

We had to wait a few minutes for the carriage to be brought around. When it stopped, and Seth opened the door, Fitzroy dislodged me from his shoulder onto the bench seat. I bounced and hit my arm against the other side. Before I'd recovered my balance, he'd climbed after me and shut the door.

The coach took off with a jerk. I lunged for the door, but Fitzroy was too quick. He barred it with his arm.

"You're a prick." I sank into the corner and pushed the hairpins that had come loose back in place.

"It's not too late to change your mind," he said. "Help me willingly and you can live at Lichfield Towers under my protection."

I snorted. "You cannot guarantee my safety once he learns what I am. He'll not stop until he catches me."

"Then I'll have to stop him *before* he catches you."

"How?"

"By killing him."

I swallowed past the lump in my throat and tore my gaze away from his icy one to stare out the window. We left the Lichfield Towers estate, and drove past Highgate Wood, onto streets lined with shops and taverns. People went about their business, blissfully unaware that a necromancer was in their midst.

"And what will happen to me if you stop him?" I asked. "What will you do with the inconvenient necromancer?"

"I don't know yet. Perhaps I'll employ you as a maid."

"I don't want to be anyone's maid."

"The work won't be too hard."

"I'm not afraid of hard work. I don't want a master. I haven't had one in years, and that's the way I like it."

"Every woman has a master."

"Lady Harcourt doesn't."

"That's different. She's a widow, and a wealthy one at that."

I said nothing as we passed by the Highgate Cemetery gates. The breeze rustled the leaves and it began to rain. A small dog scampered away from the curb, afraid of the horses thundering hooves and the carriage's clattering wheels. Its brown fur was bedraggled and knotted, its eyes weepy as it watched us pass. Sadness welled inside me at the pathetic creature.

"You're taking me to Tufnell Park," I said. "To my father."

He didn't answer.

We continued through Tufnell Park, going nowhere near Father's house. I frowned at Fitzroy, but he stared out the window, his gaze intent yet unseeing. A muscle pulsed in his throat above his collar. It would seem his thoughts had distracted him. Perhaps I should try escaping again.

I waited for the coach to slow, but by the time it did, Fitzroy was once more alert. The time for leaping from the coach had passed.

"This is Whitechapel," I said, looking around.

I'd lived there twice before, including when the Ripper had been doing his worst, but not in this street. It was a narrow lane, paved with uneven stones made slick with slops and rain. There were no shops or taverns, only crumbling, crooked buildings divided into rooms. I knew from experience that those rooms were crammed with as many people that could fit into them as possible. Barefoot children watched us, their hollow faces reminding me of my own. A group of them approached the horses and coach, but Gus's hiss sent them scurrying back.

A woman with a crying baby clamped to her hip emerged from one of the buildings. She put out a hand and mouthed *please.* Seth tossed her a coin. That only drew out more women, and some men too.

Seth opened the door and held his hand out. It took me a moment to realize he was offering to assist me down, as a gentleman would a lady. I glanced at Fitzroy, expecting him to grab my arm and pin me to the seat.

"You wished to leave," was all he said. "So leave."

"You're letting me go? Just like that?"

"It's what you want."

I watched him through narrowed eyes. "I don't trust you. You're up to something."

"Go," he said heavily. "Let's see how long you last here without my protection."

Ah. Now I understood. He was proving a point, or trying to. I laughed without humor. "This is my home," I said, nodding at the grimy faces, the filthy gutter. "I know how to survive out here. I've been doing it for years."

"Not as a woman, and a respectable, pretty one at that."

One of the men hawked a glob of spit onto the stones. The child on the woman's hip cried harder. Fitzroy was right. Although it was daylight, and women and children crowded near, it wouldn't be long before I found myself alone at night. Dressed as a woman, I would be vulnerable, a target.

"Your lack of hair might save you," he went on. "But it also means you have nothing to sell. Aside from the obvious, of course."

I lashed out, but he caught both my wrists before I connected. He drew me closer, so that I was almost sitting on his lap. His eyes were as black up close as they were from a distance.

"Reconsider." His deep, rumbling voice almost hypnotized me into saying yes.

"No. You won't leave me here. I'm too valuable to you, and you're too cock-sure to consider failure. You won't leave me," I said again.

He let me go, shoving me back onto the seat as he did so. "Get out."

I flattened my hands down my skirts and called his bluff. I climbed out, refusing Seth's offered hand. Fitzroy closed the door himself and remained inside. Seth climbed up onto the driver's seat beside Gus and the coach pulled away.

I was free. I smiled at the retreating coach, still unable to believe that I'd won. Surely it was a trick. It must be. And yet they were out of sight already, around the corner.

A child of about six came up to me and tugged on my sleeve. "Coin, miss? We be starving."

"I haven't got any money," I told her, loud enough so that they could all hear. If they thought I had money, I wouldn't get far before I was robbed.

I walked away, ignoring the stares and the occasional tug on my skirt. With no money, my options were limited. I could sell the bonnet, and perhaps the gown after I stole some boys' clothes. I'd keep the boots. They were sturdy and only a little worn. They would last some time. I smiled as I walked along the miserable streets of Whitechapel. Fitzroy had under-estimated me.

I spent the rest of the day wandering, thinking about where next to live. I couldn't return to Stringer and the others, and Fitzroy's investigation meant I was too obvious in my previous haunts now. It might be time to leave London altogether. But where to go? How close was the nearest city?

By the time evening fell, I was starving. My stomach protested, even though I'd eaten one good meal already at breakfast. And despite being summer, it was cold. I had no shawl or coat and I'd left the gloves in the coach. I'd become too used to the good life at Lichfield Towers. I'd known that would happen. I could kick myself for accepting Fitzroy's hospitality.

As darkness descended, I settled under a railway bridge. It stank of urine but it was empty of other residents. Because of the rain, no one had hung out clothes to dry, but I hadn't given up hope. There was always the morning. I just had to get through the night unnoticed.

I drew my knees up and settled my chin on them. If Fitzroy changed his mind and returned to the place where he left me, he'd find me gone. Should I make my way back so that I was easy to find? He would have to apologize before I agreed to return.

The more I thought about it, the surer I became that he would return. Lady Harcourt would send him back when she discovered what he'd done. She and the other committee members wouldn't let him just leave me here. She was much too kind, and they needed me.

But he'd made it clear that he was the leader. They did as he said. And he was a determined man, not one to back down. I hardly knew him, but I knew that. If he'd decided to throw me into the pond, then he would certainly not fish me out again at someone else's suggestion.

It would seem I'd overestimated my worth to them. To him. I was nothing, after all. A well of sadness I hadn't experienced for a long time opened inside me.

"Who're you?" came a harsh voice from behind me. "What're you doin' on my patch?"

I spun round and flattened myself against the bridge supports. There was just enough light from the single gas lamp to see by and I saw a very large man looming over me. He looked like a bear with his black shaggy beard, long hair, and big hands.

"I'm going," I said, deepening my voice. I'd already removed the pins from my hair to cover my face again, but I was still dressed in women's clothing. "I didn't know this was your place."

"Halt there." He lumbered toward me and I edged away. "I said halt!"

I turned to flee, but he lunged. He had a surprisingly long reach and was fleeter of foot than he looked. He caught my elbow and jerked me round to face him.

"Please, let me go, sir. I mean you no harm or disrespect."

"What's a girl like you doing out here all alone, eh?" He glanced around, as if expecting to see my menfolk nearby.

"I'm not alone," I said quickly. "My father and two brothers will be here soon. They're dock workers and carry big knives."

"The docks ain't near here. And I got a big weapon too." He grinned, revealing teeth as black as his beard. He groped his trousers at his crotch and licked his lips beneath his moustache. "Show me ya face, girl. I wanna see it while I fuck you."

I pushed at him, but he was too strong, too big. He laughed at my pathetic attempts. I kicked his shin and he yowled.

"You little bitch!" He hooked a leg behind my knees, making them buckle. I crashed to the ground, hitting my hip and head against the bricks of the bridge support. I scrabbled and hit out, but could get no strength behind my punches with the damned corset constricting movement and breathing. He pinned my arms above my head with one of his massive hands and swept my hair back with his other.

"Ain't you're a prize. Got lucky tonight, didn't I? Eh? First some coin, now a tasty little tart."

I tried to kick him again, but he lay half on top of me, pinning me. He pulled my skirts above my knees and his fat fingers rubbed my thigh through my drawers. I tasted bile and blood and realized I'd been biting my lip to stop from crying out. Screaming would only draw more men my way. A pack of them would be worse than just this one.

"Where's that little peach of yours, eh?" His hot breath stank. I choked down the bile in my throat and wished I hadn't. Throwing up over him might get him off me.

But I doubted it. The light caught the determined gleam in his eyes, the glisten of saliva on his beard.

I shut my eyes and willed myself to be calm, to empty my head and think of nothing. To not feel. But it was impossible. I felt every pinch of his dirty fingernails on my inner thighs, every scratch of his beard on my throat, every tear that slid down my cheek. It was hopeless. All I could do now was endure. Endure and survive.

And try not to regret my decision to leave Lichfield Towers and Lincoln Fitzroy.

CHAPTER 10

The weight of the body pressed down on me, grinding my bony hip and shoulder into the greasy ground. He tried to kiss my mouth, and I did the only thing I was capable of doing in that position. I bit his cheek. My teeth sank into flesh. I gagged as the tang of blood filled my mouth. The brute reared back, screaming and clutching his face. But he didn't get off me. He raised his massive paw to strike me.

Then suddenly he was gone, ripped off me by someone dressed in a dark hood. The newcomer punched my assailant in the stomach then shoved him away. My attacker crumpled like a doll and lay entirely still except for the blood oozing from the wound in his stomach.

He hadn't been punched, he'd been stabbed. And he was dead.

The wisp of smoky haze rising from the body told me that. It formed the man's shape, right down to the abundance of whiskers and broad hands. It was the man's spirit, yet I hadn't touched the body in order to see it. Either that had been the situation all along, or my power had grown stronger.

The spirit didn't look at me but at his murderer. He bared his teeth. "Damn you! You tricked me!" The smoky essence thinned and floated past me as if on a breeze. I leaned away from him, but he didn't touch me.

I blinked and he was gone. Only the body remained, and my rescuer. Or the man I had to fight off next.

He pushed his hood back and I gasped. "Fitzroy!" I choked on the name, relief bringing fresh tears and tightening my throat.

He crouched at my side and helped me to sit. The corset made it difficult to do on my own. He stroked my hair off my face and checked me over by the miserly light of the streetlamp. His touch was entirely clinical.

"Are you harmed?" His voice quavered ever so slightly.

I had some bruises on my thighs, but I wouldn't tell him about those. I couldn't anyway. Speaking had suddenly become the most difficult thing to do. I simply shook my head and fought hard to not let my tears overwhelm me.

But when his face softened and he picked me up, it all became too much. I pressed my cheek to his chest and sobbed. It was pathetic but cathartic too. My fear flowed away along with my tears until there was nothing left but a sense of wellbeing. It was wrong to feel grateful to be in the arms of my captor, yet I couldn't bring myself to hate him. My relief was too great, the strength of his arms too comforting. He was keeping me safe, just like he'd promised.

He did not set me down. We walked for some time through the dark streets, not speaking. His arms didn't loosen around me. If anything, they seemed to tighten. I couldn't see his face, tucked under his chin as I was, but I could hear his heartbeat. It had been erratic at first, but was now steady.

"Where are you taking me?" I asked. We seemed to have left the slums. The houses we walked past were larger, the streets emptier. It was late.

"Home."

I don't have a home. I closed my eyes and listened to his heartbeat again. The rhythm lulled me and chased away the memory of that brute's fingers, his stench and my fear. I felt more like myself again, with a clearer head and a sense of dignity that had been absent since I'd realized what he'd intended to do.

"You can put me down now," I told Fitzroy. "I won't run off." I needed to stand on my own two feet again, no matter how much I liked being in his arms. That was entirely the problem—I liked it too much.

He didn't respond immediately, but walked several more paces before finally setting me on my feet. We were between streetlamps so I couldn't make out anything more than his silhouette.

"It's not far," he said and set off again.

"How did you know where to find me?" I asked. He shortened his strides so that I could keep up easily.

"I followed you."

I frowned. "You've been watching me?"

"Yes."

"All day? Ever since dropping me off in Whitechapel?"

"Yes."

His words slowly, slowly sank in. My God. I'd been right when I thought he was trying to make a point. Only I hadn't expected him to go so far as to leave me behind. When he had, I'd assumed I'd gotten him wrong and he'd decided to let me go after all. But this…this was beyond comprehension.

I stopped. He stopped too and his gaze met mine. "You never had any intention of setting me free," I murmured. I shook my head, over and over, no longer certain of this man. He'd been so kind as he picked me up—only because he felt guilty at leaving me there dressed as a woman with no weapons or money.

I went to punch him in the chest where my tears dampened his coat, but he caught my fist.

"I needed you to help me," he said. "I needed you to see that you're better off at Lichfield."

I backed away from him, but was stopped by the low brick fence of the church behind me. "That is a horrible thing to do to a woman. To anyone!"

"Your stubbornness only makes *you* suffer, Charlie."

"I am not doing it from stubbornness. I'm trying to stay alive."

"And look how that worked out."

I pressed my lips together and crossed my arms. I could try running away, but he would catch me. Or he might let me leave entirely, and I would once again be vulnerable and alone, and I was so tired of feeling that way.

"You may be alive out here," he said, "but it's not a good life. You know that."

"Stop pretending to know what I think. And anyway, how can I trust you after that little test?"

"I give you my word. It's all I have to offer, but I hope you know me well enough to believe me."

"Ha!"

"You have to trust me, Charlie. The alternative is…that."

Tears burned my eyes again as the memory of that brute came crashing back. It had been as bad as my first night alone, taken by the man who'd tried to sell me to the highest bidder. Worse, perhaps, because now I was aware of what could happen. Five years ago, I'd been naive.

I sniffed and inclined my head in a nod. "Congratulations. You win. I give in." I marched off in the same direction we'd been heading.

He quickly caught up and we walked side by side in silence. I'd hoped for an apology but none came. At least he didn't gloat.

"Your heart is made of ice," I hissed at him.

"It was for your own good."

"If I were you, I'd keep quiet. Say the wrong thing and I might change my mind, and you are not very good at saying the right thing, in my opinion."

Mercifully, he remained silent. It was too dark to see what he thought of my snippy response, and I was too tired to care.

We strode through the Lichfield Towers gate and I sighed, not out of frustration, but contentment. I was moments away from food and a soft bed. I wanted a bath too, to wash away the grit of the street, the stink of that man. Lights blazed from every window in the house, even from the tallest room in the central tower. I wondered if I would find myself back up there, or if I were to remain in Fitzroy's rooms.

The front door was thrown open before we reached it. Seth and Gus tumbled out, grins splitting their faces. Were they happy to see me again? How odd. I smiled back. To my surprise, I was glad to see them, but I wouldn't tell them that.

They both looked me over, then with satisfied nods, stepped aside to let us through.

"Good," Seth said for no apparent reason.

"Welcome back, Miss Charlotte," Gus said, tugging on his forelock as a working man would do as a lady passed.

"Call me Charlie or I'm leaving immediately."

His gulp was audible. He shot a startled glance Fitzroy's way. "I, er…"

"It was a joke." I patted the poor man's arm. He blushed brightly in response.

"Ignore him," Seth said. He offered me his arm. "Cook has some treats lined up for you—jellies, candied fruit, even ice cream. Shall I bring it up to your room?"

"Yes, thank you. That's very kind of you to organize sweets for me."

His smile faded. "It wasn't me that ordered them." His gaze flicked to Fitzroy then away.

I frowned at Fitzroy, but he was already moving off. "Draw a bath for her," he told Gus. "And show her to her new room. There's no need to set a guard on the door. We'll talk in the morning, Charlie." He took the stairs two at a time and disappeared from sight.

We three let out a collective sigh, the tension having left with him. "Was it much of an ordeal?" Seth asked me.

"I'd rather not talk about it."

Gus smacked his friend's arm. "Idiot. Leave her be."

"Go and draw the bath," Seth told him. To me he said, "We're glad you're back, Miss— Charlie. You might not know it, but your presence has livened this place up."

I couldn't help laughing. "It must have been terribly dull beforehand."

"Aye," Gus said, casting a glance at the stairs.

I took his arm, surprising him into another blush. "Will you show me to my room now, please?"

"Right you are, ma'am. Miss. Charlie."

Seth wandered off toward the kitchens, chuckling, and I walked with Gus up the stairs. Now that I'd made the decision to stay, I felt more at ease. I would keep my promise and not try to escape.

Yet I would also try to keep my feelings in check. Fitzroy had proved he was ruthless in getting his own way; he was not to be trusted. I'd be a fool to put myself at his mercy, physically or emotionally. I'd not made the mistake of trusting someone in a long time, and I wasn't about to begin now.

***

Lady Harcourt came to my new room the following morning. She was dressed in a steel gray gown that would look grim on anyone else, but looked elegant on her, with its slender fit, large bustle and white frills at cuff and collar.

She was followed by Fitzroy. I hadn't seen him since our return the night before. His eyes seemed a little tight as he regarded me from beneath half-lowered lashes. If he was annoyed, I doubted it could be because of me this time. I'd done exactly as he'd asked.

Lady Harcourt also seemed somewhat provoked as she greeted me with a brief smile. I suspected they'd argued about something. Me? Or perhaps Fitzroy's methods?

"It's a little warm for a fire," she said, glancing at the fireplace. She gasped when she saw what was burning in the grate. "Oh, *Charlie*! You didn't."

"It accidentally caught fire."

"How?"

"It somehow found itself in the grate among the kindling with a flame put to it."

She gave me a withering glare. "If you didn't want to wear the corset, you could have simply left it off when you dressed this morning. There was no need to burn it."

I begged to differ. I felt a very strong need to destroy the damned thing.

Fitzroy added a scoop of coal to the fire. "How do you find your new rooms?" he asked, straightening.

"Very nice. Thank you." While the bedroom and adjoining sitting room were better than the tower chamber, they weren't as spacious as his suite. My new abode was located down the hall from his and was comfortably furnished. It was better than I expected.

"Do you have everything you need?"

"Seth delivered the books earlier."

"You ought to sew," Lady Harcourt said. "Do you remember how?"

"I think so." I'd never been very good at sewing, always rushing my stitches, frustrating my mother. Her needlepoint had been particularly fine, but she'd had far more patience than me.

"When you come to live with me, I'll see that you're given something simple to begin with."

"Live with you! But I thought I was to remain here?" I glared at Fitzroy, but he was looking at Lady Harcourt.

"Julia," he intoned. "That's not how we agreed to approach this."

Lady Harcourt sighed and swanned further into the room. The sitting room was small enough that the presence of three people filled it. Fitzroy, in particular, looked much too large for the room. He stood near me, making me very aware of the power contained within his tall frame. For the first time since it happened, I thought of how he'd killed the man who'd accosted me beneath the bridge. Fitzroy had not given him a chance to beg forgiveness. He'd stabbed him as he would a sack of grain, and left his body there to be picked over by thieves and rats.

As glad as I'd been at the time, today I was struck by the brutality of it—the coldness. Yet, only moments later, he'd carried me gently away from the scene.

Lady Harcourt pressed a flat palm to her stomach and seemed to be gathering herself. "Very well," she said. "Charlie, I've come to ask you, once again, to live with me. Now that you have agreed to help, there is no need to lock you up."

"No, thank you. I have no desire to wear corsets and scrub your floors."

Her fingers splayed. "You don't have to be a servant. You may be my companion."

"What does a companion do?"

She shrugged. "We sit together, talk and walk together. You can pay calls with me."

"On who?"

"My friends."

It didn't sound like something I'd like to do, but I didn't want to offend her. "I prefer to remain here."

She opened her mouth to protest, but Fitzroy cut in. "Charlie has given her decision. You promised to abide by it."

"Yes, but I'm not sure she's thoroughly thought it through." Lady Harcourt turned a winning smile onto me. "What is there for a girl to do here?"

"Gamble and play cards," I told her.

She clicked her tongue.

"Drink whiskey and smoke cigars."

"Charlie, really, now you're just being stubborn."

"Apparently I make a habit of it," I said, ignoring Fitzroy as best as I could.

"She won't come to any harm here," he assured her. "You know that, Julia. Indeed, you also know that this is the safest place for her, while we try to draw V.F. out. I won't expose her to danger because you believe she needs feminine company."

It was quite the speech, and I was surprised at his vehemence. It would seem he took my safety seriously.

"Very well," she huffed. "I'll have some embroidery sent around. And you are to keep Gus and Seth on a tight leash. If anything happens to her—"

"Nothing will happen," I said. "They're not going to…compromise me under Fitzroy's nose. He'll skin them alive."

He lifted his brows at Lady Harcourt in what I suspected was triumph, but I wasn't entirely sure.

She sighed. "Then that is that. I'll retreat. I must dash anyway, but I'd like a word with Charlie alone before I go."

Fitzroy bowed then left us. Once the door was shut, Lady Harcourt picked up the fire iron and stabbed at the burnt corset. Her vigorous thrusts quickly made her breathless. I could have told her she'd be able to breathe better if she threw her own corset into the fire, but I didn't think the suggestion would be welcomed.

"Do you have your courses?" she asked.

"Pardon?"

"Your monthly woman's courses."

"I…no. It stopped some time ago."

She eyed me up and down. "That can occur with underweight girls. I expect, now that you're eating, it will return. I'll have linens sent to you along with the sewing."

"Thank you, my lady. You're very kind." I meant it. She had thought of difficulties that hadn't even occurred to me. "I know you're worried about how a girl who doesn't like to wear corsets will behave around the men, but I can assure you, I am not interested in…those sorts of activities."

She stabbed at the ruined corset again. "Not yet."

I sighed. "Fitzroy won't allow it under his roof anyway. He'll make sure the men treat me with respect."

Stab, stab, stab.

"And I won't tempt them." I laughed. It sounded ridiculous. "As if I could, anyway."

She stopped and placed the fire iron in the stand. "You underestimate yourself, Charlie. And I think you underestimate men, too." She lifted a finger when I opened my mouth to protest. "Men, not boys. They are not the same. Well, some are, but many are not. Now, tell me something."

"What?" I mumbled, unsure if I'd been chastised or advised.

"How did Fitzroy convince you to stay and help us?"

"He didn't tell you?"

She smiled sweetly and hooked her arm through mine. "I thought I'd ask you."

"Perhaps you ought to ask him." I extricated myself, but not before I felt her fingers tense on my arm.

I headed for the door and opened it. Fitzroy wasn't there, and nor were any of the men. It took me a moment to remember that I was no longer a prisoner. I walked down the stairs with Lady Harcourt. We found Fitzroy in the library, propped against the windowsill, a book in hand.

He looked up as we came in and closed the book. "We need to talk."

I wasn't sure if he spoke to me or Lady Harcourt and whether his announcement meant the other should leave. Lady Harcourt, however, seemed to know. She gave him her hand and he bowed over it.

"I look forward to your report," she said.

"I'll be in touch with the committee soon."

He walked her out, leaving me alone in the library. I picked up the book he'd been reading—*A Guide To The Spirit*

World. How curious. I flipped it open and began to read, but didn't get very far before he returned. Outside, Lady Harcourt's carriage rolled away.

"Tea and cake?" he asked. "Cook has been baking."

"I'm not hungry."

"You need to eat."

"Breakfast wasn't that long ago."

He tugged on the bell pull in the corner of the library. The house was so vast that I couldn't hear the corresponding bell ringing in the service area.

He stood by the table while we waited, hands behind his back, and nodded at the book. "You should read that. It might help you understand your necromancy."

Seth entered. "Can I get you anything, Charlie?" His smile made him even more handsome, and not for the first time I wondered why he was working for Fitzroy alongside a ruffian like Gus.

"Tea and cake." Fitzroy's gruff manner wiped Seth's smile from his face.

Once he was gone, Fitzroy indicated I should sit at the table. I did, and a moment later, as though it were an afterthought, he did too.

"Now that you've agreed to help, I want to keep you informed," he said.

"You do? Oh. Thank you. Is there more to what you've already told me?"

"Not much. I've learned that a man has been calling at all the homes of London vicars and asking after girls living in the same house. Daughters, wards, servants…"

"I'm sure that went down well. Did he know my name?"

"I don't think so, but I didn't know it at first, either. Not until I learned about the tragic disappearance of Anselm Holloway's daughter, two days ago."

"And you investigated further," I finished. "How did you learn the piece of information about the vicar? How did V.F.?"

He sat quite still, one palm flat on the polished tabletop. I thought for a moment he would keep that secret to himself, but then he answered. "A woman we'd been watching in Paris wrote to him. Her husband had died in suspicious circumstances here in England, and she'd exiled herself to Paris to avoid the police, and us, asking uncomfortable questions."

"You think she killed her husband?"

"I think she knew the killer and was possibly present for the murder. I also believe the murderer to be the man she wrote to, this V.F. Her husband's body was cut open and the brain used to—"

"Stop!" I pressed a hand to my lurching stomach and drew in a deep breath. "So you watched this woman in Paris and waited for her to send a communication. You must have intercepted the letter."

"I did. She'd written it in code and tried to have an unsuspecting couple deliver it, since the usual postal service would be too slow and unreliable. I intercepted and decoded it. The letter claimed she'd found the girl V.F. was seeking, and that she was living with a London vicar. I don't know how she learned that. I then made sure the missive found its way to V.F's hands."

"Thereby putting the girl—me—in danger."

"You weren't in danger because you weren't living with a London vicar."

"You didn't know that at the time."

"And I would not have allowed V.F. to capture you."

"Forgive me for doubting your competence on this, Mr. Fitzroy, but you are only three men, if you include Gus and Seth, and there are many vicars living in London. You couldn't watch them all."

The fingers on the table splayed wide.

"Tea," Seth announced, as he entered the library with a tray. Behind him, Gus followed, carrying a second tray laden with plates and slices of cake.

They set the trays down and began to pour and pass out plates. There was enough for them too. It would seem they were to join us. The household arrangement was odd, and I still wasn't sure whether the two men were supposed to be servants, assistants, or something else. Not friends. Fitzroy certainly didn't treat them as equals.

"You need a maid," I told Fitzroy.

"Aye," Gus muttered, as he handed me a plate.

"Or dress these two in livery."

Seth had been about to hand me a cup and saucer, but he held it back. "I am *not* wearing livery."

"We're not bloody footmen," Gus added, pulling up a chair. He sank his teeth into his slice of cake, scattering crumbs over his chest.

"Then you definitely need a maid," I said. "And footmen too. Is money a concern?"

"No," Seth said.

I arched a brow at Fitzroy, but he didn't notice. He pushed my plate closer to me. "You should eat."

"I told you, I'm not hungry."

"Eat."

"Better do as he says," Seth warned me. "He likes getting his own way."

Fitzroy shot him a flinty glare that turned Seth's face pale. He cleared his throat and sipped his tea.

I nibbled the cake to appease them. It gave me time to think anyway. It seemed I knew something Fitzroy didn't—what V.F. looked like.

"I saw him at my father's house," I said. "V.F. I assume it was he. Father called him 'doctor.'"

"Doctor?" Gus shook his head as he swept crumbs off his jacket. "If it's the same man we're after, the one who chopped Mrs. Calthorn's husband into pieces, then he don't cure people."

Fitzroy sat forward. "When was this?"

"The day you kidnapped me. I sometimes sit in the garden of my old home." I looked into my teacup, not wanting to see what they thought of my pathetic behavior. "I overheard this doctor ask if there was a girl living there—he even mentioned my name. He must have learned about me having gone missing through neighbors or parishioners."

"Or via publicly available birth records. Either way, he'd done some research before his visit. What did he look like?"

I described the doctor as best as I could. "I would recognize him again if I saw him." *When* I saw him. I had no doubt I would be seeing him again. "I think he gave Father his name, but I didn't catch it."

Seth set down his cup in the saucer with a loud clank, and Gus stopped chewing. "Why didn't you say so?" Seth said. "Sir? Shall we go now?"

"Prepare the coach and horses," Fitzroy said.

Both men ran from the room. Their keenness unnerved me. Neither man had shown much intensity until now. It seemed I'd given them the first true clue for discovering V.F.'s identity they'd had in a long time.

"Can you learn where a man lives from his name?" I asked Fitzroy.

"Yes, particularly if he's a practicing doctor. If he's not, there are still ways." He got up and strode from the room.

I raced after him, almost tripping over my skirts in my haste. I picked them up to keep them away from my boots and caught up to him in the entrance hall as he retrieved his hat and gloves from the hallstand.

"You're going to my father's house," I said.

"Yes."

"And then on to the doctor's, as soon as you can connect his name to an address?"

"It might take some time to find the address."

"You may not need me to lure him out after all."

"Hopefully Holloway will give us the name without coercion, and V.F. will be found easily. If not, you will be required." His thumb and forefinger stroked the brim of his hat, and I suspected he was contemplating saying something else. But then he strode away toward the door, leaving me standing there by the hallstand.

"Mr. Fitzroy," I called. He paused and raised his brows at me. "Can I come with you? To Father's house, I mean."

He lowered his hat and faced me fully. "You wish to speak with him?"

"I…I think so. Yes."

"You don't need to. I'll get the information from him in my own way, if necessary."

I suspected his way meant beating the answer out of him. While I wasn't entirely against the idea, I did want to see my father. And speak to him. It was time, and I had a lot of things to say. "If you intend to scare information out of him, I think you may need me. He won't be too frightened of a mere human, but having the devil's maid in his midst will scare the stuffing out of him. Answers too, I expect."

"Then you'd better fetch your gloves."

***

I recognized the elderly women leaving my father's house with baskets over their arms. They were two of his most devoted parishioners, and a more pious pair never existed. As they passed Fitzroy and me near the front gate, I ducked my head so that I wouldn't be recognized, but I needn't have bothered. They were too intent on their conversation. I caught snippets as they walked away.

"Poor, poor man," one said.

"Will his suffering never end?"

"What has he done to deserve such a life?"

"Excuse me," I called out to them. They stopped and gave me benign smiles. Neither seemed to recognize me. "Has something happened to…Mr. Holloway?"

"The house was burgled last night, poor man," one said.

"While he was asleep upstairs!" the other chimed in with a shake of her head.

"The vicious animal gave him a solid crack on the head too. Poor man."

I bit the inside of my lip. "Is he all right?"

"He has a headache, but he's up and about, thank the good lord. And who are you, dear?" She squinted at me. "You look a little familiar."

"I'm new to the area," I said as I turned away.

One of the women sniffed at my rudeness, then I listened as their footsteps receded. I glanced up at Fitzroy, only to see him already looking down at me.

"Are you sure you want to do this?" he asked.

"Now more than ever." I needed to check on Father.

The door opened a mere crack upon our knock. Father's face appeared, not the housekeeper's. I'd expected to be taken into a sitting room, where we'd have to wait before seeing him. The delay would have allowed me to calm my jumpy nerves. I wasn't prepared for his skittish gaze to dart between us. It merely flicked over me, as if I didn't matter, and settled on Fitzroy.

"This is not a good time." He went to shut the door, but Fitzroy forced it open with his shoulder. My father stumbled back and we entered. "Who are you? What do you want?" He picked up a heavy book from the hallstand and held it aloft like a weapon. It was a bible.

He sported a gash on his temple. The red, angry cut crossed his frown lines. He looked much older than I remembered. His hair was grayer, the lines deeper, and his shoulders stooped. He hadn't been a young man when I was born, but he looked much older than his fifty-five years.

"Do you recognize me?" I said.

He looked at me again, and this time he actually *saw* me. And he knew. The mask of horror that descended over his face told me that. His eyes widened, his lips moved without speaking. "You," he choked out. "*You.*"

"Me. Your daughter. I've come to—"

"You're no daughter of mine! Get out! Get out of here, devil's spawn!" He threw the bible.

Fitzroy caught it before it hit me. "You had some trouble overnight," he said. "What happened?"

"Wh…what?" Father shuffled backward toward the stairs. His shaking hand reached out for the newel post.

"We won't hurt you," I told him. "We've come to ask you about the man who came looking for me a few days ago. A doctor. But first…are you all right?" I moved toward him, but he tripped over the bottom step in his haste to get away and landed on his rear.

I clasped my hands tightly in front of me, stopping myself from reaching out to help him. This man didn't want me to touch him. It was clear from the twist of his mouth and the fear in his eyes.

"Father—"

"Do not call me that," he snarled. "You are not my daughter. You don't belong here. You belong in hell! Get out!" He began a prayer as he scooted up the stairs on his behind.

I bit back tears, refusing to let this man see how much his hatred affected me. I thought I'd given up hope of a happy reunion years ago, but it seemed a flame had flickered in my breast the entire time. I'd promised myself I would never feel anything for him again, and yet here I was, about to shed tears for the pathetic man I wanted to love me.

"I am your daughter," I whispered, struggling to get the words out through my aching throat.

He laughed, a manic, high sound that grated on my ears. "You're not. You're adopted."

I fell back and reached out for something solid to hold on to; to stop myself losing my balance in the suddenly tilting world. Fitzroy's arm was there. His hand on my elbow steadied me.

"You…are not my father?"

The old man on the stairs stopped laughing and squared his shoulders. "No. How did you not see it? Your mother was pure of heart. I am the lord's faithful servant. And you are a creature of darkness and death. The lord sent you to us, to test me. I didn't fail. I cast you out, as the devil should be cast out. I removed the ugly cancer from my house and—"

Fitzroy's fist stopped the vomit of insults. My father's head—no, *Holloway's*—snapped back. He cried out and clasped a hand over his mouth. Blood seeped through the fingers. He scrambled further up the staircase, away from us.

Fitzroy followed him, his hands closed into fists at his sides, his shoulders rigid.

"Don't!" I shouted.

Holloway had reached the top of the stairs. Fitzroy stopped, towering above him. "The man who was here calling himself Doctor. Was it he who came last night?"

Holloway closed his eyes and began praying again. "Answer him," I said. "Or he'll kill you."

Fitzroy glanced at me over his shoulder. I shrugged.

"You won't be harmed if you tell me his name," Fitzroy said. He kicked Holloway's foot.

Holloway pulled his knees up and clasped them to his chest. He opened his eyes. "Yes, it was the same man. He wanted to know where you were." He nodded at me. "I told him you'd gone to Hell."

"You probably won't be surprised to know that Hell looks very much like the slums of London." I felt numb, like I was looking down on the scene from afar. But more than that, I felt like I was speaking to a stranger, not the man I'd called Father for as long as I could remember.

"His name," Fitzroy prompted.

Holloway eyed the fists at Fitzroy's sides and swallowed. "He's a doctor. Frank something. I can't recall."

"His initials are V.F. Is it Doctor Frank?"

"I told you, I can't recall. It was an unusual name, foreign."

Fitzroy leaned over and grabbed the front of Holloway's smoking jacket. He lifted him until he was no longer sitting. "Think."

His eyes widened to the size of saucers. "Frank…Frank-in…star."

"Doctor Frankinstar?"

"Frankenstein! That's it. Doctor Frankenstein. First name Victor."

CHAPTER 11

I traced the letters on the headstone with my fingernail, from top to bottom. *Loving Mother to Charlotte* read the final words, right beneath *Devoted Wife to Anselm.* She *had* been loving toward me, but she had not been my mother. I'd accepted it immediately when Holloway told me. Perhaps it was the numbness of shock, or perhaps I'd given up thinking he cared for me long ago. But now, sitting on the grass near my mother's grave, I felt like my chest had opened up and I was bleeding over the ground.

She'd loved me during her lifetime. I'd felt sure of that. And yet what if she'd lived to see me perform my necromancy as he had done? Would she have continued to love me regardless, or would she have called me names and cast me out too? A mother was supposed to love her children unconditionally, no matter what they did, but perhaps adoptive mothers didn't feel the same degree of love.

It felt so strange, sitting there, as I'd done so many times before, and yet this time I felt more alone than I ever had. I used to have her memory for warmth, the feeling that I had once been loved. But now, I wasn't entirely sure of that love.

It was like mourning her loss all over again. Fighting tears, I scooped up a handful of dirt and sprinkled it over her grave.

Something moved behind me. I sprang to my feet but it was only Fitzroy, standing as still as the angel statue marking a nearby grave. I quickly turned away and dashed my damp cheeks with the back of my hand.

"You made a noise," I told him. When he didn't answer, I added, "Just now, you made a noise as you approached. Usually I don't hear you coming."

"I know," was all he said.

"How did you know where to find me?" I hadn't told anyone where I was going upon our return to Lichfield. Seth and Gus had dropped us at the front door and then taken the horses and carriage to the stables. Fitzroy had said something about speaking to Cook. I'd wanted to visit my mother's grave, so I'd just walked out. It wasn't until I'd arrived at the cemetery that I'd wondered if he would assume I'd run away.

"I asked a grounds keeper for directions. He boasted that he knew the location of every grave. Seems he knew this one."

"I mean how did you know I'd be at the cemetery?"

"A guess."

I looked down at the headstone and the words *Loving Mother to Charlotte*. "She was ill for a long time and stipulated what she wanted on her headstone. It was completed before her death. Before I…displayed my true colors. I'm surprised he didn't have another one made. One that leaves off that line."

"Headstones are expensive."

"His won't say *Loving Father*, of that I'm quite sure." I pointed down at my feet. "He bought the plot next to hers when it became clear she wouldn't survive. Their headstones will be side by side, but they won't match now. It'll look odd."

He didn't respond, but I hadn't expected him to. I was rambling, trying to fathom what it all meant for me. A few hours ago I'd had one living relative who hated me. Now I didn't even have that. I wasn't sure if I was better or worse off. I supposed nothing had changed. I was still on my own.

"Historians will wonder about the discrepancy in years to come," Fitzroy said.

I blinked at him. What an absurd thing to say. Yet he was right. It would be confusing for anyone unfamiliar with the story. I smiled, despite myself.

"If you want to stay longer, I can wait," he said. "You shouldn't be out alone. Not while Frankenstein is after you."

"He wouldn't know where to start looking."

He arched one brow and glanced at the headstone.

"Oh. Yes, of course. I wasn't thinking." I rubbed my forehead. I felt exhausted, despite doing nothing all day. It would seem learning one was adopted was a trying experience. "I'm ready to go now." I walked away from the grave and did not look back.

"Luncheon will be ready upon our return," Fitzroy said, as we walked through the cemetery gatehouse.

"I'm not hungry."

After a moment, he said, "Cook will be offended if you don't eat."

"Cook knows I don't have a large appetite. And since when do you care if he's offended or not?"

We passed the costermonger's cart, the one I had been caught stealing from. The scruffy fellow watched me from beneath his hat, a frown on his face. Surely he didn't recognize me now. I frowned back and he quickly set about rearranging a pile of wilting lettuces.

Fitzroy and I walked back toward the house in the sunshine. It was a pleasant day, although clouds crowded on the horizon. I found it difficult to appreciate the sun, however. My mind still felt like it was stuffed with cotton wool.

"I wonder if I'm an orphan or if my parents are alive," I muttered, more to myself than him.

"If they are, it's likely they couldn't care for you. Mothers have to give up their babies all the time. Some don't want to."

"Poor, unwed mothers, you mean."

He stared straight ahead with hard eyes.

"Are your parents still living?" I asked.

After a moment, he said, "I believe so. Like you, I never knew them."

"You're adopted too?"

"No."

I frowned. How could he not know his parents but not be adopted? And yet he did know that his parents lived, so he was a step ahead of me. "Who raised you? General Eastbrooke?"

"He had a hand in my upbringing."

"Were you his ward?"

"I was nobody's ward."

Nobody's ward and nobody's child either, it seemed. Lady Harcourt had told me Fitzroy was specifically chosen to be leader of the ministry from birth. Did that mean the committee had raised him? "If I ask any more questions, will you answer them?"

"Will any of those questions be about lunch?"

"No."

"Then it's unlikely."

I sighed. "You say I'm stubborn, but you are positively obstinate."

We walked back to the house in silence, slowing down as we drew closer. Four carriages were stopped in front of the steps, two of which I recognized as belonging to Lady Harcourt and General Eastbrooke. The other two escutcheons were new to me, although I wouldn't be surprised if the one with the serpent coiled around a sword belonged to the snakelike Lord Gillingham.

"I'd hoped they wouldn't be here yet," Fitzroy said, his face dark.

"You invited them?"

"A meeting of the committee has been called. Not by me."

"You sent word about the man known as Dr. Frankenstein?"

"Not yet. I haven't had time. This meeting is in response to you agreeing to help."

"Ah. It seems you'll have a lot to discuss then. What a lark."

"You'll be present too."

I pulled a face.

"After you've eaten, of course."

I sighed. "Very well, I'll eat. If I indulge too much, however, Lord Gillingham will only have you to blame when I vomit over his shoes."

"I'll have Cook double the quantity on your plate."

We got no further than the front steps when the door burst open. "You found her!" Seth stood with hands on hips, alternately smiling and frowning at me as if he couldn't make up his mind if he were pleased or mad. "Are you all right, Charlie?"

"Fine, thank you."

Gus pushed past him, his heavy brow scrunched into a frown, his arms folded over his chest. "What'd you think you were doing, leaving without telling anyone where you were headed?"

His vehemence surprised me. "I…I'm sorry, Gus."

"Sorry! That's all you got to say for yourself?"

I shrugged.

"Be sure not to do it again or you'll find yourself locked in the tower room."

"Enough!" Fitzroy growled.

Seth smacked Gus in the shoulder. "We're not going to lock you up," he said to me.

"We been looking everywhere for you," Gus hissed at me as I passed him. "Me and Seth been out of our minds with worry."

They were worried? About me? No one had worried about my wellbeing in so long that I wasn't sure how to respond. Nor was I sure I liked being monitored, now that I was supposedly free.

I patted his cheek. "That's very sweet of you. I simply wanted to be by myself."

A growl rumbled from the depths of his chest. "Be sure to take someone with you, next time you want to be alone."

Seth rolled his eyes and I smiled tightly. "I will."

With the two of them appeased, I thought my ordeal was over. I didn't see the four stiff, regal figures until I entered the house. They stood as one, a wall of dark austerity—three men in black suits and Lady Harcourt in her mourning crepe. Lord Gillingham was there, along with General Eastbrooke and another man aged fifty or so who was as tall and well-built as the general but considerably rougher in appearance, thanks to the scar on his temple and another slicing through his gray beard.

"There you are." Lady Harcourt broke ranks and held her hand out to me. I hesitated, then took it and allowed her to lead me to the men. "Gentlemen, may I present Miss Charlotte Holloway, daughter of Anselm Holloway. Charlotte, you know both General Eastbrooke and Lord Gillingham." Lady Harcourt waited, but I wasn't sure what for. Me to curtsy to them?

"You look better as a girl," the general said, offering a gruff nod as he gave me a thorough once over. "On the small side, but I dare say Fitzroy will fatten you up."

"Now that your lies have been exposed, I expect you've seen the error of your ways." Lord Gillingham leaned on his walking stick. If I kicked it out from under him, he would topple forward. "Do not lie to us again or there will be consequences. Is that understood?"

I stepped forward and touched my toe to his stick. I gave it a nudge so that he knew I could have done more if I'd wanted to. "Do not behave like an in-bred half-wit, or I might refuse to co-operate."

His eyeballs almost popped out of the sockets. "You can't speak to me that way!"

"Can't I? I'll try to remember that next time."

Eastbrooke placed his hand on Gillingham's shoulder as the lord's face turned an apoplectic shade of purple.

"And this is Lord Marchbank." Lady Harcourt pulled me away from Gillingham so roughly that I stumbled and bumped into her. Her smile never even wavered as she presented me to the new man.

Another lord. I'd thought the scarred man was an old soldier, but it seemed he was just another tosspot like Gillingham. My opinion was confirmed when he didn't offer me a smile. He merely looked down his crooked nose and said in the blandest voice, "Miss Holloway."

"My lord," I said in the same bland voice.

He met my gaze with a somewhat cool one of his own, but there was no obvious animosity in his eyes as there was in Lord Gillingham's. He seemed…indifferent. Indifference was fine with me. I felt the same toward him and the other committee members.

"Let's get on with it." Lord Gillingham's walking stick click clacked on the tiles as he headed toward the parlor. When he realized nobody followed, his fingers tightened around the knob. "Well?"

"Charlie needs to eat," Fitzroy said.

"So?"

"We're not starting without her."

"She doesn't need to be present! Indeed, she *shouldn't* be present."

"We are not starting without her." Fitzroy nodded at Gus, who left us.

Gillingham marched back, proving he didn't need his stick to walk. "You fly too close to the edge, *Fitzroy*." Only his lips and jowls moved. His jaw remained clenched. "Push us too far and you *will* see how things lie. You are not indispensable."

Fitzroy turned his back to him, as if he couldn't be bothered wasting his breath on an argument, and indicated I should walk on ahead. Gillingham spluttered his protest at the insult.

"It's only lunch, Gilly," the general said quietly. "We'll wait in the parlor."

"She shouldn't be privy to ministry business." Gillingham raised his voice, insuring I could hear.

We headed to the kitchen, where Cook stood over the range, stirring something in a pot. "Charlie," he said with a nod at me. "Hungry?"

"No, but I've been ordered to eat something."

Gus handed me a plate with lettuce, a slice of bread and a sliver of beef on it. "Sit. Eat."

"You are all so demanding." I sat and accepted the plate.

"They be staying, sir?" Cook asked Fitzroy.

"Not for lunch." Fitzroy stood by me as I ate, which would have been enough to put me off my appetite if I'd had one. "Have tea brought in."

Cook set the wooden spoon aside and handed Gus a pot. "Fill it."

Gus left with the pot just as Seth arrived. "Lord Gilly's in a fine mood today," he said. "What set him off?"

Fitzroy's gaze met mine. "Me," I said, cutting up my beef. "He seems to have something against lying, thieving necromancers. Can't think why."

"Ignore him." Seth placed a hand on my shoulder and squeezed. I was so surprised at the intimate gesture that I pulled away. A blush infused his cheeks. "My apologies," he mumbled. "I forgot that you're a…"

"Lying, thieving necromancer?"

"Woman."

I smiled to let him know I wasn't offended. "It takes some getting used to." I wanted to tell him that his touch hadn't upset me—just that I wasn't used to it. However, there seemed no easy way of broaching the subject, so I remained silent.

I finished my light lunch, including the scoop of jelly afterward, and joined the committee members in the sitting room with Fitzroy at my side. He even remained standing by me as I sat. He must think me at risk of running off again.

"How much have you told her?" Lord Gillingham asked, before anyone had even taken a breath.

"Everything she needs to know," Fitzroy said.

"Is that wise?"

"Yes."

Lord Gillingham snorted. "I'm not sure your judgment is one we should trust."

The silence that descended was as smothering as a shroud. Lady Harcourt opened her mouth to speak after a moment, but Fitzroy got in first. His voice was as cold as ice.

"Whether you trust my judgment or not is immaterial. Charlie is an integral component in my plan, and she must be kept informed. You are not integral to any part of my plan. If you disagree with my decisions, see yourself out. My men are busy."

Gillingham's jaw dropped like an unhinged trapdoor. "I say! You dare speak to me in such a manner!"

"May we please discuss the situation?" Lady Harcourt looked distressed, and I felt a little sorry for her. These gentlemen were her peers, perhaps her friends, and Fitzroy her lover. It put her in an awkward position, particularly as the only female member of the committee. Not for the first time, I wondered how a beautiful young woman had ended up part of the body that oversaw the Ministry of Curiosities. Particularly now that I'd met the final member, another aged lord.

"See how he repays you, General!" Gillingham crossed his legs and settled into the armchair. "You should have had him disciplined more as a child."

Lady Harcourt, sitting beside me on the sofa, stiffened and pressed her gloved hand to her lips.

"That's enough, Gilly," Lord Marchbank said. "You're upsetting the ladies."

"Lady," Gillingham muttered. "There is only one present."

I sighed. This was going to be a long afternoon.

"Tell us about Charlotte Holloway, Lincoln," the general said quickly. "How did you learn the boy Charlie was, in fact, her?"

Fitzroy told them how he'd traced me back through the years, then went on to inform them that I'd seen a man visit my father. He finished by telling them the vicar had revealed the full name of the man they sought.

"Then you know where he lives!" Lord Gillingham said.

"I've not had time to investigate."

Gillingham looked as if he were about to chastise Fitzroy, but a glare from Marchbank kept him quiet.

"Good progress," said the general. "We're very pleased. Having a name at this point is more than we'd hoped for."

Seth and Gus had entered with the tray of tea things during the speech and now served cups to everyone. Seth also took one, but Gus did not. He fell back to the door, removing himself from our presence. Only Gillingham eyed him as if he didn't belong in the parlor. Seth, however, escaped his snobbery.

Lady Harcourt touched my hand. "Your assistance has already proven valuable. Thank you, Charlie, on behalf of not only the ministry, but the entire realm."

"The empire really is in danger from this man?" I asked.

"Yes, unfortunately. If he manages to reanimate an army of superior bodies, then we are all at his mercy."

"He will turn that army on the members of parliament," the general said. "That includes the three of us." He indicated the three gentlemen.

"And the court, too, would be in danger," Lady Harcourt finished. "The queen and her family are vulnerable to an attack from someone intent to do harm."

"How do you know that's his intention? You know him to be a murderer, but committing treason is another crime altogether."

"That is none of your affair," Gillingham snapped. "Leave these matters to your betters. You wouldn't understand them."

"Gillingham!" the general snapped. "You forget that we need the chit's help."

"Do we?" Gillingham drawled. "We have the man's name. Fitzroy doesn't need her to find this Frankenstein fellow. It seems to me we can dispense with her now."

"And leave her for Dr. Frankenstein to capture?"

Gillingham didn't answer. He sipped his tea calmly. I set mine down, unable to swallow it. Fitzroy, who'd not accepted tea, took a seat and addressed me.

"You recall we told you about the woman in Paris, whose letter to V.F. I intercepted," he said.

"I do. Her husband was murdered and you suspected she had a hand in it, or knew the murderer—Dr. Frankenstein, I assume."

He nodded. "Her husband's head was cut open, the brain removed."

My stomach rolled, threatening to toss my lunch onto the rug, but I willed myself not to throw up. Somehow I suspected that would work in Gillingham's favor. "Frankenstein wanted to put his brain into a body made up of parts from others?"

"Superior parts taken from athletes. But it was the brain of Mr. Calthorn that was crucial to his plan."

"Was Mr. Calthorn an intelligent man?"

"Yes, but it wasn't merely his cleverness that Frankenstein wanted. It was Calthorn's knowledge. He was England's spy master."

I gasped. "England has a spy master?"

"Not anymore," the general said. "Calthorn is yet to be replaced."

"You ought not tell her all that." Gillingham sniffed. "If this information gets into the wrong hands…"

"Calthorn is dead," Marchbank said. "All the girl knows is that England has a spy network. Our enemies already know that too. It's hardly news."

Gillingham sipped, watching me over the rim of his cup.

"Calthorn knew a great many important secrets," Lady Harcourt said, taking over the story. "After we were alerted to his murder, and the missing brain, we began to piece everything together. We'd already heard about the missing body parts of other murder victims, all of them physically superior in one way or another. We questioned Mrs. Calthorn at the time but she could prove she was elsewhere at the time of the murder. We didn't believe that she was entirely innocent, but we couldn't pin anything on her."

"Then she went and exiled herself to Paris," the general said. "Blasted woman."

"How did she know about me?" I asked. "It seems that Frankenstein had been searching for me, and she found out enough clues to point him in the right direction. How?"

"We don't know," Fitzroy said. "Nor do we know how Frankenstein learned of your existence. It's only clear that he failed to reanimate his monstrous creation on his own and realized he needed a necromancer to perform the deed. I think he's been seeking you ever since, corresponding with his friend, Mrs. Calthorn, in Paris. The first I learned about a necromancer is from her letter. It became a race to find you before he did."

I almost blurted out that I was glad he'd got to me first, but bit my tongue. For some reason, I didn't want Gillingham to hear my gratitude. I didn't want any of them to hear it. Not even Fitzroy. I didn't even like admitting it to myself.

"Mrs. Calthorn's information was out of date," Lady Harcourt said. "You haven't lived with your father since you were thirteen."

"He's not my father." I picked up my teacup and concentrated on not looking at anyone, even though I could feel their gazes on me. "I'm adopted, or so he informed me this morning."

"Adopted!" General Eastbrooke sat forward. One of the lords gasped as Lady Harcourt's hand touched my arm. "Then who is your real father?"

"I don't know."

"Did Holloway know? Did you question him, Lincoln?"

"No," Fitzroy said.

"Why not?" Gillingham snapped. "My God, man, this is of utmost importance! If the girl inherited her ability, we need to know who he is."

"Or she," Lady Harcourt added. "Lincoln, I agree with Lord Gillingham. You need to question Mr. Holloway."

"He won't tell us anything," Fitzroy said. "Questioning him will only produce lies or total silence. His state of mind is delicate, his fear absolute."

"It's unlikely he knows anyway," Lord Marchbank said. "Orphanages don't give out that information to the adopting parents."

"We won't know if Fitzroy doesn't ask." Gillingham slammed the foot of his walking stick on the floor. "To hell with the fellow's state of mind. I don't care if your questions turn him into a blathering idiot, unable to function in society. It's an oversight on your part, Fitzroy."

"Not an oversight," Fitzroy said in a voice so quiet that Gillingham's swallow was audible. "It was a deliberate decision."

"One that I protest."

"You can protest all you like. It changes nothing."

"I command you to ask him!"

Fitzroy stood, very slowly, his hands curled into fists. Gillingham lifted his chin as Fitzroy stepped closer. "You don't command me."

"I bloody well do. We *all* do. You work for us, Fitzroy."

"I work for England. I can also stop working for England."

Gillingham snorted. "You were born to do this, Fitzroy. It's your entire life. You won't leave."

Several moments passed, in which I expected Fitzroy to either deny it or punch Gillingham in the nose. He did neither. "If you disagree with my decision, you're welcome to question the vicar yourself."

Gillingham's gaze slid away and his hands increased their rapid rubbing over the head of his stick.

"Don't wish to get your hands dirty, I see," Fitzroy said.

Gillingham's fingers flared then closed around the knob again. He pointed his stick at me. "I wager her real parents were sewer rats, just like her. Breeding always reveals itself in the end, you know. Bad blood breeds only more bad."

Fitzroy's knuckles turned white.

"I'm famished," I said quickly, rising. "Unless I'm needed, I think I'll find something to eat in the kitchen."

Seth set down his tea. "I'll escort you. Gus?"

Gus shook his head and nodded at Fitzroy. Fitzroy, however, took a step back. It wasn't until Gillingham tugged on his tie that I realized he'd been anxious.

Lady Harcourt clasped my hand before I walked off. "Everything will be all right. You'll see."

"I'm not worried," I said with a shrug. And I wasn't. I didn't care if Fitzroy gave Gillingham a bloody nose. I just didn't want to see it.

"You ought to be," Lord Marchbank said. "Of everyone here, I'm the only one who saw the crime scene. I know what this Dr. Frankenstein is capable of."

He was right, and I should have been more concerned about the murdering doctor. He wanted me, and he seemed desperate enough to go to great lengths to get me.

"Was that necessary?" Lady Harcourt said to Lord Marchbank. "You've scared her now."

"Good. Fear will keep her safe."

He was correct there. It was a sentiment that had helped me get through five long, hard years relatively unscathed.

I hadn't decided whether I liked Lord Marchbank. He spoke less than the others, only talking when he needed to impart an important point. In that, he reminded me of Fitzroy. It was a trait that made it very difficult to read either man.

Gillingham pushed himself to his feet. "Good day, gentlemen, Lady Harcourt. I've got business to attend to."

I stepped aside to let him pass. The other committee members also made their excuses. They, at least, addressed me in their farewells.

"Remember what I said," Lady Harcourt whispered as she took my arm. "There will be a place for you in my household, if you wish, when this is over. You won't have to live on the street anymore."

"Thank you." I decided not to go through the ritual of refusing her offer again, but I knew I could never live with her, either as a servant or her companion. Indeed, I couldn't imagine living anywhere other than Lichfield Towers.

The admission shocked me and left me speechless as the carriages rolled away. I'd only resided there less than a week, and most of that as a prisoner, and yet I felt more comfortable there than anywhere. Perhaps that had more to do with the fact that I had no home now. Not in the Tufnell Park house I'd grown up in, or any of the derelict buildings I'd lived in with the boys' gangs. Dr. Frankenstein would be looking for me in all those places. I wasn't safe there. I was only safe at Lichfield.

Seth confronted me at the foot of the stairs, arms crossed over his impressive chest, making him seem even broader. "You didn't wish to eat more, did you?"

"No. I needed to leave the parlor."

He sighed. "I thought as much."

"I'm sorry. I didn't realize you believed me."

"I was hopeful." He lowered his arms. "At least you ate all your lunch."

"And I promise to eat all of my dinner, as long as the plate isn't piled too high or Cook serves sprouts."

He pulled a face. "I'll boycott the sprouts too, if he does." His gaze slid to a point past my shoulder. He cleared his throat, gave me an uncertain smile, then moved away.

I turned to see Fitzroy hovering. "I'm not going to try and escape." At his small frown, I added, "Your constant presence…you seem to think I'll run away at any moment. I won't. I gave you my word and I intend to keep it."

"I never doubted it." Still, he did not leave.

"Is there something you wished to speak to me about?"

"No." He went to walk away but stopped. "Yes. Are you comfortable here? Is there anything you require?"

"I'm not sure. I haven't resided here as a free woman for very long yet." At his blank face, I added, "I have everything I need for now. Thank you."

It was a strange, awkward conversation, which seemed to be leading onto a further question, perhaps the one I suspected he truly wanted to ask, yet he merely said, "I will be out all afternoon, searching for Dr. Frankenstein."

"Without me?"

"Your presence isn't required."

"I suppose not." I was relieved, on the whole, yet a part of me wanted to go with him. Or wanted, at least, to *be* with him.

I forced myself to walk up the stairs. I didn't like my growing feelings for someone who'd kidnapped me without qualms and held me prisoner until I'd made myself useful. I doubted *he* thought about *me* in the same way I thought about him. He'd certainly given no indication that he did. Such an imbalance of feelings between two people was never a good thing.

I read *A Guide To The Spirit World* in my small sitting room and learned more about my power in thirty minutes than I'd discovered in eighteen years. Most of it chilled me. A necromancer was different to a spirit medium, in that mediums could only speak to ghosts that had decided to remain and haunt their place of death. They could summon spirits into the living body of another through possession, but the spirit had a will of its own and a medium could not control it. A necromancer could raise a spirit that had already crossed over *and* control it—any spirit, no matter how long ago they'd died. The spirit could go anywhere in its ghostly form and not be confined to their place of death. That made necromancers much more powerful. Frighteningly so. The only limitation was that a spirit raised by necromancy couldn't be placed into a living body, only a dead one. The book didn't specify whether the body had to be its own or could be any cadaver.

I re-read the page three times then shut the book and folded it against my chest. It seemed I'd only scratched the surface of my capabilities so far. What unnerved me was that Fitzroy already knew this information, and so, perhaps, did the others. It was no wonder he wanted to keep me away from madmen and evil ones.

I set aside the book and read a novel to lighten my mood until Gus and Seth coaxed me outside for a walk. I'd been surprised to see them, having assumed Fitzroy took them with him in his search for Frankenstein.

"If Fitzroy finds him, do you think he'll confront him alone?" I asked as we ambled through the orchard.

Seth, who'd been striding ahead, slowed to walk alongside me again. "He might."

"That's rather foolish. He ought to have you two as support."

"He don't need us," Gus said, picking off an unripe apple and throwing it at a trunk. It missed.

"Fitzroy works better alone," Seth clarified. "Especially when he's following someone."

"We ain't that bad!"

"No, but he's better. If he's following you," he said to me, "you'll never know it. A hunting cat makes more noise than Death."

I could attest to that all too well. "What do you know about him? His background, his family, where is he from?"

"Wouldn't know." Gus snapped another apple from the tree and threw it as hard as possible. It split when it hit a nearby trunk and he gave a whoop of delight.

"We know very little about him," Seth said. "Neither of us has been employed by the ministry for long."

"How did you end up working for him?"

Seth picked an apple and threw it at the same tree, but missed. Gus snorted. We'd stopped altogether, both men distracted by their sport. I thought they wouldn't answer my question, but after three misses, Seth did.

"I found myself at a loose end one evening. Death was there and offered me a job."

"Bloody liar," Gus said with a shake of his head. "Seth were gambling and drinking like there ain't no tomorrow. He had nothing left to lose, except his own person, so he staked it."

"What do you mean, 'staked it'?"

"Himself. His body."

"That's enough," Seth growled. "She's a lady. She doesn't want to hear the particulars."

"I'm no lady, and I certainly do want to hear the particulars. They're the best part."

Seth's face turned a bright crimson as he glared at Gus. Gus ignored him. "Some old, fat lord took the wager. Said his wife would like to lie with a young, handsome fellow again." He leaned closer to me, his grin splitting his face. "Only I think the old lord wanted Seth for himself. The look on his wrinkly face when Seth removed his shirt to prove—"

"I did not remove my shirt!" Seth rolled his eyes. "It's not true, Charlie. That part isn't, at least. Anyway, how would you know, Gus? You weren't there."

"You told me, you blathering idiot. That first night you arrived at Lichfield, feeling all sorry for yourself. You got rollicking drunk and tossed up your guts and your story."

"That doesn't explain how you wound up here, working for Fitzroy," I said. "So you lost to the lord at cards."

"Got soundly beaten," Seth said. "Fitzroy was there and offered to pay my debt in exchange for coming to work for him."

"The gentleman accepted?"

"Not at first, but Death offered him a large sum." Seth puffed out his chest. "He realized my worth."

"Realized how desperate you were," Gus said, pulling off another apple. "You were available at just the right time too, and had some skills he could use." He slapped his colleague on his brawny shoulder. "He ain't just a pretty face, Charlie. He can shoot straight and bare knuckle box with the best of 'em. I saw him defeat Toothless Tom in the ring."

"Why were you fighting in a bare knuckle boxing match?" I asked Seth. "It's not the sort of thing a toff does." Attending the illegal matches was, but I'd never heard of one actually getting his hands dirty.

"I like to fight," Seth said with a shrug.

"He were desperate, and the pay were good. Everyone in the city came to see the toff in the ring. Including me, and maybe Death. That's probably where Fitzroy first saw him." Gus threw his apple, not at a trunk but into the middle distance.

Seth picked off another and threw it in the same direction. It passed Gus's. He gave his friend a smirk. Gus took that as a challenge and got another apple. He threw it hard, and it traveled so far I couldn't see where it landed.

"Ha! Beat that," he said.

Seth's next apple also disappeared from sight.

"Wait a moment." I hiked up my skirts and climbed the nearest apple tree. It felt like an age since I'd scrambled over a fence or wall. It was something I used to do several times a day. That and run, usually away from my pickpocket victim or the police.

"Charlie! What you doin' up there?" Gus cried, tilting his head back.

"Seeing who won. I think it was Seth."

"Get down before you hurt yourself," Seth called up.

"I'm not going to fall."

"If you get hurt, Death'll kill us," Gus said. "Come down now or we'll come up and get you."

I sighed and began to descend. "I was just having some fun. Turn away so you can't see up my skirt."

Both men dutifully turned their backs. I took the opportunity to pluck two apples and drop them on their heads.

"Oi!" Gus cried, rubbing his head.

I landed on both feet beside him and grinned. He frowned, but Seth laughed. "You're unlike any girl I know," he said.

"That's because I'm not used to behaving like a girl."

"That be true," Gus muttered. "You shouldn't be climbing trees. Lady Harcourt would have a fit."

"I don't care what Lady Harcourt thinks. Or anyone, for that matter. If I want to climb a tree, I'll climb a tree. Girls should be allowed to."

"Ain't proper," Gus grumbled, striding off. "Besides, you ain't a girl, you're a woman."

I stared at his retreating back, as rigid as a plank of wood. Why had my behavior upset *him* so much?

"Don't mind him," Seth said as we followed at a slower pace. "He's still not sure what to make of you. Sometimes he thinks of you as a lad, and other times he becomes aware of your femininity and he gets embarrassed."

"Why?"

"Because he doesn't know how to act around females. They scare him."

"Why do we scare him?"

"I'm not sure. Why don't you ask him?"

Perhaps I would, but another time. Gus didn't look in the mood to talk to me.

We headed back inside the house, where I spent a dull afternoon waiting for Fitzroy to return. The day stretched into the evening, and Seth, Gus and I dined in the kitchen with Cook. Afterward we played cards and I learned some new games from the men. If we'd been playing for real money instead of dried broad beans, I would have lost a fortune. I couldn't concentrate. Every creak of the house made me glance at the door. Every chime of the long case clock in the entrance hall set my teeth on edge. When it finally chimed ten, I couldn't stand it any longer.

"Where is he?" I tossed my cards down on the table and got up.

The others watched me pace back and forth with bemused expressions. "There's no need to worry," Seth said. "He'll be fine. He always is."

"You don't know that. He could be lying injured or dead somewhere."

Gus swept the cards up in his big paw and began shuffling them. "Come sit down and stop worrying. For one thing, he don't deserve it. For another, he can take care of himself. You ain't seen what he's capable of, yet."

Cook and Seth both nodded in agreement. When I refused to sit and continued pacing, Seth got up and intercepted me. He clasped my arms and dipped his head to peer into my eyes. He was about to say something when a shadow blocked the doorway.

I gasped at the sight of Fitzroy looking as unruffled as always. "You're back!" I wrenched free of Seth's grip, but stopped myself rushing to Fitzroy like I wanted to. "Did you find him?"

"Yes." He came into the kitchen and immediately the space seemed smaller. His gaze flicked over me then settled on Seth.

Seth swallowed heavily and sat at the table again.

"I'll warm up dinner," Cook said, rising.

"And?" I asked, as Fitzroy poured himself a glass of water from a jug. "What happened after you found him?"

"I lost him."

That had everyone staring, even Cook.

Fitzroy set the glass down and regarded each of us in turn. The men returned to their tasks, but I met his gaze directly. "Go on," I said.

"I learned where he lived, but when he didn't show up there, I returned to Holloway's house."

"Father's? Why?"

"I suspected he would visit again in a desperate attempt to find you. Holloway is his only link to you. I was right. He did."

I bit my lip to stop myself voicing my fear that Frankenstein had injured the man who'd raised me. Fitzroy, however, must have understood my concern. "He realized Holloway couldn't help him and left without harming him. I followed but lost him."

The other three men exchanged glances but made no comment. I suspected that was wise. Fitzroy seemed frostier than usual. His failure probably frustrated him.

"I'm sure it wasn't easy to follow him in the dark." My attempt to mollify him earned me the full force of that icy glare. I cleared my throat and forged ahead anyway. "I'm sure you'll find him again soon."

He didn't respond. Instead, he took his dinner to his rooms. The others resumed their card game, but I yawned and said goodnight. Upstairs, I contemplated knocking on Fitzroy's door, but I had nothing to say to him and I would only embarrass myself by asking after his wellbeing.

I prepared for bed, then lay under the covers listening to the silence. An hour later, I could no longer stand it. I got up, threw a shawl around my shoulders, lit a candle, and padded along the hallway to Fitzroy's rooms. I was about to knock on the door when it opened. Fitzroy seemed as surprised to see me standing there as I was to see him dressed for going out.

"Where are you headed at this time of night?" I blurted.

His eyebrows arched and I pressed my lips together. The corner of his mouth twitched. "Out."

"But it must be almost midnight. What can you possibly— Oh." Where else did a gentleman go at such a time, but to visit his lover? Thank goodness the light from my candle flame wasn't strong enough to show my reddening face. "I was concerned for your welfare," I mumbled pathetically.

He paused. "Why?"

I shrugged. "I don't know. I just am. You were out for so long tonight, and now you're going out again." I lowered my candle. "Of course you must want to see her, and she you."

"Who?"

"I don't know. Lady Harcourt, I presume."

His eyes briefly flared.

"It's none of my affair who you see in the evenings, secretly or otherwise," I went on. "If it is her, however, I can think of no one more lovely. You're both interesting people and you make a handsome couple." *Ugh*, strike me down before I say something even more humiliating. I turned to go, but Fitzroy grabbed my hand, the one holding the candlestick at a slight tilt.

"You're dripping wax on the floor." He righted the candle, but didn't immediately let go. His hand remained over mine, his warmth seeping through my skin to my bones. "I am not going to see Lady Harcourt." He spoke softly, his voice a deep purr.

"Oh," I said on a breath. I angled my face to peer up at his, only to be caught in his black, fathomless gaze as thoroughly as an insect in a web. I couldn't pull myself free, no matter how much I wanted to. "Another, then."

"You're bold, Charlie." His thumb stroked my knuckles and his head dipped closer to mine. It was such a small move, yet I'd noticed it. It gave me hope and courage to ignore the voice within me shouting at me to stop.

Another voice was louder. It urged me to kiss him.

CHAPTER 12

I reached up to touch Fitzroy's cheek. I didn't know what I was doing. It was like someone else lifted my hand and angled my head. I'd never flirted with anyone, never kissed a man, yet here I was behaving as if it were something I did all the time.

What must he think of me?

What did I think of myself?

I lowered my hand at the same moment he let my other go. We both took a step back. I pulled my shawl up my shoulder where it had slipped down.

"Return to bed," he said, gruffly.

Too full of swirling emotions to think of something clever to say, I simply turned and walked back to my rooms. I was about to close the door when he stopped nearby. I hadn't realized he'd followed.

"Please accept my apologies," he said with a curt bow. "That was unforgivable."

I wanted to shout at him that it wasn't, that feelings ought to be acted upon. But I didn't know if he had feelings for me. Nor did I think acting on them was the right thing to do in our situation—not when I was being honest with myself. "You have nothing to apologize for," was all I could manage.

"I do. I—" His face turned stony. "Goodnight, Charlie."

He walked off and I closed the door, still none the wiser as to where he was headed. My jangling nerves didn't allow me to fall asleep until it was almost dawn.

***

When I awoke late morning, I quickly dressed and hurried down the stairs. I found Seth and Gus in the scullery, helping Cook with chores.

"You missed breakfast," Cook said without glancing up from the pot he scrubbed.

"Can't you fry a little bacon for her?" Seth asked.

"I'll do it," I said. "Is Mr. Fitzroy here?"

"He came back two hours ago," Gus said. He sat on his haunches on the floor, scrubbing brush in hand, and rubbed his back. "He's probably sleeping."

"If he sleeps." Seth grinned and winked at me. "I'm not sure he requires any."

"You mean he's been out all night?" I looked from one to the other and received only shrugs. "Does he do that often?"

"On occasion." Seth indicated I should walk ahead of him out of the scullery. "When the need arises."

I was about to ask what he meant, but decided it was best not to ask. He might mean the sort of needs only a woman could satisfy.

He followed me into the kitchen and showed me where Cook kept the pan and bacon. I wasn't overly familiar with cooking, but Seth taught me how to add more coal to the range, although it was still hot enough for my needs. The actual cooking part was easy. He made some tea while I worked and we chatted as I ate.

By the time I finished, I'd learned about his love of all things equestrian and the details of every horse he'd ever owned. I learned nothing about himself or his family, except that they must have been wealthy to afford all those horses. My father had not owned one.

"Good morning." Fitzroy's sudden appearance caught me by surprise. As usual, I'd not heard him approach. "Did you sleep well?"

"Abominably," I said. "I hear you didn't sleep at all."

He unwrapped the bacon I'd carefully rewrapped and placed two rashers in the pan I'd used. "I managed a little."

I was diverted from my own food by the sight of a gentleman cooking his own breakfast. I supposed in a household without servants he occasionally had to do things for himself. When he finished, he tipped the bacon onto a plate and accepted a cup of tea from Seth. He sat opposite me and ate.

"Did you find him, sir?" Seth asked.

"Yes, but I lost him again."

"Again!"

Fitzroy's sharp glare pinned Seth for a brief moment before releasing him. He continued to eat but the air in the kitchen had become chilly, despite the heat thrown out from the range.

"You were looking for Frankenstein last night." My words came out in a rush, followed by a bubble of laughter.

Fitzroy watched me from beneath lowered lashes while continuing to eat. Seth shrugged. "Where did you think he was?" he asked.

"That…never mind. So you found him again?"

"And lost him in the same spot," Fitzroy said. He sounded more bemused than angry. It was as if he couldn't fathom *how* he'd lost Frankenstein. Perhaps it had never happened before.

"The man must be a magician to get away from you twice," Seth said.

"The thought had crossed my mind."

I blinked at him. "Magic? Surely that's a joke?"

"I don't joke."

"Amen," Seth muttered as he picked up the empty pan.

"But…magic…" I shook my head. "That's something only children and fools believe in."

"As are necromancers," Fitzroy said.

"Point taken." I finished my bacon and pushed my plate aside. "You said you lost him in the same place. Where precisely was that?"

"You think you can help?" Seth asked, taking my plate. "Best leave this to us, Charlie."

I flattened my palms on the table. "Don't treat me like a child. My knowledge of London's streets likely exceeds yours. I doubt you found yourself in too many dark, crowded lanes during your pampered life."

"You'd be surprised," he said with a harsh laugh. "My life hasn't been all that pampered of late."

I rubbed my temple and winced. "I'm sorry, Seth, I didn't mean to let my temper get the better of me."

He chucked me under the chin and smiled. "Don't fret. I deserved it."

Fitzroy shoved his plate at Seth. Seth's face fell. He took the plate and wandered out of the kitchen toward the scullery.

"Totten Lane," Fitzroy said to me. "Do you know it?"

"In Clerkenwell? Yes, I do." I frowned and chewed on my lower lip. The lane bled into a small, miserable courtyard, where several families occupied the tenements. There were buildings on all sides, and there was no other exit except through a manhole that led to the underground sewers. It was located behind a brick wall that seemed to belong to one of the buildings from a distance, but up close, it became obvious that the wall was once part of an old well that had once stood there. "I know how he disappeared."

One of his brows lifted. "Go on."

"It's easier if I show you. Shall we go now?"

I stood and he stood too. "I don't think that's wise."

"Why not? You need to find Frankenstein, and I can help you." I crossed my arms in what I hoped was a show of defiance but felt more like pettiness.

"You were afraid before, and with good reason."

"I was. I still am. But I know that helping you will mean he's caught sooner. When he's caught, I can stop being afraid."

He blinked slowly and nodded. He walked off and I had to race to catch up to him.

"Wait, sir."

He stopped in the narrow, dark service corridor and waited until I was alongside him.

"I want to help. I owe you for taking me in."

"You don't. The circumstances under which you came here…were not ideal. It should negate any gratitude you feel. It's I who should be thanking you."

"True," I said lightly.

He huffed out a breath that might or might not have been a laugh. "Thank you, Charlie, for not shooting me in the head."

I shivered at the memory of having nearly killed him. A few inches to the left and the bullet would have pierced his heart. I folded my arms against the chill.

"Charlie," he said softly. "It was a joke."

"Not a very funny one."

He sighed. "I'm unused to making jokes. I apologize. I'll hold my tongue next time."

"No! Don't do that. I prefer your unfunny jokes to none at all." I liked that he was telling jokes when he ordinarily didn't. It felt like he was trying just for me.

"You'll change your mind soon enough."

I wasn't sure if that was meant as a joke too, so I laughed anyway, just in case. "Sir," I said, peering up at him, "what will happen to me after Frankenstein is caught and this is over? I don't wish to live with Lady Harcourt, and I can't go back to the streets."

"No, you can't."

"I'd like to stay here."

"That has yet to be decided."

"Who decides? You?"

"I make all the decisions regarding the ministry and Lichfield Towers."

"Don't tell Lord Gillingham that. He seems to think you're an underling."

"Don't be afraid of Gillingham. He's an old goat in an expensive suit, nothing more."

"I don't want you to incur his wrath if I stay here."

"I can cope with Gillingham's wrath, and anyone else's censure. If I decide that you are to stay, that is."

"Don't send me away," I whispered. It was suddenly so hard to hold myself together. Mere days ago, all I'd wanted was to get away from Lichfield. But now, the thought of leaving was unbearable.

We stood so close that I could feel the heat of him. I was aware of his every breath, every shift of muscle, and my aching response to him.

"Charlie," he said on a sigh, "staying here may not be in your best interests."

"How can it not be?"

His gaze wandered over the top of my head, toward the scullery where three deep, quiet voices hummed in conversation.

"You are entirely wrong, Lincoln."

His gaze flew to mine.

"I know what you're thinking, and you're wrong." I thrust my hand on my hip, angrier now. Good. I preferred anger to the pathetic whine I heard in my voice moments ago. "I am capable of taking care of myself, and I am also not going to succumb to teasing flattery from the men. I'd hoped you thought me better than that."

His lips parted and I was gratified to see that my words had slapped him into giving a facial expression. If I wasn't mistaken, my outburst had shocked him. Perhaps he hadn't expected me to be aware of his thoughts on the matter.

"Now, have someone prepare the horses and carriage. We're going to Clerkenwell." I picked up my skirts and sailed off down the passageway, out of the service area. I didn't turn to see if he watched or not, but if the heat in the back of my head was an indication, he couldn't take his gaze off me. I only wished I knew if I'd shocked him in a good way or bad.

***

We walked down Totten Lane rather than take the coach. The road was narrow, being only a little wider than the width of the brougham, and turning would have been impossible. Besides, it made us too conspicuous. Although Fitzroy didn't say it, I suspected he wanted to arrive undetected. Unfortunately, the sight of four well-dressed strangers drew stares anyway.

"Should've worn disguises," Gus muttered. He and Seth seemed tense, their arms and fingers rigid as if they were ready to draw weapons at the slightest sign of trouble. Where they'd hidden their weapons, I couldn't say, but I strongly suspected they possessed a knife or two and perhaps a pistol on their person.

"Where precisely did you last see him?" I asked Fitzroy.

He walked beside me. Outwardly, he seemed calm, his body less stiff than the others, his movements as fluid as always. But when he came so close to me that our arms brushed, I sensed him clench. "In Black Water Yard." He nodded ahead where the lane ended at an archway that led through to a small courtyard.

"Our exit will be easily blocked once we enter," I said.

He looked at me and arched a brow.

I shrugged. "I remember Black Water Yard well. I was almost caught after stealing a shirt from a washing line."

He nodded gravely.

Up ahead, Seth peered back at me over his shoulder, a small smile on his lips. "It's easy to forget that you were a thief, looking as you do now."

Gus and Seth went through the arch first, then me, and finally Lincoln. Gus and Fitzroy had to duck beneath the ancient bricks of the arch, and Seth's head skimmed it. He was hatless, as were the other men, whereas I wore the small bonnet set back on my head, my hair pinned off my face. I felt much too exposed as people stared at us, and me in particular. Did they recognize me as that boy thief of mere weeks ago?

A group of children stopped their game of tag and watched us through wary eyes. Washing strung from lines between buildings flapped overhead. It would take an age for it to dry; the sun struggled to pierce the dense air and the courtyard was filled with shadows layered upon shadows.

"That wall there is false," I said, nodding at the bricks on the far side of the courtyard. "From here it blends in with the wall of the building behind it, but if you get closer, you see that it's separate. Between the two walls is a manhole that leads down into the sewers."

"Bloody dangerous, having a manhole near where children play," Seth said.

"I don't think the authorities cared much about the slum children when they put it there. They think there are too many mouths to feed in these parts anyway. Losing a child to the sewers from time to time won't keep them awake at night."

Fitzroy eyed his surroundings before striding to the wall and disappearing behind it. He reappeared moments later. "Take her back to Lichfield."

Gus nodded. "Yes, sir. Both of us?"

Fitzroy nodded.

"Shouldn't one of them stay with you to help?" I asked him.

He shook his head. "Go."

Seth placed his hand at my lower back and both men flanked me as we walked out of the courtyard. I glanced over my shoulder, but Fitzroy had already disappeared behind the wall again. Whether he was lying in wait or going down into the sewers, I didn't know.

"We'll be out of here in a moment," Seth said, splaying his fingers wide on my back. "Miserable place."

"It's home to some," I told him, hotly. "Not everyone can live in a mansion."

His mouth opened, closed, and opened again. "I'm sorry if I offended. It wasn't my intention."

I sighed. "I know. I'm sorry too."

"Blimey." Gus stopped a few paces ahead of us. "Don't look now but there's a toff coming our way. You don't think it's—"

"It is," I muttered. "Frankenstein."

I recognized the slim man with the short whiskers in the gray suit. His gaze settled on us and he slowed, just as we did. He'd never laid eyes on me before, and he couldn't know what Charlotte Holloway looked like, yet my instincts screamed at me to run.

Seth and Gus fell into step alongside me. Did they sense my anxiety? Seth took my hand and placed it on his arm, then folded his own hand over the top, trapping me. If we were in Hyde Park, we would have looked like any other couple taking a stroll on a warm summer's day. But no well-dressed couple strolled through the filthy lanes of Clerkenwell for entertainment.

I tried not to look directly at Frankenstein as he passed, but I couldn't help myself peering through my lowered lashes. He touched the brim of his hat, but neither Seth nor Gus offered a greeting in return.

Later, I wondered if that had tipped him off.

I breathed out a long breath as he passed us by, but another caught in my throat when he called out. "Miss Holloway?"

My heart stopped dead. How did he know?

Seth shoved me behind him and I stumbled into the wall. I whipped around, gathering my skirts at the same time. But I lowered them again when I spotted Frankenstein backing up, hands above his head. My two protectors aimed pistols at him.

"Miss Holloway," he said, eyeing the pistols. "Charlotte. I know it's you."

"You don't know me," I said.

"I saw a photograph of you at the Holloway residence. You were younger, but you haven't changed so much that you're unrecognizable."

"I'm not going with you."

"Please, listen to me before you make that decision."

Seth straightened his arm and aimed the pistol at Frankenstein's temple. "Don't speak."

"I must. Charlotte, these people have lied to you about me. They've made you afraid of me, when it is them you should fear."

"Shut your mouth!" Gus shouted.

Frankenstein swallowed heavily and directed his gaze at me. He had bright blue eyes, and where his jaw had been hard that day I'd seen him storming away from my father's house, it was now slack. He didn't appear in the least harmful, particularly as Seth and Gus were so much bigger.

"Listen to me, Charlotte. Whatever these people have told you is false. Lies. They've been seeking out my secrets for some time now, and wish to use my knowledge for their own gain."

"I don't know what you're talking about," I said, chin up.

"Good girl," Seth said. "Don't believe him. He's a liar and a murderer."

"I've not murdered anyone!" Frankenstein took a step toward me, but Seth and Gus blocked his path. The doctor's lips curled in frustration. "It's not murder to put suffering, dying men out of their misery. Those poor souls were terminally ill. They were in pain. They begged me to end their suffering."

"You used their body parts!" I covered my mouth and swallowed bile. It was one thing to hear of his deeds second hand, it was quite another to come face to face with such a monster. Yet he looked nothing like a monster. He looked like a normal gentleman. He was in earnest, yes, but I wasn't afraid of him.

"Calthorn wasn't dying," Seth said.

"Calthorn was a wicked man." Frankenstein spoke to me. His entire focus was directed at me. "He hurt his wife. He beat her daily. Not on her face, where the bruises would be seen, but in the stomach and chest. She couldn't have children because of the beatings. He used the secrets he gained through his position as head of the nation's spy ring to bully and harm those weaker than himself. He was a cruel man, yet no court would have convicted him. He was above the law and he knew it. You tell me, Charlotte, if you think a man like that ought to get away with his crimes. Perhaps I acted rashly, and should not have killed him for his wife's sake, but I am not always a rational man when I'm riled. And that man did rile me."

"You took his brain!"

"I found another use for it. But that's not why I killed him." He slowly pressed his hands together above his head then lowered them. "I have begged God's forgiveness every day, and I know I will be punished for my sins in the afterlife. But while I live, I can do good here. My experiments are not to be feared. I have done England a service by creating new life. Superior life. Once the bodies have spirits, you'll see them for what they are, Charlotte. Wonderful, amazing humans who deserve to live."

I screwed up my face, unable to hide my disgust. Did he think I would believe he was doing something good for the country? For human-kind? He was mad. "They are abominations. They're not humans, they're monsters."

"They are no more an abomination than me. Or you. We are all made, one way or another. Have you yourself not been called an abomination by the very man you thought was your father?"

"He is *not* my father."

"I know." He smiled gently. His eyes shone—familiar, blue eyes.

My stomach plunged. My throat tightened and it suddenly felt too hot in the lane, the air too close. I backed away and hit the wall. I pressed myself into the cool bricks, but couldn't take my eyes off Frankenstein.

"I'm your father, Charlotte."

"Bloody hell," Gus muttered, lowering his weapon.

Seth cocked his gun.

"Don't!" I cried. I raced up to them, but stopped short. I wasn't sure what to do or say. All I did know was that I didn't want Frankenstein to be shot.

If he was my father, I had a million questions I needed answered. But I could ask none of them. I could only stare. I took in his appearance, his slender frame and oval face, so like mine. His eyes were the same shade of blue too, although not as wide. The more I looked, the more certain I became that he spoke the truth. This man had fathered me.

He lowered his hands altogether and smiled at me. "Charlotte. That's a pretty name."

I swallowed again, but the lump in my throat was too great for me to speak. I blinked back hot tears and simply nodded like a halfwit.

"I never knew you existed until very recently," he said. "Your mother never confided in me."

"Who…?" I managed to whisper.

"A kind, gentle woman. Her name was Ellen, and I'd like to tell you all about her."

I nodded. I wanted that too.

"But you have to come with me. Together we'll find out what happened to her. Yes?"

My tears hovered on my eyelids. One blink and they would spill. I nodded.

"Charlie," Gus snapped. "Don't listen to him. He's no better than a turd."

"He only wants to lure you to his laboratory and use you to resurrect his monsters," Seth said. "Don't believe a thing he says." He jerked his head toward the entrance to the lane. "Come with us, Doctor."

Some of the residents gathered near the archway, their eyes wide as they watched the scene play out between the toffs. Children clung to their mothers' aprons, and men murmured among themselves. None seemed too concerned about stray bullets.

Frankenstein held out his hand to me. "Come with me, Charlotte. Please. I mean you no harm. I'm your father, after all. I want to get to know you. I've always wanted a child to love, and a daughter most of all. I have the means to give you material things you desire, and the immaterial too. Those which only a parent can give."

My tears spilled down my cheeks. He said everything I'd ever wanted to hear. For five years, I'd lived in hope that Anselm Holloway would say such words to me, but that hope had been dashed when I learned of my adoption. Yet it rose again now, and bloomed like a flower in the dessert, with everything Frankenstein said.

"Charlie," Seth begged, "don't fall for it."

Gus cocked his weapon. "Death never said he wanted the turd alive."

"No!" I shouted. "Don't shoot him! Please."

Frankenstein backed away toward the arch and the courtyard where the crowd milled. Seth growled low in his throat.

"Death will get him in there," Gus muttered, lowering his weapon. "There're too many witnesses here."

Too many innocent bystanders who could get hurt.

The crowd parted for Frankenstein, but he did not pass through the arch. He held out his hand to me again. "Come with me, Charlotte."

Seth raised his gun again. "She's not going anywhere with you."

Frankenstein appealed to me and stretched his hand out further. Seth took my hand in his, but I snatched it free. To Frankenstein, I said, "I…I'm not sure. I need time."

His jaw stiffened, and his lips pressed together, then his face slackened once more. "I'll see you very soon, my dear sweet daughter." He turned and disappeared into the crowd, who closed around him.

"He must be paying them." Gus swore. "Bloody fools are protecting him."

"Come on." Seth took my elbow. When I tried to pull free this time, he didn't let go. "We have to get you away from him."

I planted my feet apart and resisted. "I don't—"

A woman's scream tore through the thick, hot air. Gus and Seth let me go and ran toward the arch. I followed close at their heels, but got no further than the crowd gathered in the courtyard. The woman was no longer screaming, but her sobs echoed around the clearing. I couldn't see her, but could just make out her spluttered plea. "Don't hurt 'im, sir."

"Drop it!" Frankenstein shouted, from somewhere beyond the wall of bodies blocking my sight.

"What is it?" I asked Seth. "Can you see?"

He didn't answer but pushed through the crowd, his strong arms shoving people aside. Gus joined him, and once again I followed in their wake.

I peeked past Gus to see Frankenstein standing near the false wall, a child in front of him, his gaze dead ahead on something I couldn't see behind the wall, but I knew was Fitzroy. Frankenstein held a knife at the boy's throat. The sobbing woman must be his mother. Her menfolk held her back, but the anguish on her face made my heart ache for her.

"Now do you see what sort of character he is?" Seth growled at me.

"Drop the gun down there," Frankenstein snapped. "Do it now, or I'll slit his throat."

A hush fell over the crowd as we waited for the clank of the gun being dropped down the unseen manhole. But the only sound was the woman's uncontrollable sobs.

Frankenstein's arm tensed and the boy cried out in pain as the blade bit into his neck.

I was about to open my mouth, to scream at Fitzroy to do it, when Seth's hand clamped over it. He jerked me against his chest, blocking my view. "Quiet, Charlie," he hissed. "If he knows you're here, he'll use the boy to force you to go with him."

Perhaps I could force an exchange, the boy's life for mine...

"Do it!" the mother screamed before I'd made up my mind.

The distant splash of something hitting water was a relief to hear. The crowd seemed to take a breath all at once.

"Get away from the hole." The edge in Frankenstein's voice wasn't quite as harsh anymore.

I pulled free of Seth's hard embrace and peered past him. Frankenstein moved toward the manhole behind the wall, the child still locked in his arm with a knife to his throat. As he disappeared behind the wall, Fitzroy reappeared. He did not have his hands raised, but his intense focus zeroed in on Frankenstein.

"Let him go!" shouted one of the men holding back the sobbing mother.

Everything seemed to happen at once. The boy was spat out from behind the wall, propelled into Fitzroy's waiting arms. At the same moment, while everyone's attention was distracted, the knife flew at the boy.

Several women screamed, including me. But Fitzroy spun the child out of the way and put his own body between blade and boy.

The knife buried itself in his side.

CHAPTER 13

"Lincoln!" My shout was swallowed up by the now rowdy crowd. They surged forward, surrounding the boy and Fitzroy. "I can't see him." I tried to pull free of Seth, but he held me. His gaze wasn't on me, however, but on the spot where Fitzroy had been standing.

Gus went ahead and tried to part the crowd, but they would not let him through. They jostled him and one another, their angry, vengeful shouts drowning out all other sounds.

Until a gunshot brought sudden silence. The echo left no doubt that it had come from down the sewer. Seth's hands tightened around me, and no matter how hard I tried to pull away from him, I couldn't.

"Sir!" I heard Gus shout. "Take this!"

"What's he doing?" God, how I hated not knowing. The ball of frustration growing inside me became too much and it burst out. I kicked Seth's shin then kneed him in the groin. His grip loosened and I pulled free. I was too fast once I was out of his reach.

"Lincoln?" I called as I pushed through the crowd to where I could see Gus standing over the manhole. "Gus! Where is he? What's going on?"

"Fitzroy's chasing him."

"But he's injured!"

"He's got my gun." He straightened. His breathing came hard and fast as if he were the one doing the chasing. "Where's Seth?"

"Gus, I saw the knife in his side."

"Seth got stabbed?"

"Fitzroy!" I punched him hard in the ribs and he coughed. "He's gravely injured." The drops of blood on the cobblestones were testament to that. The knife, lying forgotten near the manhole, was covered in blood. "He needs to dress the wound."

"He needs to catch Frankenstein. It's our best chance."

I went to punch him again, but he caught my fist. "That hurt," he said, rubbing his chest. His gaze lifted above my head. "Bloody hell, what happened to you? You look like you seen a ghost."

"I got embroiled in a melee."

"Why the white face?"

"My sword got in the way."

"You ain't carrying— Ah." Gus snorted. "Dagger, more like."

Seth peered down the manhole. "Where's Fitzroy?"

"Gone after Frankenstein. He's armed." He tapped Seth's shoulder. "I think it's time we left."

Three of the local men glared at us, their teeth bared. Behind them, the rest of the crowd still gathered around the boy and his family, offering comfort.

"We didn't do anything," Seth grumbled. "Fitzroy *saved* him."

"They want someone to blame. We're here, Frankenstein isn't." Gus took my elbow and tried to steer me away, but I refused to go.

"We can't leave Fitzroy down there!"

"We can and we will," Seth said. "He won't necessarily resurface this way, anyway. It's a warren of tunnels down there. We have no idea which one he's taken or where he'll end up. Come home with us, Charlie. He'll want you to be safe now."

I allowed them to escort me out through the arch. Seth dropped some coins and the crowd pounced on them instead of us.

We hurried up Totten Lane and returned to the stables, some blocks away, where we'd lodged the horse and carriage. Seth drove and Gus rode in the cabin with me. His gaze flicked to me often but he didn't speak, mercifully. I wasn't ready to talk about what had happened. About Frankenstein being my father.

Back at the house, I sat in the library where I could watch the driveway. Seth joined me, but not near the window. He sat at the central table, one foot on the chair opposite, and crossed his arms. I felt his eyes on me, but I didn't engage him in conversation. Gus delivered tea then left again to get cake.

When we were alone again, Seth finally spoke. "He's not worth it."

I said nothing and continued to look out the window.

"You're better than that. Better than him." He sounded annoyed. I supposed getting kneed in the family jewels can upset a man. "This is your home now, Charlie. You don't need him. You have us."

I frowned. "What are you talking about?"

"Frankenstein. He may be your father, but he's lying about wanting you. He doesn't even know you."

"Oh. Frankenstein. Yes, of course." I turned back to the window, somewhat more distracted from my vigil than I had been before. Frankenstein had almost duped me, until he'd endangered the life of the child. What sort of man did that?

A desperate one. One I shouldn't want to associate with. Nevertheless, I wanted to talk to him, and discover everything there was to know about my ancestry—my mother.

"You don't believe anything he said, do you?" he went on.

"I believe he is my father."

"Yes. Well, that, I suppose. Now that I've seen him, the resemblance is remarkable, I'll admit. But that doesn't mean he wants to be a loving father."

But Frankenstein knew who my real mother was. No one else did.

A movement between the trees at the base of the drive caught my attention. I rose and leaned closer to the window. A hansom cab rolled up to the house and Fitzroy emerged from the cabin. He held his arm close to his body. His side was damp with blood.

I picked up my skirts and ran out of the library then flung the front door open. "Lincoln!" It wasn't lost on me that I used his first name to greet him.

It seemed it wasn't lost on him either. He blinked at me from the bottom step. His face was a little pale, his eyes circled by shadows. I trotted down the steps as the cab pulled away.

"Thank God you're all right. I've been sick with worry." I went to take his arm to help him, but he kept his distance.

"You shouldn't have concerned yourself." He strode past me.

I stood there, staring at his back, dumbfounded by his snub. What had I done to deserve that? "You cannot tell me what I can and can't be concerned about!"

My protest might as well have fallen on deaf ears. He didn't slow down, didn't acknowledge me at all.

Seth, standing in the doorway, moved aside to let his master pass. "Did you catch him, sir?"

"No."

Seth gave me a sympathetic smile. "He'll be in a foul mood for the rest of the day," he whispered when I drew closer. "Don't mind him."

"Why will he be in a foul mood? Because he failed?"

"Yes, and he's worried that Frankenstein will get the better of him and harm the royal family."

"You got all that from the few curt words he spoke?"

Fitzroy headed straight for the stairs, just as Gus came down them in the opposite direction. "Thought I smelled you." He wrinkled his nose. Fitzroy did indeed stink of the sewers, and his trousers were wet and filthy from the knees down. "At least you're balanced now, sir," he said cheerfully. At Fitzroy's hesitation, he added, "Charlie shot you on the other side, didn't she?"

Fitzroy glanced back at me, and I froze at the coldness in his eyes. If looks could kill, I would have been turned into an icicle. I gulped and dipped my head, hoping he didn't see the color rise to my cheeks.

When I looked up again, however, he was no longer there. He'd gone quietly up the stairs.

"Better get some clean bandages to dress the wound," Seth told Gus. "I'll boil the water."

"You're going to dress his wound?" I asked. "Not a doctor?"

"If it's not too deep, he'll do it himself. He has some medical knowledge. We're just delivering the supplies."

"I wonder how Frankenstein got away," Gus mused.

"Probably lost him in the sewers," Seth said.

I left the two of them pondering that and headed toward the service area at the back of the house. "Where are the bandages?"

"Leave it to us," Gus said. "He'll prefer it."

"That's too bad. Besides, everyone knows women make the best nurses. You two lugs are too rough." They protested some more, but I refused to listen.

Cook gave me some warm water in a jug and Seth found bandages. "I'll see to the rest," he said.

"You sure you want to face him now?" Gus asked me. "He'll be a bloody-minded bear."

"He's less likely to lash out at me than you."

"True. Good luck."

I headed up the stairs, only to realize Fitzroy was in the bathroom. I could hear water spilling in the tub. I waited in his sitting room for his return, and he arrived some fifteen minutes later, looking damp, disheveled and delectable.

Thick straps of muscle stretched across his shoulders and chest. His hair hung loose, brushing the nape of his neck, and blood smeared his side. He stopped in the doorway when he saw me, his eyes huge. He seemed startled, not at all his gruff, cool self. The change threw me a little off balance and I remained rooted to the spot, uncertain how to proceed.

"Where are Seth and Gus?" he asked, recovering before I did.

"Fetching supplies." I moved close enough to him that I could smell the sharp tang of the carbolic soap he'd used. "Let me look at the wound."

"It's fine."

"It's not fine. There's fresh blood."

"The bleeding has almost stopped."

"Let me see. Is it deep?"

"It requires suturing."

Every time I came close, he either turned or moved away so I couldn't inspect the cut. After three attempts, I'd had enough. "Stop behaving like a child, and let me see."

He squared up to me and looked down that imperial nose of his. It was a pose that was probably meant to intimidate but failed miserably. It made him even more appealing, a wounded yet defiant warrior.

"A child?" he intoned.

"Yes."

"I am merely trying to protect your feminine sensibilities."

I burst out laughing. "I don't think I have any feminine sensibilities." At his flattening lips, I thought it best to be more serious. My laughter seemed to offend him. "Thank you for your consideration for my wellbeing, sir, but I'm not going to swoon when I touch you."

"That is not the point," he ground out.

I stamped my hands on my hips. "Do you honestly prefer Gus or Seth to do this instead of me?"

"I can do it."

"You can't."

He tried to prove me wrong by inspecting the wound. While he was able to reach it, he couldn't see it very well; he certainly wouldn't be able to suture it himself. "Seth can do it," he finally said, giving up.

"Seth is all thumbs, and Gus's fingernails are so dirty he's probably growing mushrooms under them. I'm gentle, methodical and can sew a stitch." Without waiting for his next protest, I dipped the cloth into the warm water.

To my surprise, he allowed me to clean the blood away without protest. The cut wasn't too deep, thank goodness, but it was important to keep it clean and avoid infection. I concentrated on my task, circling ever closer to the cut itself. I almost forgot that I was playing nurse to a very handsome man until that man sucked air between his teeth.

"Sorry," I said, glancing up at him.

He watched me from beneath lowered lashes. His face flushed when he realized that he was caught staring.

"Did I hurt you?"

He shook his head then stared straight ahead. He drew in a ragged breath. "Continue."

He stood as stiff as a statue while I finished cleaning the wound. Not even his chest rose and fell with his breathing. He only moved away when Seth and Gus arrived. I hadn't quite finished cleaning, but it would have to do. It seemed he didn't want the men to see me tending him. That would make stitching him up somewhat difficult.

He inspected the supplies the men had brought up. "Is everything sterilized?"

"Steamed the needle and thread in the kitchen," Seth said. To me, he added, "Surgical thread. We keep some just in case."

"You get wounded often?" I asked.

"Enough that we need a supply of it on hand. Mr. Fitzroy does all the stitching, though. Never had to do it myself."

"Nor me," Gus chimed in. "I'm happy to try my hand."

"Try your hand?" I shook my head. "I may not be much of a lady, but I've been sewing and embroidering since I was old enough to hold a needle. I'll do it."

"Were you any good?" Seth asked.

"Adequate." I shot Fitzroy a reassuring smile. "The wound is straight. Unless you want me to embroider *Home Sweet Home*, I can manage."

Gus laughed so hard his eyes watered. Seth couldn't hold back his grin either, until Fitzroy's glare withered it.

"Stand still and keep your arm out of the way," I told him.

Gus handed me a pair of sterilized gloves and I threaded the needle. Despite my bravado, I was nervous. Stitching a sampler was one thing, a human being entirely another. I didn't want Fitzroy to see my apprehension, however, and managed to steady my shaking hand enough to proceed, under his guidance. He calmly informed me how deep I ought to go and how wide apart the stitches needed to be. It was over in a few minutes. He hadn't winced, flinched, groaned or hissed once. I wasn't sure he felt pain at all.

"Where did you pick up your medical knowledge?" I asked as I handed the needle back to Gus.

"A surgeon taught me," Fitzroy said.

"Your lessons included surgery?"

Out of the corner of my eye, I caught Seth shaking his head at me in warning. I frowned at him, but Fitzroy caught it and arched a brow. Seth cleared his throat and followed Gus out of the room.

"My education was more varied than a regular student's," Fitzroy said.

"Why?"

"So that I could fulfill this role," he said matter-of-factly. "It's been my destiny since birth. The ministry is new, but its origins are ancient. I was chosen early as a future leader."

"At birth," I muttered.

"Before."

I laughed, then realized he was serious. "How could you have been chosen before your birth?"

"It happens." He picked up the gauze and placed it over his wound. "The bandage, Charlie."

If he had been chosen before birth, that implied there was something special about his parents. Perhaps a combination of characteristics that were deemed important in a future leader of the ministry. I wanted to ask, but he seemed to not want to talk about it. I gave up, for now, but I intended to find out more about his parents and childhood. It was thoroughly intriguing. *He* was intriguing.

I wrapped the bandage around his torso. It brought me close to him, my face just below his shoulder height. If I leaned a few inches forward, I could kiss him. I dared not look up into his face, but staring at the hollow of his throat did nothing to settle the blood raging through my body. Where before my ministrations had been clinical, now they were anything but. Every part of me was aware of him and how close we stood; how easy it would be to close the gap between us, tilt my head, and receive his kiss.

As I wrapped the bandage around him, my fingers brushed the smooth skin of his back and sides. I slowed, not wanting the connection to end. Wanting only to touch him more, to feel the muscles twitch with restrained desire, the thud of his pulse, the heat of his skin.

He wanted those things too. I could sense it, rather than see it or feel it. It was in the way he didn't move when I fastened the bandage in place, and how he lowered his face to my hair and drew in a deep breath.

With my hands still resting over the bandage, I dared to glance up at him. His eyes were closed, his jaw slack, making his face a little softer and even more handsome. I wanted to capture him in that moment, so I lifted my hand and cupped his cheek.

His eyes flew open and his face hardened. He turned away.

"Lincoln," I whispered.

He gathered up his ruined, bloody clothes. "Mr. Fitzroy," he snapped. "Or sir."

I stepped back as if he'd pushed me. "I—I thought—"

"You thought wrong." He stalked into the adjoining bedroom but didn't shut the door. He emerged a few moments later wearing a clean shirt. If I'd thought his jaw was rigid before, now it was positively rock-hard. His eyes were as black and bleak as I'd ever seen them, and his gaze didn't waver from mine. "I've decided. You can't stay here."

"Wh—what?" He was talking too fast. My head was still fuzzy from desire and his brutal rejection.

"When Frankenstein is caught, you'll go to live with Lady Harcourt."

He might as well have slapped me. My head was suddenly clear again. "No! You said I don't have to live with her if I didn't want to."

"I've changed my mind. It's the best place for you."

"Here is—"

"You can't stay here." He moved to the door, as if to see me out.

I stayed put. "Why not?"

"Because your infatuation with me is inappropriate."

My face burst into flames, or it might as well have, it felt so hot. I crossed my arms, as defiant as I could possibly be when utter humiliation ate me alive. I wanted to shout at him that he desired me too but, in truth, I wasn't sure. If he'd liked my touch as I bandaged him, it could have been because the fingers touching him belonged to a woman. Any woman. The look on his face may not have had anything to do with me.

"It's unhealthy," he went on. "And not in either of our best interests for you to live here."

Tears stung my eyes and tingled my nose. I had to hold myself very tight to keep from unraveling. "I understood your point. There's no need to pour salt on the wound."

"This is the way it has to be. You will be well taken care of at Lady Harcourt's house. She's kind."

"And if I don't wish to go there?"

"You would be a fool not to."

"I think we've already proven that I am indeed that." I sniffed, but fortunately my tears didn't spill. I didn't want him to see how pathetic I was, crying over a man I hardly knew.

"It's that or a house of charity," he said.

"I hate you, Fitzroy."

"No, you don't," he said stiffly. "That's the problem."

His cruel words were enough to shock me out of myself, and forced me to see what I was doing and saying. A small flame of anger burned in my chest, and I fueled it with thoughts of how he'd abducted me, treated me like a prisoner, and callously ridiculed my affections. I took a deep breath and felt quite a bit better; more determined than ever to conquer my feelings for him.

He was right when he'd called it an infatuation. What I felt for him was quite possibly fleeting, and certainly foolish, brought on by living in the same house and my gratitude at being rescued from poverty. I could conquer my feelings, given a little more time.

There. Better. Admitting that my affections were misplaced was the first step.

"I'll miss Seth and Gus, and Cook too," I told him with a tilt of my chin. "Perhaps more than I'll miss you, in the long term. They've shown me nothing but kindness, whereas you…have not."

I never got to see what he thought of that. Seth and Gus returned, their steps full of bounce, and they asked for an account of Fitzroy's chase through the sewer tunnels. They lapped up the details as eagerly as the boys from the gangs did, when I told them stories in the evenings. I sat on a chair and listened too. The distraction was a welcome relief.

"He exited the sewers near the docks in Wapping," Fitzroy said. "He was far enough ahead the entire time that I couldn't catch him or get close enough to throw my knife."

"Why didn't you shoot him?" Gus asked.

"The gases in the tunnels are volatile. Shooting would have been hazardous. Once above ground again, there were too many people. I followed him to a small warehouse, tucked away behind the larger ones along the docks. I decided to return here instead of entering."

"Why?" Seth asked.

Fitzroy hesitated before continuing. "In the brief glimpse I caught as he slipped inside, I decided I needed to be better armed and have a plan of attack."

Seth and Gus glanced at one another, perhaps wondering if they were going to be part of the plan. "What did you see?" I asked him, sitting forward.

"A half dozen others, perhaps more."

"Men?"

He paused. "In a way."

I gasped. "They were his monsters, weren't they? His creations, as he calls them?"

"Bloody hell," Seth murmured. "What did they look like?"

"I saw them only briefly, and from a distance. They bore scars across their foreheads, necks and chests. They wore trousers but nothing else, and appeared to be strapped to large chairs."

I was about to remark at the horrible inhumanity of chaining someone to a chair, but remembered that the creatures weren't entirely human. "Were they…alive?"

"I'm not certain. They sat very still and their eyes were closed."

I shivered. "Thank God." I remembered how horrid it had been looking into the dead eyes of the bodies inhabited by the spirits of my mother and my savior from the holding cell. I wouldn't want to see the eyes of Frankenstein's creations open.

"Did you see anything else?" Gus asked in a hushed voice.

Fitzroy shook his head. "He closed the door, and all the windows were covered. I returned here."

"That might have been the best chance to capture him," Seth muttered, half to himself. "While his monsters were strapped to their chairs."

Fitzroy just looked at him.

"He's injured!" I said on his behalf. "Indeed, he ought to be resting and regaining his strength."

"Right. Yes." Seth jerked his head at Gus. "We should go. Is there anything you need, sir?"

"No."

"Come on, Charlie," Gus said, escorting me out with a hand at my back.

I stopped in the doorway. I found it difficult to meet Fitzroy's gaze, but I managed it. What I had to say had nothing to do with our earlier conversation, and I shouldn't let that stop me. "There's something you ought to know. Frankenstein claims to be my father. Having seen him face to face now, I admit there's a strong resemblance."

His lips parted and for several long heartbeats, he didn't speak.

"The news has shocked you as much as it did me," I said with a wry twist of my mouth.

"That's his shocked face?" Gus grunted. "Looks like his normal face, to me." He quieted when Seth elbowed him in the ribs.

"Why didn't you say before?" Fitzroy said.

I shrugged. "I was going to. Stitching you up was more important."

"But I—" He shook his head. "You should have told me. I wouldn't have spoken so harshly to you."

"What does the news about my real father have to do with…anything else?"

"The day has been ordeal enough for you. I might have been kinder. Or left our conversation for another day."

"That would only delay the inevitable. Besides, you were simply being honest, in that uniquely cool way of yours."

"I'm—"

"Don't trouble your conscience over it. A kinder delivery probably wouldn't have achieved the same result anyway. I'm grateful that you chose to enlighten me on your thoughts today rather than a point in the future. It allows me to plan ahead." I turned away quickly so that I couldn't see the impact my words had. I expected he would be relieved, since he'd managed to achieve precisely what he wanted—my willingness to leave Lichfield when this was over.

"What was that about?" Gus asked as he caught up to me in the corridor.

Seth drew alongside too. "What were you two discussing before we returned?"

"The future," I told them, pausing outside my bedroom door.

"And?" Seth placed his hand on the doorknob but didn't open the door.

"And he decided that my future does not lie at Lichfield Towers."

"You're going to live with Lady Harcourt?"

"No. I'll find somewhere else."

"Where?" Gus blurted out. "There ain't no work in the factories, you ain't trained for domestic work, and you're too bloody stubborn besides."

"Perhaps I'll offer to speak to the souls of the dying as they pass away. I wonder how much one ought to charge for such work."

"That's not funny," Seth growled. His face was surprisingly grim.

I patted his arm. "I'll think of something. Don't worry about me."

"Don't you think about goin' back to live on the streets," Gus warned. "That ain't no life for you. I'll hide you in the stables myself, if necessary."

I took his hand. "Thank you, Gus, but it won't come to that."

"I'll speak to him." Seth pointed his chin over my head back up the corridor. "He won't throw you out."

Gus snorted. "He won't listen to you. Or me. He don't even listen to Lady H."

"It's all right," I told them. "I just need some time to think up a plan."

"And what if he don't give you time? He's just as likely to toss you out the minute Frankenstein is caught. That could be as soon as tomorrow."

"I'm sure he'll give me more time. He's not *that* heartless."

"Isn't he?" Seth shook his head. "I'm not so sure." He opened the door and offered me a grim smile. "I'll bring you some tea, shortly."

I thanked him and entered my room—my cozy room with the pile of books, clean clothes, and soft bed. I sighed as they shut the door and left me to contemplate my uncertain future.

***

Fitzroy had recovered enough to leave the house the following morning with Seth and Gus. They were going to investigate the warehouse where Frankenstein kept his creatures. He wouldn't be drawn on whether they would attempt to capture him today or simply investigate.

I tried to read but my mind kept wandering. When I did manage a few pages of the new book, however, I had to set it down altogether. It was about a girl who learned she was adopted. At least *her* father wasn't a murderer.

I closed my eyes. Perhaps that wasn't fair. Frankenstein had seemed to genuinely care for his creatures. And what if the men whose parts he'd used *were* dying, as he claimed? Some deaths were prolonged and painful, and I could well see why the dying would beg him to end their pain. Did it really matter that he'd then used parts of them to create something else, something akin to another life?

And what of Mr. Calthorn, the spy master, the man with the knowledge to bring down the government and the crown? The brutal man who'd hurt his wife. If Frankenstein told the truth—and that wasn't a certainty—was he a bad person for ridding the world of such a monster?

I didn't know what to think. The little boy he'd used as a shield came to mind, and so did Frankenstein's blue eyes—so like mine. I knew in my heart that *I* wasn't a bad person, despite what Holloway said, so how could the man who'd fathered me be bad?

It didn't make sense, and my mind spun around in circles, trying to think it through. I needed a distraction, so I ventured to the kitchen where Cook was attacking a leg of mutton with a cleaver.

"Can I help?" I asked. "Chop some vegetables or clean pots?"

"Vegetables are all chopped, but there be some dusting to do and dishes to clean. There's a pile of 'em in the scullery. Gus'll be right pleased if he finds them all done. It be his turn, today."

"Cook, why are there no maids or footmen here? The house could do with a few."

"Aye, it could. Gus and Seth manage a little, here and there, but the house is too big for 'em to do things proper. You be only a little thing, but if you be a few inches taller, you'd see the dust on top of shelves."

I chuckled and he smiled.

"The master don't like no maids and footmen snooping about, so he says. The ministry got too many secrets."

"Unless those secrets are written down, I don't see why employing some staff would cause problems."

He merely shrugged and returned to the range.

I fetched a duster from the utility cupboard and dusted everything I could reach in the entrance hall. The floor was filthy from the comings and goings, so I scrubbed the tiles with a bristly brush I found. I moved on to the sitting room next. The work wasn't difficult. Indeed, I found I enjoyed sprucing the house up. I took the liberty of rearranging a few pieces of the furniture in the parlor, and hiding some of the uglier knickknacks behind other things. A stuffed rat-like creature was the first to go. Who thought that ought to be displayed in a parlor?

By the time I returned to the scullery, I felt content with what I'd achieved. Perhaps I *could* do a maid's work. It wasn't as awful as I'd expected, and although I would have to work with other maids, the company of women was something I needed to get used to. Perhaps I would ask Lady Harcourt for a reference. She might feel that the ministry owed me enough to lie for me. I couldn't work for her, however, no matter how often she asked. I would be forever expecting to see *him* there, and disappointed when I didn't, or when he ignored me, as a gentleman should ignore a maid. Besides, seeing Lady Harcourt every day would be a constant reminder of their relationship and how he found her tempting and not me.

It was a thought I entertained as I picked up the empty pail and headed outside, to the water pump in the courtyard.

I saw the flash of movement out of the corner of my eye too late. I was knocked to the ground, landing heavily on my knees and one hand. The other still held the pail. I whipped around and smashed the pail into my assailant, hitting him in the legs. His knees buckled and he fell on top of me, pinning me. I tried to push him off, but he was too heavy. He grabbed one of my wrists and squeezed so hard my hand went numb.

With his other hand, he held a knife to my throat. "Be still so I can remove the devil from you."

"Father! Please," I sobbed, "let me go."

"I told you." Holloway bared his teeth, and I noticed for the first time how long they were, how like a rabid dog he looked with madness brightening his eyes and saliva dripping from his lower lip. "I'm not your father. You're the devil's daughter."

Yes, I almost told him. *I am.*

"I'm going to save you, child. I'm going to release the devil from your body and bring you back to God's light."

"How?" It sounded strangled. The knife at my throat dug into my skin. I felt a warm trickle of blood slide past my ear and into my hair. I dared not swallow, lest that make his blade dig in further.

"The devil is well entrenched in you." His voice wasn't normal. It was raspy, harsh, and pitched low. It was the voice of a madman. "It must be gouged out."

The knife pressed into my throat. I struggled again, pushing and kicking out, but nothing dislodged him, not even clawing at his cheek. Flesh scraped off in my fingernails, and blood poured down his face, but he didn't seem to notice. He was too intent on removing the devil from me. Too intent on killing me.

And I was too weak to stop him.

CHAPTER 14

"*Our Father, who art in Heaven, hallowed be thy name.*" Holloway's body shook. His lips curled back from his teeth. If there was a devil inside anyone, it was inside him.

I pushed and struggled, but it did no use. He didn't budge. I tried to scream, but either fear or the blade at my throat made it come out weak, strangled. I was pathetic, and soon I would be dead.

"*Thy kingdom come. Thy will be done, on—*" His eyes suddenly widened, the pupils mere pinpricks in the sea of white. His face twisted as he arched backward, his mouth open in a silent scream.

He sat back, alleviating the pressure of his weight on me. The blade was gone too, I realized. I pushed him off and he stumbled aside. He clutched his shoulder where a meat cleaver was lodged.

The moonlike head of Cook appeared above me. He held his hand out and I took it. He inspected my throat. "It ain't too deep."

Perhaps not, but it stung.

He reached down and, as calmly as he'd helped me to stand, he pulled the cleaver out of Holloway's shoulder. The man screamed and clutched at the wound, but it didn't staunch the gush of blood.

Cook sighed at his cleaver. "Have to throw this out now. Shame. Good knife, that."

I touched the cut at my throat and my hand came away bloody, but it was nothing compared to the blood covering Holloway's shoulder. "He needs a doctor," I said.

"He be needing a miracle when Fitzroy learns what he done."

Holloway curled into himself and sobbed into the dirt. He was pathetic; a small man with a closed mind. I couldn't believe I'd looked up to him, yearned for his love and respect. For the first time since discovering I was adopted, I was glad he wasn't my father.

"We'll put him in the cellar." Cook hauled Holloway up by his good arm. Holloway wailed in protest but didn't fight. He couldn't win anyway, not against a big man holding a meat cleaver. "Fitzroy can decide what to do with him when he gets back."

"We can't let him bleed to death."

"I'll patch him up best I can. I ain't calling the doctor until Fitzroy says to."

"Will he be mad if you let him go?"

"Furious. I'd rather have this cur's death on my conscience than be dismissed from Lichfield. Or worse."

He half-dragged half-carried Holloway to the house. I picked up his forgotten knife and followed. Cook unhooked a large key from inside the kitchen door then descended a set of stairs nearby. He unlocked a heavy oak door and marched his prisoner into the cool, musty room beyond.

Wine bottles lay on shelves to the left, most covered in dust. Sacks of flour huddled in the back corner, some empty crates beside them. Cook sat Holloway on one.

"How did you know where to find me?" I asked.

"You thought yourself clever." He laughed harshly. "You were seen leaving the cemetery."

"By whom?"

"By someone you have wronged before. Did you visit my beloved? Did her spirit talk to you, tell you that you revolt her?"

"That's not how it works." I wasn't going to try to explain my necromancy to him. Besides, I was curious about the person I'd wronged before. "Do you mean the costermonger?"

"He recognized you. You think a dress changes you, but it doesn't. The devil's creature is always recognized by the pure."

I snorted. "If this is the same costermonger who alerted the police to me, then he's anything but pure. I saw him fondling a whore one night, behind his cart. I believe he's married." It didn't surprise me that the costermonger recognized me that day when I left the cemetery with Fitzroy. He knew me well; I'd walked past his cart many times and stolen from him more than once. Holloway must have realized I would visit my adopted mother's grave and questioned him.

"Wait here," Cook ordered.

"The devil get you," Holloway hissed.

"One day. But not today. I be too busy."

Holloway's teeth ground audibly. "You'll burn in hell for this."

"No," I told him. "The bible preaches forgiveness. I will forgive you for this, in time, but you seem unable to forgive me for being born differently. Which of us deserves God's love?"

I walked away. It was only then that I saw the iron chains dangling from rings attached to the walls. I wondered if Cook had the keys to them. If so, he didn't chain Holloway up, but simply locked the door.

"I'll see to his wound," Cook said. "You rest."

Rest. I was too on edge to rest. Cook found a salve for me to use on my throat and I tied a clean bandage around the cut to protect it from my collar. I washed the dishes next, while he tended to Holloway's injury. I had to remember to thank him. If it hadn't been for the burly cook, I'd be dead.

That thought troubled me for the rest of the day. Holloway wasn't a large man, yet he'd completely overpowered me. And then there was the homeless fellow who'd almost raped me, the men in the holding cell… Too many times, I'd come close to either losing my life or my virginity. Today was one time too many. I couldn't rely on someone else being nearby to help me. One day my luck would run out, and I would be alone and helpless.

It was time to stop being helpless and learn to fight off attackers. Somehow.

The day went by slowly. Fitzroy and the others didn't return for lunch or dinner, and when darkness fell, I was sick with worry. Cook was no help. He insisted they always returned after such ventures, occasionally harmed and exhausted, but always alive.

But what if today was the day *their* luck ran out? What if Frankenstein had discovered them and captured them? While it seemed unlikely—three against one—I couldn't shake the anxiety needling at me.

I told Cook I was going to bed early. Instead, I changed into my boys' clothing when I returned to my room. Sometime in the previous days, the trousers, shirt and jacket had been cleaned, folded and put away in my dresser. I unpinned my hair and dragged the long fringe over my face. A familiar boy stared back at me in the mirror, and I offered him a smile. Charlie wasn't as afraid as Charlotte. He was tougher, more resourceful, and fleet-footed. It was good to walk in his boots again.

Cook kept to the kitchen so it was easy to sneak out the front door. It was a long walk to the docks, over an hour, but the night was dark, and nobody saw me as I crept through the shadowy lanes to Wapping.

It wasn't an area I knew particularly well and there were more warehouses than I realized. Fitzroy had said Frankenstein's was behind the larger dock-side ones, so I ran down streets and looked for windows that were covered. At each one, I paused and listened. When I heard nothing, I moved on.

After another hour, I was beginning to think I'd missed the right warehouse altogether, but then I spotted one at the end of a lane with a crack of light edging the window covering. I squatted beneath the window and listened. Only a faint humming came from inside. Not human, musical humming, but machine-like.

The window was locked; the door, too. A quick check showed there was no other way in through the front. I traversed back up the lane, past the row of joined warehouses, until an even smaller lane cut through the row. I scrambled over the gate and landed softly on the other side. The rear of the row was fenced off with gates providing access to loading yards behind each warehouse. I ran to the last one and tried to open it. Locked. Using a discarded crate as a step, I climbed over the top. My landing was as silent as all my movements had been so far. I may not have been able to fight off an attacker, but I'd been the best thief in the gang. None of the boys could match my combination of agility, speed and lightness. Dressing as a boy again reminded me of that. It was a skill I must remember to harness and use when necessary.

Now, it was vital.

The rear window was covered like the front. I squatted beneath it and listened. The humming sounded louder, like an engine coming to life. Then suddenly there was a crack, like lightning without the light.

I peeked through the window and had to cover my mouth to smother my gasp. Fitzroy had told us about the bodies of Frankenstein's creations, but seeing the six pale, scarred forms strapped to the chairs was far more gruesome than anything I'd imagined. The flickering light from a dozen candles revealed raw, ridged cuts across their chests, throats and foreheads, sewn up like seams. Blue veins formed intricate webs beneath their ghostly skin, and dark bruises circled their eyes. They were alive. I knew that much from the veins, yet they were utterly still.

So why the thick leather straps pinning their ankles and wrists to the chairs? And what kinds of chairs were made entirely of metal and had wires connecting them to a central machine? The humming and cracking came from that device. It was so loud now that any noise I made would not have been heard by Frankenstein inside.

He bent over another body, lying on a table at the far end of the warehouse. There were two more bodies on separate tables, their feet pointed toward me. Their ankles were strapped down too, but I couldn't see if their wrists were bound from my squatting position at the rear window.

I dared to stand on my toes, but still I couldn't see the faces. There were three bodies, and I could tell from their large bare feet that they were all men. No. No, no, no. Surely Fitzroy was too clever—too strong—to have been caught. But the coincidence was too great for me to dismiss it.

Bile burned my throat. My stomach rolled and heaved. I squatted down again and sat with my back to the wall. I drew in large breaths and steadied my nerves. Then I began to plan.

I found crates and stacked them, then climbed up to peer through the smaller, high window, used for ventilation near the roofline. From that angle I could see all three faces of the bodies on the tables. They were bloodied and bruised, but I recognized Seth and Gus immediately. The third had his cheeks smashed in, and the rest of his face was swollen and covered in blood. His hair was matted too, but it was clearly black. Unlike Seth and Gus, the third figure struggled to breathe. His chest barely rose with each gasp of air, and once, a bubble of blood formed on his lips. He was unconscious. They all were.

I stumbled down from my makeshift ladder and threw up in the corner of the loading dock. Oh God. No, please no. Don't let them become a body farm for Frankenstein. Don't let Fitzroy die.

I pressed the heel of my hand to my heart, where it felt like a sharp blade pierced me. Tears cascaded down my cheeks, but I dashed them away. They weren't dead yet.

I steeled myself and climbed back up the crates. Frankenstein had moved away from the tables and was checking the machine. Candlelight picked out a cut on his lip, the swell of a bruise on his cheek, but they were nothing compared to the injuries on my three friends. How had he overpowered them with only minimal harm to himself?

His face was slick with sweat, his hairline damp. He'd discarded hat, coat and gloves and stood in his shirt and trousers, rubbing his hands together as he inspected a glass panel on the machine. With a satisfied nod, he twiddled a dial and tapped the glass. His gaze flicked between his six creatures, then he turned the dial again. The sudden crack and snap of lightning made me jump. Bolts of light flashed at the points where the wires met the chairs, causing the bodies strapped to them to twitch and jerk as if they were alive.

My rapidly beating heart in my throat, I leaned closer to the window, unable to believe what I saw. I'd heard about electricity but never seen it in action before. Even so, I knew that I witnessed electricity at work. The engine must be generating it and sending it through the wires and into the chairs to animate the bodies.

If he had a machine to bring them to life, why did he need me?

The motor's hum began to slow, and the lightning bolts generated by the electricity ended. Yet the bodies still jerked and twisted.

The eyes of the one facing me opened, and I fell backward in surprise, landing on the hard ground. Thankfully the crates remained in place, and I'd not cried out. I was sore but nothing seemed broken. When I realized Frankenstein wasn't coming out to investigate, I climbed back up.

He wasn't there. I couldn't see the whole room from where I crouched on the top crate, so it was possible he was simply out of sight, or he could have left without snuffing out the candles.

The motor had wound down and stopped. Now that the humming had ended, the silence seemed unnatural. The creaking of boat timbers carried on the breeze, but otherwise, there were no sounds. The starless sky above was a vast, black sea. The only light came from the flickering candles inside the warehouse. They lit up the cloudy, soulless eyes of the creature facing me. He didn't seem to see me, but that could have been because he didn't see anything.

His head moved from side to side and every part of him jerked or twitched. Then, as if it were nothing, he pulled free of the bonds strapping his wrists to the chair arms. His bound ankles freed next and he sat a moment, as if he wasn't sure what to do with his newfound freedom. Then he rocked forward and finally stood.

The other five bodies came alive too, each of them releasing themselves using unnatural strength. They stood on unsteady legs and checked their surroundings with blank eyes. I kept low, and thankfully my window was above their head height. They did not look up or down, only from side to side.

The first one, the one nearest me, tore the leather straps off the chairs and threw them. The others did the same, and even tried to pick up the chairs themselves, but they must have been bolted to the floor. One of the creatures took a candelabra and stared into the flames. He tried to catch one, and the fire didn't seem to hurt him, even when his skin began to burn. Then he snapped each candle in two, and threw the pieces to the floor where one of the others stomped on them, mashing the wax into the wooden boards with his bare heel. The first creature then slammed the metal candelabra against the chair until it too broke.

If I had any thoughts about these creatures being human, they were quickly dashed. They might have the appearance of men, but they had no conscience, no thoughts beyond violent instinct. They couldn't be allowed to roam free.

"I knew you would come, Charlotte."

My heart leapt at the familiar voice behind me. Slowly, slowly, I turned away from the warehouse, where the creatures progressed ever closer to the three bodies on the tables.

"I hoped you would be here to witness this." Frankenstein smiled up at me. He held out his hand, but I refused it. "Come away from there. If they see you, neither of us will be able to stop them."

I climbed down. I could run now. He didn't appear to be armed, and I'd wager I was faster than him. It was the only way to keep myself out of his hands, to keep myself safe. I was dressed in boys' clothing again, and it would be easy to lose myself among the network of narrow lanes leading away from the docks.

It was so tempting to dash past him. I'd not kept myself out of danger for the last five years only to throw myself into the pit now. If I stayed, there may never be another opportunity to change my mind. It was unlikely that I could save myself once caught. I'd proven my ineffectiveness in fights several times over, of late.

No, I needed to make a choice now. Run, or stay and try to save Seth, Gus and Fitzroy.

Yet it was no choice at all. I could never live with myself if I left them to the mercy of this man. Fitzroy's callousness toward me hadn't stopped me from caring about all of them, including him.

"You must stop those things!" I cried. "They're going to kill them."

He held up his hands. "I can't. They don't listen to me. I learned that the hard way."

I frowned. "Then why did you animate them again?"

"Because I saw you there, watching, and I wanted you to see why I need you."

He'd seen me?

"Admittedly, I was looking out for you." He smiled gently. "I hoped that when your captors didn't return you would come to investigate. I had everything prepared—"

"My friends! You have to get them out!"

"They're not your friends, Charlotte. You can't trust them."

I went to shove him, but he caught my arms. "I see that they've succeeded in brainwashing you." He sighed. "Ever since meeting you, I've been wondering if that's what happened. It's understandable."

"Listen to me," I growled. "Get. Them. Out."

He let me go and turned me toward the lower window. "It's all right, dear daughter. Their energy will dissipate before they can do any harm. Look."

Two of the creatures had fallen to the floor in crumpled heaps, while the other four seemed to be winding down, like automatons having run their course. Only one had reached a table. I watched as the remaining four stopped altogether then stumbled as if their legs could no longer hold them. Their expressions didn't change as their eyes closed and they too slumped onto the floor.

Tears of utter relief clogged my throat.

"The electrical currents only animate them for so long." Frankenstein sounded disappointed. "And even when it does bring them to life, they're not controllable. They won't even listen to me, their maker."

"That's why you came outside."

"It's too dangerous in there when they're alive. They're uncommonly strong, stronger even than the original men whose parts I used to make them."

"They're not alive," I spat. "They're not human. They're monsters."

"At the moment, you're right. But once they have souls, they'll be perfect. They'll think and feel—"

"Stop it," I hissed. "I'm not going to help you." Fitzroy had been right. Frankenstein wanted to use me to reanimate his creations, to bring them fully to life. To bring them under his control.

"You're sounding like them again." He jerked his head at the bodies through the window. "Charlotte, listen to me." He grasped my shoulders but I shook myself free. He sighed. "With your help, we can control them. They'll be absolutely perfect. There might not even be a need for the electricity. Imagine that!"

"I am, and it's sickening."

"Come now. Disregard what the ministry have been telling you and think for yourself. I know you're a smart girl. You're my girl, after all." He smiled again, and it was patient and understanding. It was how a loving father smiled upon his daughter when she said something silly. "Together, you and I will have created life. How is that a bad thing? It's not. It's beautiful. You'll be a part of something amazing, and innovative too. Something that no one else in the world has done."

"Why are you doing this?" I asked. "So you can build an army and take over the government?"

"No, no, nothing like that. Once again, you've allowed yourself to be brainwashed. I'm a scientist, a doctor. I don't destroy life, I create it."

"Shouldn't doctors *save* lives?"

"Save, create…it's all balanced out. One sick, dying man's life is taken and given to another so that he may live and breathe again. It's not something to recoil from—it is something to embrace. It's the way of the future, Charlotte. It's where modern medicine is heading, and you and I are at the forefront of new and exciting things. They'll write about us in books and newspapers. They'll remember the name Frankenstein forever. I'll be the father of half the world—perhaps all of the world one day. Imagine it, Charlotte."

"I am, and I'm sickened. I won't help you."

His smile finally wavered, but not for long. "Come now. Don't be like that. I've been hoping to find another necromancer for so long and—"

"*Another* necromancer?"

"Your mother was one. She was a wonderful woman, but she had her reservations too."

My head began to spin. I pressed my hand to my temple. "My mother…that's why I'm like this?"

He frowned and his mouth flattened. "I don't want to talk about her. I was…upset when she left me." He touched my chin. "But now I have you. To think that I've gained both a daughter and a necromancer in one day…it's beyond my wildest hopes. You are special, Charlotte. Never forget that. Special and loved."

"I…I can't…"

"Hush, child." He stroked my hair, my cheek. His hands were cool, but I didn't pull away. No one had touched me like that since my adopted mother, and it felt so wonderful. Whatever his motives, this man was my father. He loved me. He wouldn't hurt me.

"You will come to live with me, of course," he said, smiling again. "I live in Chelsea, in a nice house. You'll have your own room and dolls."

I almost told him I was too old for dolls, but stopped myself.

"We'll search for your mother together." He spoke faster and his smile turned harder. "She will love you instantly too. I know she will."

"She's alive? Tell me about her. What is she like? Who are her family? Perhaps she's living with them."

He pressed a finger to my lips. "All in good time. After you help me, we'll find her. I promise you."

"Doctor, I—"

"Call me Father."

I shook my head. "I can't help you. What you're asking is wrong. Dangerous."

"Stop it!" He thumped his fist against the wall, startling me. It must have hurt, against the bricks, but he showed no sign. "I'm telling you that they're wrong. They've fed you lies, brainwashed you. They are not your friends, Charlotte, no matter what they said. They're our enemies. They plan on stealing my creations and using them for themselves."

"That's ridiculous."

"It's not." He clasped my shoulders again and dipped his face to look into my eyes. "I'm sorry, Charlotte, but that's the truth. You can't trust them. Everything they've told you that I plan to do, it's *they* who plan to do it, only with *my* creations. They're simply waiting for me to complete the science and reanimate the bodies before stealing all my work. But I've suspected all along, and I'm not going to give up my creatures without a fight."

"You're wrong, Doctor."

"Am I? My dear, I would never hurt the queen. I don't care for power. What would I do with an entire nation to run? I'm a scientist."

The truth of that struck me in the gut. He may be mad, but he was a man of science, not politics or the military. He was obsessed with simply seeing his work come to life, and being remembered for it in years to come—not with taking over the country.

"Listen to me," I said, taking his hands in mine. He squeezed them, and it was as if he could sense that I was about to give in and agree. How wrong he was. "Has someone from the ministry been in touch with you about your creations? Is someone paying you?"

He pulled away and patted my cheek. "Come on. Come inside. Let me show you what you need to do."

He grabbed my hand and opened the back door. He pulled me inside to the scarred bodies on the floor. "We have to get them back in the chairs first." He grabbed one under the arms and began dragging it.

I didn't help. I inspected the bodies on the tables. Seth and Gus breathed normally, but Fitzroy didn't. He labored for every breath, and only managed shallow gasps. I couldn't look at his battered face, once so handsome and now a pulpy mess. It made me want to throw up again.

"Did you do this to them?" I whispered.

"Those two are merely sleeping for now." He grunted as he worked to lift the body onto the chair. "I've given them enough diethyl ether to keep them unconscious for now."

"And Fitzroy?"

He looked up sharply then lifted the body and began dragging. He locked that one into a chair too then joined me by the bed. "He won't survive."

A sob bubbled in my throat. I couldn't hold it in, no matter how hard I tried.

Frankenstein touched my shoulder. "I'm sorry, Charlotte. I see that you cared for him. Your affections are misguided, but I understand why you have them. He saved you from the streets, I believe. It's easy to mistake his actions for caring. He was simply doing his job—a job with the sole aim to rid the world of people who want to live outside the acceptable boundaries of an unyielding society. People like me. And you."

I swiped at my tears and turned away from Fitzroy. I couldn't look at him anymore; couldn't bear to see him struggle for breath. Such a virile, strong man, and now this. It was too much.

"Why do you want them?" I asked.

"You don't know?"

I shook my head.

"To complete the final component of our project. Your part."

I blinked at him. Blinked again. And then it sank in. He wanted me to use their spirits to reanimate the bodies of his creations. To do that, they had to die.

"I…I can't," I choked out. "I want nothing to do with it."

He slammed his fist on the table near Fitzroy's leg. A leg that was covered with dirty trousers, frayed at the cuff. I frowned and inspected the rest of the body. It was still fully clothed, yet they weren't the same clothes Fitzroy usually wore. I'd not seen him leave that morning, but I'd never seen him dress in ragged, untailored trousers. They hung loose on the body—a body that was considerably smaller than Gus's.

It wasn't Fitzroy.

Another sob burbled within me, but it was one of utter relief. I felt giddy with it. Wherever Fitzroy was, he wasn't here, half dead on Frankenstein's table. So who was? And where was Fitzroy?

I glanced around the warehouse, but saw nowhere for him to hide. I must be careful not to let Frankenstein realize that I knew it wasn't Fitzroy. He hadn't corrected me earlier. Either he didn't know who was on his table, or he didn't want me to know that it wasn't Fitzroy.

"Listen, Charlotte." Frankenstein's voice had gentled again. "I know you're frightened, but there is nothing to be afraid of. You've controlled spirits before. You have nothing to fear from the dead, and they have nothing to fear from you." He turned me to face him. The reflection of a candle flame flickered in his eyes and deepened the shadows, making him look hollow cheeked and cadaverous. "This poor man will pass on soon, and when he does, you'll talk to his spirit. Guide him into one of the bodies. Along with the electrical current, it will be a spectacular reawakening. You and I will experience the dawning of new life. *Real* life. Come." He put his arm around my shoulder. "I want my guest of honor to turn the generator back on."

"I…I can't. Please, don't do this. I'm begging you—"

"No, *I* am begging *you*." He grasped my shoulders and pain shot down my arms as his fingers speared me. "It will be marvelous, Charlotte. Why can't you see that?" He shook me. "Why can't you see the good I can achieve?"

I jerked my head toward the bodies on the tables. "I doubt they think you're doing good."

"They're my enemies. *Our* enemies. They want to keep our nation—the entire *world*—in the dark. They want nothing to do with the fantastical. They think anyone who isn't like them is unnatural, wrong. If that were so, then *you* would be a monster, and you're not. You're beautiful. Different, yes, but that's what makes you perfect."

Tears burned again. Nobody had ever said such kind, loving things to me. Things I'd spent years dreaming of hearing. And here was my real father, calling me perfect, wanting me in his life. It was almost too much for my fragile heart to hold.

And yet my head wasn't so easily swayed. It didn't fall for a few longed-for words. I looked at the two men who'd been good to me in recent days, trapped and vulnerable on the tables, and I knew what I had to do.

"What will happen to them?" I asked.

"What does it matter?" he snapped, letting me go. "They care nothing for you, why do you care for them?"

"Answer my question. What will happen to them?"

"I need their souls for you to do your work."

"You're going to kill them," I said flatly.

He pressed his lips together, as if he were summoning some patience. "The life of three enemies with vile intentions is worth exchanging for three of my creations."

"What if the souls refuse to help?"

"They cannot refuse." He frowned. "Do you not know the extent of your power? Charlotte, *you* control the spirits. They may have minds and wills of their own, but you command them. They must obey you."

I'd learned that much from Fitzroy's book, and now I knew that Frankenstein knew it too. He did not appear to realize that any spirit could be raised, not simply a newly deceased one. "Do you know that from my mother?"

He nodded. "She was a powerful necromancer."

I folded my arms and glanced at Seth and Gus, unconscious and unable to help me even if I managed to free them from their bonds. The third man's breath rattled in his chest, the skin surrounding the bruises paler than ever. Death clung to him, waiting.

Frankenstein checked the man's pulse. "It's almost time." He pushed the tables closer to the chairs and switched on the generator. It hummed to life. The three bodies on their iron thrones sat ready to receive their new souls—three dead bodies and three soon-to-be-dead ones, with only me to connect them.

"I'm not doing this."

Frankenstein didn't hear me over the increasing noise of the generator. He checked the glass panel and spun one of the dials. I glanced around again, searching for any sign that Fitzroy was near; that he was lying in wait to capture Frankenstein before the bodies became animated.

What if my arrival had ruined Fitzroy's plans? What if he had intended for Seth and Gus to be caught and he was right now lying in wait? But where?

Or was he already dead and therefore useless for Frankenstein's scheme?

"Come, Charlotte." Frankenstein had to shout over the drone of the generator as he moved to the tables. "Stand closer, so the spirit can hear you." He nodded at the dying man on the table while he stood between Seth and Gus. "It's almost time."

Electricity flashed and crackled along the wires like blue, life-giving veins. The fingers of all three creatures twitched, their arms jerked. Their eyelids fluttered. They would soon be awake.

"Charlotte! Now!" Frankenstein opened a medical bag sitting on the floor behind Seth's table and pulled out a dagger. When he turned back to me, his eyes were bright with fevered excitement and his lips battled with a triumphant smile. He pointed the dagger at the dying man. "Stand there!"

I moved to the side of the third table, and caught sight of the bloodied face. I gagged on my own bile and quickly turned away again.

"He is almost gone," Frankenstein shouted, "but you must help him on his way. Press down on his throat. It'll be over in a moment. Hurry! The first is rising."

One of the creatures got to its feet. Where before it had rampaged around the room, and used up all its energy before reaching the tables, this time it focused on the tables first.

And they were closer. We were closer. We couldn't control it, or the other two that had opened their dead eyes and turned toward us.

The only way to control them was by investing souls into them. But that would condemn Seth and Gus to death.

"Charlotte!" Frankenstein screamed. His smile had slipped and his face was now distorted with uncertainty and fear. "Do it, or we will be torn apart!" His gaze flicked to the monster, now advancing with lumbering, loping steps toward me.

Frankenstein pressed the blade of his dagger to Seth's throat.

CHAPTER 15

"No!" I cried. "Don't kill him!"

I dodged behind the table, away from the monster, and peeked out from behind the table legs. The creature had turned toward Frankenstein. Its blank eyes focused on its maker.

Frankenstein fell back, the blade still in his hand. I couldn't see if he'd used it on Seth, but I saw no spirit rise from the body. He must be alive.

I fell to my knees, partly from relief, but mostly because I'd spotted the medical bag. I rummaged through it until my fingers connected with something long and sharp. I pulled out a blade.

"Charlotte! Charlotte, you must do it now!"

He stumbled away from the table and his creature. I slipped under the table and came up on the other side. The sharp medical knife cut through the leather bonds easily, but Seth was still unconscious. I would never get him and Gus out while they slept.

Frankenstein's bellows drowned out the hum of the generator. He alternated between ordering me and begging me, as the monster backed him into a corner. I raced to Gus and cut through the straps trapping him too, and then I hoped for a miracle.

My movement caught the creature's attention. It lunged and fingers circled my arm so tightly it almost cut off the blood flow. I winced and tried to pull away, but the creature was too strong. The second monster loomed at my side too. The stench of rotting flesh and foul breath swamped me, but it wasn't its stink that brought vomit to my mouth, or the blistered, red scars. It was the pale eyes, devoid of life.

I tried again to wrench away, but it was no use. He was unnaturally strong. His other hand circled my throat, over the cut inflicted by Holloway, and began to squeeze. It felt like my windpipe was being crushed. I couldn't breathe. Couldn't speak. Even if the unknown third man died, I wouldn't be able to command the spirit, because not a sound would escape my mouth.

Tears slipped down my cheeks. The cut stung, but it was nothing compared to the pressure on my throat. I closed my eyes, so that I didn't have to look into the creature's anymore, as I felt my life force slip away from me.

A soft thud had me open them again. I barely registered the black figure amid the shadows before it leaped onto the monster and dragged it off me. Everything was a blur and I hardly knew what happened until it was all over. The creature lay on the floor, its throat cut so deeply that the head was almost severed from the neck. Blood poured out, slicking the shadowy man's boots.

The figure approached. It was Fitzroy. "Are you all right?" he asked.

I nodded, even though my throat burned and my chest ached. I gasped in air, the effort bringing a fresh wave of panic. I couldn't breathe. My throat was too tight. No matter how hard I tried, my lungs didn't fill.

Fitzroy removed his bloodied gloves and dropped them on the floor. He clasped my face, stroking his thumbs along my jawline. "It's all right," he said in that soothing, commanding voice of his. "Look at me."

I stared into the black pits of his eyes and he stared back at me, as if there was nothing and no one else in the room but us. It was a dizzying thrill to have his full attention, to feel like I mattered, and I didn't want it to end. I slipped into the deep pools of his eyes and could have stayed there forever.

"Concentrate on my hands," he murmured.

Those hands with the long, strong fingers that could confidently wield a knife to slice through a man's throat then be so gentle and comforting a moment later. His caress traced the ridge of my cheeks up to the corners of my eyes. He dabbed away a tear with the pad of his thumb then tucked my hair behind my ear.

I drew in a steady, deep breath that filled my chest. It hurt my throat, but I didn't care. I could breathe.

Frankenstein's grunts drew Fitzroy away from me. He let me go but did not try to help as one of the creatures picked up his maker. It slammed Frankenstein against the wall, again and again, as if the doctor were a tool to be used to break through the bricks.

"Help me," Frankenstein whimpered after the third hit. He sounded weak, groggy. After the fourth slam, he groaned in pain. "Please, kill it! For God's sake!"

But Fitzroy didn't move. He turned his attention to the third creature. That one picked up a lifeless Gus in his arms and went to throw him.

Fitzroy attacked. He leapt at the creature, a knife in his hand. I hadn't seen him retrieve it. He went to stab the creature, but it swung Gus like a shield and Fitzroy had to duck or be swiped.

"Get outside!" he shouted at me. "Go, Charlie!"

I edged to the door, but didn't leave. The two remaining creatures were now both targeting Fitzroy. Frankenstein, the lesser threat, lay forgotten on the floor, spluttering and coughing. He got to his hands and knees then to his feet. With a glance at me that I couldn't decipher, he stumbled toward the dying man on the table, and calmly plunged the knife into his throat to the hilt.

I smothered my cry with my hands, not wanting to distract Fitzroy. He heard me anyway, and one of the creatures smashed its fist into his stomach. With a grunt, he fell back against Gus's table, then had to quickly duck to dodge another fierce blow.

The wispy spirit was almost invisible in the poor light. The tendril of smoke drew together and formed the shape of a man's face. He blinked down at his badly damaged body, then at Frankenstein, and shook his head.

Frankenstein couldn't see it. "Do it," he snapped to me. "Or your friends will all die." He turned to the central table and pressed his knife to Seth's throat.

Fitzroy couldn't go to his man's aid. He fought off the other two creatures, his swift movements cutting them, but not deeply enough to kill them. One by one they attacked, and each time he managed to escape their massive fists, but for how long?

"Three," Frankenstein chanted, his eyes on me. "Two. One."

"I'll do it!" Saying the words hurt my damaged throat, and they came out faint, but Frankenstein heard me. He nodded, but did not lower his weapon. To the spirit I said, "I can see you there, ghost." The smoky form looked around then his gaze settled on me. I moved closer so that only he could hear me, not Frankenstein. "Yes, you. Please, listen to me."

"What d'you want?" The spirit seemed a little surprised that he could speak, and even more surprised when I answered.

"You have to save us, save my friends, by doing as I say," I whispered. "I'm going to ask you to re-enter your body."

"Blimey! That even possible?"

"Yes. It won't hurt you, and it will only be for a moment. You will then cross over to your afterlife, where you will find peace." Whether that was true or not, I didn't know, but it seemed like the best thing to say.

"Why would I help him?" He jerked his chin at Frankenstein who was staring at the body. His knuckles were white. "He did this to me. He killed me."

"You won't be helping him, you'll help me. He's going to kill my friends if you don't. Please, sir. I'm sorry for your death, but it had nothing to do with me."

"Why should I care?"

I rubbed my temple. Why couldn't he just do it?

"Now, Charlotte!" Frankenstein screamed from behind me. "Do it now! Command him! You have the power." His urgency was perhaps increased by Fitzroy defeating another one of his creatures. It lay in a pool of its own blood on the floor, and with only one left now, Frankenstein's options of a successful reanimation were limited.

"I'm sorry, but you have to do this," I whispered to the spirit. "Lie on top of your body to re-enter it. I command you," I said, louder for Frankenstein's benefit.

The eyes of the spirit widened and then the faint ghost settled on top of his body. "Oi! Blimey, what's happening? Stop it! Stop it! Let me go, witch!" The dead body rose from the table. Unlike Seth and Gus, he hadn't been restrained. There hadn't been a need to.

His swollen eyes turned on Frankenstein. His bloodied lips parted, revealing broken teeth. He seemed to be speaking, but only a whistling, thin breath came out.

"That's the wrong one!" Frankenstein shouted at me. "He was supposed to go into one of mine! You tricked me!"

The body sat up unsteadily, then slowly swiveled its legs around until they dangled off the table. It moved no further.

"Blast it!" Frankenstein's eyes gleamed as he pressed down again on the blade. A thin line of blood striped Seth's throat.

"No!" I shouted. "Stop, or I will direct him to kill you."

"Kill your own father?" Frankenstein laughed. "No, you won't. You love me, just as I love you, dearest daughter. You're precious to me, remember? My own perfect necromancer child. We'll live together in my—"

The knife struck him in the right eye. He made no sound as blood streamed down his cheek and he crumpled to the floor. Fitzroy strode around the head of the table, leaned down and removed his knife from Frankenstein's eye.

I stumbled all the way back to the door, my hands on my stomach. I stared unblinking at the man who claimed to love me. The man who said I was perfect as I was.

"You killed him," I whispered. "You killed my father."

Fitzroy stood over the body, his arms rigid at his sides, a bloody dagger in each hand. His loose hair fell to his eyes in ragged tangles. He was covered in blood, some of it probably his, and looked very much like an avenging devil. Or angel. I wasn't yet certain which. He peered at me through his hair but said nothing. It didn't really matter. There wasn't anything to say, and I wasn't sure what I even wanted him to say.

All I knew was that I'd had a father and he was gone. Nothing had really changed from the last few days—the last five years.

Except everything had.

"You witch." The reanimated corpse glared at me. His voice had strengthened and his movements were steadier as he stood on the floor. "You are vile," he spat at me. "As vile as that man there. Look at what you've done to me. Look!"

All I could see was the smashed face, the broken teeth and bones, and a man walking toward me. This wasn't a good man, as the one who'd saved me in the holding cell had been. This was a man I'd never met in life but who'd undoubtedly lived on the streets. In my experience, few good men lived on the streets.

Fitzroy circled him and plunged his knife into the base of the man's neck. The corpse stopped and then turned to his attacker. The knife stuck out from between his shoulder blades, but no blood dripped from the wound.

He laughed. It sounded brittle, broken. "You can't kill me, Fool. I'm already dead." He reached back and pulled the blade out.

Then he lunged at Fitzroy.

"Get out of the body!" I shouted as Fitzroy dodged the knife. "Leave this place. Go to your afterlife."

"Why would I want to—" But his words were lost, as if carried on a breeze, although the air in the warehouse was stuffy and still. The spirit emerged and flew away without a glance back at the body now crumpling to the floor.

I folded in on myself, using the door for support against my back. I drew in deep breaths and dragged my hands through my hair. It was over. I was alive.

A hand touched the back of my neck, resting there. I wasn't startled. I knew it was Fitzroy. He said nothing, but remained standing beside me, his bloodied boots in my line of sight. I swallowed a sob but not very successfully. I covered my face with my hands and let a few tears escape, but not too many. They were more from relief, but a little from loss too. I may not have liked Frankenstein but he was my father, and it felt wrong not to mourn him.

Fitzroy's thumb stroked my hairline on the back of my neck. His warmth seeped through my skin, infusing me with a little of his strength. I didn't stand up straight in fear that he might take it as a signal to stop touching me.

After several more heartbeats, he pulled away anyway. "Stay here," he said simply. "I'll be back soon."

I snapped to attention. "Where are you going?"

"There's a horse and cart in one of the neighboring yards. We need to get them home." He nodded at Seth and Gus.

"Oh. Yes, of course." I moved away from the door and he slipped out.

I avoided the bodies and as much blood as possible and checked on Seth first, then Gus. Both breathed normally and none of their injuries appeared too terrible.

Fitzroy brought the horse and cart to the rear door then carried Gus and then Seth to it. I sat beside him on the driver's side and we headed back to Highgate.

"Are you injured?" I asked him.

"A few cuts only. They'll heal quickly."

I splayed my fingers on my knees and breathed deeply. "Where were you hiding?"

"On a ceiling beam."

"But…how did you stay up for so long, and undetected too?"

"The beams were black and I lay on the most shadowed one."

It must have been uncomfortable. "I suppose you had a plan in mind, to save Seth and Gus. Did I ruin it by arriving?"

"Your arrival changed my plan to capture Frankenstein. It worked out well enough in the end. Perhaps better."

'Capture Frankenstein', not save Seth and Gus. Surely he hadn't been going to sacrifice them? I dared not ask. I wasn't sure I wanted to hear the answer.

I did want to know the answer to my other burning question. "What happens to me now?"

"I haven't decided."

"What do you mean you haven't decided? The situation has come to an end. Frankenstein is dead. You no longer need me." I swallowed the lump in my throat. "I need to know."

"I've been too busy to think about it since we last spoke."

I stared down at my hands, twining together on my knees. I stilled them.

"We'll discuss it tomorrow," he said.

We drove north, through the quiet streets of London, not encountering a soul. Gus and Seth slept behind us. I wondered when the effects of the ether would wear off. I hoped they'd be back to their cheerful selves in the morning. I might need their support in my petition to remain at Lichfield.

"Your throat is bandaged." Fitzroy's voice startled me.

I touched the strip of cloth covering the wound Holloway had inflicted earlier in the night. "There'll be a prisoner waiting for you in the cellar. Anselm Holloway." I couldn't bring myself to call him Father.

He glanced at me out of the corner of his eye. "He hurt you?"

"Not as much as Cook hurt him. He's quite the knife thrower."

He lowered the reins, but the horse kept up its plodding pace. "Are you all right?"

"The wound isn't deep and doesn't hurt much now."

"I wasn't referring to the wound."

I blinked at him and almost reached across the gap between us and took his hand. Instead, I clutched my own hands tighter. "My nightmares will be different ones for the next little while." I laughed but he didn't join in. He continued to watch me with that blank face of his. "You must have heard me when we were sleeping in the same room. I've been told that I cry out. I was merely trying to lighten the mood by making a joke about it."

"I noticed." He'd noticed my nightmares or my attempt at a joke? He looked forward again and urged the horse to quicken with a light flick of the reins. "So you got to see the dungeon after all."

I blinked. "Er, yes, and once was enough. I hope never to have to go down there again."

"You won't." He said it with such surety that I wondered if he meant he'd made up his mind that I was leaving, and that's why I'd never see the dungeon again.

***

Cook emerged from the rear of the house when we arrived back at Lichfield. He met us near the stables before we pulled to a stop, and lifted his lantern. His eyes widened when he saw me jump down from the driver's seat. They widened even further when he spotted Gus and Seth in the back. He shook Seth's foot.

"Are they…?"

"Asleep," was all Fitzroy said.

"What'll we do with 'em, sir?"

"They can sleep in the stables tonight. The fresh air will do them good."

Cook nodded. "You know about our prisoner?"

"Charlie told me. Is he alive?"

"Aye, but he needs a doctor."

Fitzroy handed the reins to Cook. "Give Charlie anything she needs from the kitchen." To me, he said, "Will you be having a bath now?"

"Bloody hell, yes." My gutter language elicited neither a smile nor a frown.

"Then I'll see you in the morning." He walked off, but I raced after him.

"What are you going to do with Holloway?" I asked.

"Turn him over to the authorities."

I blew out a measured breath. "Oh. Good."

"You assumed I would kill him?"

"I…may have."

"I only kill those who threaten the queen and her family."

"Just the royal family? Not the government, prime minister, or those you care about?"

"I don't care about anyone. I can't afford to."

I halted but he continued. His stark words spun in my head. How could he not care about anyone? Even I'd cared about Holloway, right up until I learned he wasn't my father. In the gangs, there'd always been a boy or two that I'd tried to look out for, simply because I liked their company and didn't want to see them harmed. And in recent days, I'd come to care for Seth and Gus. And Fitzroy, although he didn't seem to want me to.

Perhaps it made it easier for him to do his job if he didn't care. A job that involved protecting England and the royal family from people like Frankenstein, who could do them harm using supernatural methods.

I frowned at his retreating back until he disappeared into the house. Something Frankenstein had said nibbled at the edges of my memory. I'd been so distracted with his declaration of fatherly love, that I'd almost forgotten it. But now his words came flooding back. I wracked my brain, until I finally remembered.

'They think anyone who isn't like them is unnatural, wrong. If that were so, then you would be a monster, and you're not…'

A monster. To some people—perhaps many—I was little better than the creatures Frankenstein had created. I'd been of service to Fitzroy and the ministry, but now Frankenstein was dead and I was no longer needed. What if the decision about my future wasn't merely a matter of whether I would stay on at Lichfield?

What if Fitzroy needed to decide whether I—a necromancer, an abomination—should be allowed to live?

CHAPTER 16

I slept late. I wasn't sure how I'd managed to fall asleep at all, with so many thoughts buzzing around my head, but I felt refreshed enough to confront Fitzroy in the morning. If he refused to give me a direct answer about my future, then I would sneak away from the house and never go back. His avoidance of my questions seemed to be his way of not saying something he knew I'd dislike. I would take his silence as a sign this time, instead of finding out his intentions too late.

I opened the door to see both Seth and Gus in the corridor, leaning against the wall opposite.

"'Bout bloody time you woke up, sleepy head." Gus's craggy face creased even more with his grin. "We were thinkin' we'd have to check if you were still alive."

Seth thumped him in the arm then stepped toward me. I was swept up into a hug before I knew what was happening. He let me go, only for Gus to take over. He took longer to release me, and I had to gently shove at him before he stepped back again, a slight flush to his cheeks.

"Who're you calling sleepy head?" I teased him. "You two would have slept through the end of the world last night."

"We had a good reason." Gus grinned again. "Hear we missed all the action."

"You did."

"You saved us," Seth said, his eyes glistening. "We owe you."

"I think Fitzroy exaggerated." I laughed. "I'm not really sure who saved the day, but everyone's alive, and that's all that matters."

"You'll have to tell us the full story," Seth said. "Death told us so little."

"Ain't too chatty this mornin'," Gus said. "Committee's here."

My heart dove. I wouldn't get an opportunity to talk to him alone until after they left, and that could be hours. His decision might also be swayed by them. Or perhaps not. He'd been adamant that he alone made all the ministry's decisions. Whether that would work in my favor or not was yet to be determined.

"Is Holloway still in the cellar?"

Gus shook his head. "Death took him this morning." At my raised brows, he added, "Fitzroy handed him over to the police."

"He'll be charged with attempted murder against Cook," Seth added.

Not me. Was that because I wouldn't be at Lichfield for much longer? Or was there another reason?

I couldn't fathom it all. Not without knowing where my future lay.

"Where is the committee convening?"

"The library."

"It seems I'll have to wait to speak to Fitzroy. Would you mind bringing me up something to eat? And some fresh water for washing too. Thank you." I touched their arms. "I'm so glad you two aren't any worse for your ordeal."

"Wouldn't want my pretty face smashed in, eh?" Gus chuckled as he walked off.

I shivered, reminded of the third man, whose soul I'd coaxed back into his body.

Seth leaned down and pecked my forehead. "I'll bring up fresh bandages for your wound too."

I fingered the cloth at my throat and watched him retreat along the corridor. His footsteps finally receded enough that I felt safe to follow at a distance in bare feet. I had only minutes before they returned, so I quickly crept to the library door. The hum of male voices on the other side was unmistakable, but I couldn't make out what they said.

Until Lord Gillingham, in his distinctive sneering growl, said, "She's of no use to us now!"

I cracked the door open just enough for the voices to tumble out to me, but I couldn't see anyone. "You can't send her back to the streets," Lady Harcourt said. "It's our moral duty to see that she has a home to go to."

"Why?" Gillingham countered. "She's not our responsibility."

"Gilly," the general chided.

"She's alone in the world." Lady Harcourt's usually serene voice turned crisp. "She needs guidance at this vulnerable age."

"She refused your offer of guidance, Julia," General Eastbrooke said. "I must admit, the chit doesn't seem to know what's good for her."

"We can't force her to live with me."

"But *why* doesn't she want to live with you?"

"I don't know."

"She's not used to living in a grand household," Fitzroy said. "There are rules and a specific way of doing things, whether she comes to you as a maid or a companion. It'll stifle her and she knows it. She's used to doing as she pleases."

"Then it's time she learned some discipline," Gillingham barked.

"Lincoln's right," Lady Harcourt said on a sigh. "More discipline will send her running away."

"I don't see a problem with that. Either she takes you up on your offer or we get rid of her. That's my advice."

"Get rid of her?" Fitzroy asked, tone icy.

"You know what I mean."

"No. I don't."

The leather of a chair creaked. "She's a magnet for madmen, a danger to everyone. Frankenstein may be dead, but there will be others. You know that, Fitzroy. She cannot be allowed to fall into the hands of unscrupulous types who'll use her as a weapon against us."

"Gilly, are you saying what I think you're saying?" the general asked.

"I am," he said darkly. "There's no need to spell it out."

Oh God. He meant to have me killed!

I sat back on my haunches and blinked through the small gap into the library. My heart had stopped beating. My sore throat ached more. I rose to my feet, steadying myself with a hand on the doorframe.

Run. Get away.

The round of protests from the other committee members made me pause, then Fitzroy's voice stopped me altogether. His harsh growl cut through the heated discussion.

"You won't touch her. None of you. And I will not do your dirty work on this. Is that clear, Gillingham?"

Someone—Gillingham?—made a strangled sound.

"Is that clear?" Fitzroy snarled.

"Yes, yes!"

The leather creaked again. Footsteps paced across the floor, but not near the door. Waiting for someone to speak was painful.

"Then what is to be done with her?" Lord Marchbank's calm words broke the tension. "Gillingham is right, in that she cannot be allowed to fall into our enemies' hands. For that reason alone, I don't think sending her to Lady Harcourt's house is a good idea. There are too many people coming and going."

"What do you propose, March?" the general asked.

"The village near my Yorkshire estate is far from civilization. She'll be out of harm's way there. I know a kind, elderly couple who will take her in, as long as we pay them a sum each month."

Yorkshire! That was so far away!

"Exile," Lady Harcourt said flatly. "I think that might work."

"Agreed," the general said. "But not Yorkshire. It's too close. And what if she is seen performing her necromancy?"

"She won't *perform* necromancy by accident," Fitzroy said.

"I do think exile is a good idea," Lady Harcourt said. "But perhaps in another country."

Another country! Why not just send me to the wilds of Africa and let the lions feast on me?

Eastbrooke agreed with her. "Leave it to me. Have her pack a few things now, Fitzroy. She can come with me today, and I'll have her on a ship by nightfall."

Today!

"To where?" Fitzroy asked.

"It's best if you don't know. The fewer people who do, the better."

"I disagree."

"An asylum would suffice," Gillingham grumbled. "That's where the freaks and deranged go. Hide them away, that's what I say. Does anyone know of an asylum in another country? Somewhere they don't allow visitors, preferably."

I gasped then shut my mouth. I listened for signs that they'd heard me, but none came. Lady Harcourt was speaking again.

"She doesn't belong in an asylum. General Eastbrooke, I like your idea of exile. I trust you have somewhere in mind?"

"I do. Pleasant little island I came across in my time in the army. It'll do nicely, but that's all I'll tell you about the place. Best if you don't know any more."

"I'll see that she's ready to—"

"No." Fitzroy's tone chilled me to the bone, even as my heart lifted to hear him speak out for me.

"No?" Gillingham sneered. "You dare to refuse the general's suggestion? If you ask me, she's getting off lightly."

"I'm not asking you. I'm not asking any of you for your opinions. Exile is not a good idea in this case."

"What?" Eastbrooke exploded. "Have you gone soft?"

"Let him speak," Marchbank said. "Go on, Fitzroy. What do you propose?"

"You're all correct in that our enemies will try to use her against us," Fitzroy said. "That's why we need to keep her close, not push her away. We can't keep her out of their hands if we can't see her."

"Don't tell me you want to keep her here," the general scoffed.

"I do, for two reasons. To protect her from anyone who would use her, and to study her."

"Study her! You have gone mad."

My sentiments precisely. Study me? As in subject me to tests and interrogation? I wouldn't be a party to that.

"No reason an asylum can't do the same thing," Gillingham said. "They have effective methods for *studying* patients."

"She will remain here," Fitzroy said. "Where I can keep an eye on her."

"I'm not sure that's a good idea," Lady Harcourt said. "This is a house full of men, for one thing."

Gillingham snorted. "You're worried about the virtue of a vile little whoring necromancer? My dear lady, there is no need for charity in this instance. The girl is an aberration."

"That is quite enough," Lady Harcourt snipped. "She is a human being, and an attractive girl. Living with a group of men is asking for trouble."

"I would hope, Julia, that you know me better than to think I would allow something unfortunate to befall her under my own roof." Fitzroy's frosty words were followed by silence.

The door suddenly opened and I fell backward onto my bottom. Fitzroy towered above me, blocking my view. I couldn't see anything past him, but more importantly, the others couldn't see past him to me either.

He shut the door, reached down and grabbed my arm. He hauled me up and marched me toward the service area at the back of the house. His grip was hard but not bruising, but his strides were long and I had difficulty keeping up. He didn't slow his pace as we passed Seth and Gus, carrying trays and linens. They stared at us, but didn't ask for an explanation. Perhaps Fitzroy's glower silenced them.

He marched me out to the rear courtyard, but didn't stop until we reached the orchard where he finally let me go. I rubbed my arm and glared at him. He glared back.

"Hear enough?" he snapped.

"I was only there a moment."

"Liar."

I bristled. "Very well. I heard sufficient to know that Lord Gillingham wants me dead, the others think I ought to be exiled, and you want to dissect my brain for science."

The corner of his mouth lifted slightly. Surely he couldn't be smiling at me. I had been entirely serious. "Your brain will be safe from me."

"So, you have decided. Will they abide by your decision?"

"Yes. The real question is, will you?"

I blinked at him. "It's not as if I have too many other choices."

"There is always a choice."

"Then I choose to stay."

A few heartbeats passed before he said, "You haven't asked me what you'll do here."

"Very well. What will I do? Aside from be your scientific experiment."

"Be my maid. There'll be a great deal of work. It won't be easy. I require you to dust, mop the floors, do the laundry—"

"I know what a maid does, and I accept the position. I don't expect to live on your charity. I'll work hard. You won't regret the decision."

"I never have regrets."

"Lucky you."

"Don't agree, yet. Not without knowing everything."

"Everything? Are there rooms I've yet to see that are filled with mud?"

"I meant everything about me."

"I know you'll be difficult to live with." I tilted my chin, daring him to counter me. He didn't. "I know you have terrible moods, and I'll do best to avoid you when you're in a temper."

His eyes narrowed. "I admit that I have a temper, but I think I'm able to keep it in check."

I snorted, earning a glare from him.

"There is something aside from my temper that you need to know." He crossed his arms and shifted his weight from one foot to the other. "Do you recall that man who accosted you the day I set you down in Whitechapel?"

"He's difficult to forget. What about him?"

"I paid him to scare you."

My mouth flopped open. "Paid him? You mean…" I thought back to that night. The brute had mentioned receiving money, and his spirit had accused Fitzroy of tricking him. Bloody hell…

"I needed you to change your mind and help me find Frankenstein. I needed you to see that you were better off with me than living on the streets."

I slapped his cheek as hard as I could. It stung my hand and left a satisfying red mark on his skin, but not enough to quell the rage boiling within me. "He tried to rape me! What's wrong with you, that you would do such a thing?" I shouted.

He merely watched me from beneath long, thick lashes, but his face didn't change. Nor did he speak.

"You killed that man." I pressed a hand to my churning stomach. "You stabbed him to death, and yet he had done exactly as you asked."

"No, he didn't. He went too far. He was only meant to scare you."

"He succeeded."

"He wasn't supposed to go through with it and hurt you."

"Is that so? You thought you could control such a man?"

"Yes," he said quietly.

"Perhaps it's your fault that he almost succeeded," I snapped. "Perhaps he misunderstood you. Or were you just slow in reacting and rescuing me? Rescuing," I sneered before he could answer. "My God, Fitzroy." I leaned back against the trunk of an apple tree and drew in deep breaths to steady my frayed nerves. "How *could* you?"

Not only had he paid a monster to *scare* me, he'd then gone on to kill him. If he was capable of such things, what else was he capable of doing?

He didn't speak as I tried to gather my wits. It was impossible to tell what he was thinking, with the mask in place, his eyes hooded. He held himself very still and seemed to be waiting for me to do or say something.

"Why're you telling me this?" I finally asked.

"So you can make an informed decision. If you choose to stay, that is the sort of person you'll be living with."

A cold-hearted killer. A man whose moral lines were blurred, and who'd do anything to succeed. The leader of an organization whose members didn't want a necromancer in their midst.

Yet he was also a man who'd never failed to protect me, and who'd offered me a safe home among friends.

"Do you want me to stay?" I asked.

"I want you to make a choice based on the facts. If you decide to stay, there will be a place here for you."

It wasn't the answer I'd wanted, but I knew it was the best he would give. He certainly wasn't trying to make it easy for me to decide, telling me I would be nothing more than a maid, as well as opening my eyes to the sort of person he could be. It was an odd way to induce me to stay, and yet I was grateful that he'd been upfront and that he left the decision to me.

"I'll give you time to think about it," he said, turning and walking off.

I pushed off from the tree. "I'll have an answer for you tomorrow." I raced after him and he slowed his steps to match mine. "You could have caught my hand," I told him.

His gaze slid sideways to me.

"I know your reflexes are fast. You could have caught my hand before I slapped your cheek." When he still didn't speak, I added, "You'll be gratified to know that it hurt me too."

"Will I?"

"I assume that now I'll be working for you, I can no longer use violence against you when you do or say something ill-conceived."

"You assume correctly."

"Then you'd better not do anything ill-conceived. I have a temper too, and controlling it isn't easy."

"I'll be sure to catch your hand next time."

I didn't tell him I had a good kick on me. We walked back to the house together. The committee had all departed, and the delicious scent of baking bread wafted out of the kitchen. I was starving.

"There you are!" Seth called from the landing. He came down the stairs and grinned at me. "It's safe to come back inside now. The dragons have departed."

"They're not all dragons," I said, smiling.

"True enough. Some are snakes."

I laughed.

Seth's gaze flicked to Fitzroy and his smile died. "Luncheon will be ready soon." He left us and headed toward the kitchen.

Once he was out of earshot, Fitzroy said, "If you remain here, there is only one rule that I require you to abide by."

"Don't steal the silver?"

"No fraternizing."

I arched my brows, then glanced in the direction Seth had gone. I laughed. He was friendly enough but certainly not in a way that tempted me. "I'll cross that off my list of morning chores."

Without waiting for his response, I hurried toward the kitchen. It wasn't until I saw Cook, Seth and Gus chatting quietly near the range that I wondered if Fitzroy was actually referring to me fraternizing with *him*.

I didn't find that notion the least amusing.

***

That afternoon was different to all the others I'd spent at Lichfield Towers. It was as if the four men finally relaxed, now that Frankenstein was caught. Well, perhaps Fitzroy wasn't all that relaxed, but the others were. We played some cards after luncheon, while Fitzroy remained in his rooms, but by mid-afternoon, Seth and Gus had grown restless.

"There be some cleaning for you to do," Cook told them. "The scullery's a pig sty."

"We're saving it for Charlie," Seth said with a wink at me.

"I haven't given my decision yet," I said. Fitzroy had briefed them on my future, and told them he'd given me until tomorrow to decide. Seth and Gus had treated me as a regular member of the household ever since. To them, it seemed natural that I would stay.

Perhaps I would, but I wanted to take the full time Fitzroy had given me. I wanted to make a decision with a clear head, after thinking through all the implications. I was, after all, giving up my freedom to become a servant.

"Want to spar?" Gus asked Seth after he lost all of his beans at cards. "I'm feeling restless."

"Sparring will be good. Meet me on the lawn."

The men left to change and I headed out to the lawn to wait. They showed up ten minutes later, stripped to the waist. I glanced at the house, expecting Fitzroy to storm out any minute and order them to dress when around me, but he didn't. I didn't want the men to change their habits because of me, so I said nothing. I just sat on the grass and watched.

They were good, but Seth clearly had the upper hand. I could well believe he'd been a bare-knuckle fighter when Fitzroy had discovered him from his hard punches and nimble footwork.

When they finished, they sat alongside me to catch their breaths. Cook brought out tea and cake and we ate sitting on the grass. I glanced up at the second floor and caught Fitzroy watching us from his window. He turned away, and I waited for him to join us. He didn't come.

I tried talking to him that night, but he told me he was busy and that unless it was urgent or I'd made my decision, he had no time for idle chatter.

"All work and no play will make you even grumpier," I retorted.

"It's a risk I'm willing to take."

He shut the door on me and I signed a rude gesture at it before going to my own room. I picked up a book and read into the night. As I drifted off to sleep, I wondered if I would be allowed to remain in the guest suite or be moved to the servants' quarters in the attic if I decided to stay at Lichfield as a maid.

The following day, I needed some time alone, away from the house. I'd not seen Fitzroy all morning or afternoon, so I informed the others that I was heading to the cemetery for a while. I promised to return before dusk.

The day was warm, thanks to the blanket of cloud smothering the city, and my skin felt damp by the time I reached my mother's grave. No, not my mother. I must stop thinking of her in that way.

An ache settled into my chest. She might not be my mama, but she had loved me up until her death, and that's what I would hold onto. I may never find out anything more about my real mother, but at least I'd experienced a mother's love in my childhood. Some children never had that.

I sat beside her grave and leaned back against the headstone, my legs stretched out in front of me. I breathed deeply. The scents were so much earthier and cleaner than in the rest of the city.

I must have dozed at some point, because I awoke with a start to the sounds of digging. The groundskeeper must be preparing a new grave nearby. Odd, because dusk had already settled. I was about to get up and leave when voices stopped me.

"Hurry up!" hissed a man. "We're sitting ducks out here."

"You were the one who wanted to come in daylight," said another, also male, but a little deeper than the first.

"You want to go wandering around the cemetery at night?" The first man snorted.

"What does it matter? If you're worried about ghouls, you should be worried about digging up this blighter. His ghost won't be happy to find his body missing."

I peeked around my mother's headstone and saw two men dressed in dark coats, both with shovels and a mound of dirt piled beside them. It was a fresh grave that I'd seen on my way in, one that hadn't been there on my last visit. What were they doing opening it up again? Whoever they were, I was certain they weren't supposed to be digging there. I couldn't see their faces, but they were both solid men, with brown hair visible beneath their caps.

The digging resumed at a faster pace until the second man spoke again. "We've got to be deep enough now, surely."

The sound of a shovel striking wood made them both laugh. "There. Come on, let's get him out."

I watched as they removed more dirt and then one jumped down into the hole. The other unraveled a blanket and tossed it down. The scraping of wood on wood made me cringe.

"Blimey!" the man down in the grave said. "That bloody stinks."

"What'd you expect? Roses?" He glanced around, and for one sickening moment, I thought he'd seen me. "Hurry up."

I breathed out a measured breath and remained still. They wouldn't notice me if I didn't move.

The man in the grave pushed something up. It was wrapped in the blanket, and shaped like a human. His companion reached down and hauled it further out then gave a hand to his friend. He then picked up the wrapped body and tossed it over his shoulder.

"Go on ahead," he said. "Signal if you see anyone."

I watched them leave, my heart in my throat. I ought to do something to stop them, but what? They were bigger than me and stronger than me. I silently cursed and wished I knew how to fight. I'd been at the mercy of others so often, and I was tired of it. Tired of being pathetic and weak. Being fast wasn't enough; I needed to learn skills to help me fend off an attacker bigger than myself. I'd seen Fitzroy do it. The brute under the bridge had been bigger than him, and Frankenstein's creatures were stronger.

I waited several minutes before leaving my mother's grave. I kept vigilant for the body snatchers, but didn't see them. In the morning, I'd have to give an account of what I saw to the police, but there was little they could do to stop such a practice, unless they caught them in the act. For now, the robbers were long gone.

I walked swiftly back to the house and was a little breathless when I pounded on Fitzroy's door. He opened it, a frown on his brow.

"Is there an emergency?"

"No. Yes. Not really."

His brows rose and he stepped aside. "Then you'd better come in."

He indicated I should sit on the sofa, but I couldn't. I was too wound up, too eager to say what I wanted to say.

"Stop pacing, Charlie, and tell me what the matter is."

I stopped. "I've made my decision."

"And?"

"And I'll stay, on one condition."

He paused, then said, "No conditions."

"Hear me out. It's not a terrible condition. I think you'll find it a good one, actually."

"Go on."

"I want you to teach me to fight someone bigger than myself."

He leaned against the chair behind him and crossed his arms. "What brought this on?"

"Everything! All my life, I've been vulnerable. My size and gender has seen to that. I've had to be continually vigilant to protect myself. I know how to avoid most situations, and I can run away fast, but running becomes exhausting, and I don't wish to run away from here. I want to stay, and staying means I must learn to defend myself."

A vein in his throat throbbed above his collar. "You won't need to protect yourself," he said quietly. "That's for me to do—if you agree to live here."

"I don't want to rely on you, or anyone else. What if you're not home and there is an attack? It happened with Holloway. Or what if you die and I find myself alone in the world again? In your line of work, all manner of unfortunate things could befall you."

His eyebrow quirked. "You think me incapable of protecting you?"

"I think you're human." I closed the gap between us and clasped his arms. He jerked at my touch, perhaps taken by surprise, but I didn't let go. "Please, Lincoln. Please teach me. You can have Seth and Gus oversee my training."

"No," he growled. "I'll do it."

I squeezed his arms. His muscles tensed. "Is that an agreement?"

He nodded then moved away. "Maids don't address their masters by their first names," he tossed over his shoulder. "You will address me as Mr. Fitzroy or sir only."

I saluted the back of his head. "Is that another rule?"

"Yes."

"So no fraternizing, and no first names. Anything else?"

"I'll let you know as I make them up." His voice sounded amused, as if he were laughing at me, but when he turned to face me, he wasn't smiling. I wasn't sure why I expected him to be. I'd not yet seen him smile, and I wasn't sure what it would take to produce one.

"Good. Then I'll start tomorrow. Sir." I gave him a little curtsy that almost unbalanced me.

"You'll do your chores in the mornings, and in the afternoons I will train you. Is that clear?"

"Yes." I beamed. I couldn't help it. *This* was what I wanted. Being able to fight off an attack was the ultimate form of liberation. I might be about to enter servitude, but I felt freer than I had in years. "Oh, I'll have to take some time off to visit the police. Or perhaps you can do it." I bit my lip and cringed. Speaking to the police went against every grain of my being. What if they recognized me as Fleet-foot Charlie the thief?

"Is this to do with Holloway's attack?"

I shook my head. "I went to the cemetery this afternoon and saw some grave robbers stealing a body."

He stalked across the room to me. "Was the grave fresh?"

"Only a day or two old."

His lips flattened. "This may not be a matter for the police."

"You're just going to let them get away with it? What if they come back?"

"I'm going to investigate myself. There are two motives for removing a body. The first is medical, to provide doctors with cadavers to use in their research. That's harmless."

"I'm sure the body's spirit would disagree, and the family members."

"The second is supernatural."

I gasped. "To create super humans like Frankenstein wanted to do?"

"Among other reasons."

I pulled a face. "I wish I'd followed them now and seen where they'd gone."

"You did the right thing. Following them would have been dangerous."

"All the more reason to begin my training immediately. Tomorrow afternoon," I said as I headed to the door. "Do not forget. You promised."

The frown he gave me as I shut the door was one that I had no trouble deciphering—resignation. It was the closest thing to an expression he'd ever shown. It would seem he didn't always wear the mask after all. That glimpse into his thoughts made me more determined than ever to see him shed the mask again, perhaps altogether.

Now that I was living at Lichfield, I could plan how to draw out more of his expressions and the emotions that underpinned them. It was fortunate that I had nothing else to do, and nowhere else to go, because I had a feeling it would take some time.

THE END

LOOK OUT FOR

Her Majesty's Necromancer

The second MINISTRY OF CURIOSITIES novel.

Somebody is stealing bodies from the cemetery, and it's up to Lincoln and Charlie to find out who and why. But when their investigation leads them into the bowels of Victorian London, Lincoln's protective nature brings him into conflict with the independent Charlie.

To be notified when C.J. has a new release, subscribe to her newsletter at http://cjarcher.com/contact-cj/newsletter/

ABOUT THE AUTHOR

C.J. Archer has loved history and books for as long as she can remember. She worked as a librarian and technical writer until she was able to channel her twin loves by writing historical fiction. She has won and placed in numerous romance writing contests, including taking home RWAustralia's Emerald Award in 2008 for the manuscript that would become her novel *Honor Bound.* Under the name Carolyn Scott, she has published contemporary romantic mysteries, including *Finders Keepers Losers Die*, and *The Diamond Affair.* After spending her childhood surrounded by the dramatic beauty of outback Queensland, she lives today in suburban Melbourne, Australia, with her husband and their two children.

She loves to hear from readers. You can contact her in one of these ways:
Website: www.cjarcher.com
Email: cjarcher.writes@gmail.com
Facebook: www.facebook.com/CJArcherAuthorPage

Made in the USA
Coppell, TX
22 January 2020

14811347R00157